RONAN BENNETT

HAVOC,
in its third year

A NOVEL

Simon & Schuster
NEW YORK · LONDON · TORONTO · SYDNEY

SIMON & SCHUSTER
Rockefeller Center
1230 Avenue of the Americas
New York, NY 10020

This book is a work of fiction. Names, characters, places, and incidents
either are products of the author's imagination or are used fictitiously.
Any resemblance to actual events or locales or persons, living or dead,
is entirely coincidental.

For information about special discounts for bulk purchases,
please contact Simon & Schuster Special Sales at
1-800-456-6798 or business@simonandschuster.com

Manufactured in the United States of America

1   3   5   7   9   10   8   6   4   2

Library of Congress Cataloging-in-Publication Data
Bennett, Ronan.
Havoc, in its third year: a novel / Ronan Bennett.
     p.   cm.
1. Great Britain—History—Puritan Revolution, 1642–1660—Fiction.
2. West Riding of Yorkshire (England)—Fiction. I. Title.
PR6052.E5315H385 2004

823'.914—dc22   2004045200
ISBN 978-0-7432-5857-9

To Finn-Tomás

Mistrust all in whom the desire to punish is imperative.

—GOETHE

Author's Note

In early seventeenth-century England—the time and place of this novel—men of property were gripped by fears. They feared enemies without and within. Massing at the gates were the fanatical, brainwashed followers of the pope and the Catholic armies of Spain and the Holy Roman Empire determined to extinguish their liberties, religion, heritage and institutions—what today we would call their very way of life. Since peaceful coexistence was unthinkable, there had to be wars, and when there were not wars, there was the inevitability of such. Vigilance was paramount; there were spies, traitors and fifth columnists among the very highest of the land and among the lowest, biding their time, waiting for the opportunity to strike.

England's external enemies greatly benefited from the lamentable condition into which the country had been allowed to sink. At least so the godly believed. Looking balefully about, they saw the poor living idle, morally suspect, semicriminal lives; women raising bastard children on the parish; disrespectful youths and apprentices shirking work and challenging authority. They viewed with a mixture of alarm and disgust the landless laborers and masterless men, mixed with impoverished Irish, Gypsies and other incomers and foreigners, who wandered in vagrant gangs through their towns and villages begging for food, searching for shelter. They were outraged by the law's failure to control thieves and robbers or punish wrongdoers with the severity their crimes merited. They wanted things settled and known.

For this new leaders were required, not the jumped-up, scandal-prone small men so indifferent to the breakdown of society and its values. And, in towns and parishes up and down the country, new men did indeed emerge as magistrates, mayors and aldermen, masters and governors. Inspired by Scripture, with a burning vision of a just, godly, disciplined community, they determined to uphold the law, reform the manners and habits of the poor, protect true religion, and maintain orthodoxy in thought and deed. They were often sincere, energetic and compassionate; they were also intolerant and merciless (their principles demanded no less). Their ideal was uniformity, and they brought to their great project fearsome dedication.

What follows is a fictionalized imagining of one such experiment in the remodeling of a community in the north of England in the early 1630s. I have seen no evidence to support the assertion that when history repeats itself it does so as farce. Tragedy, it seems, comes round again and again.

One

When the women found milk in her breasts, and other secret feminine tokens, Scaife, the constable's man, an archdolt, was dispatched across the windswept moors and icy mountains to fetch Mr. John Brigge, coroner in the wapentakes of Agbrigg and Morley.

Brigge was reluctant to answer the constable's summons. His wife was pregnant, she was bleeding, and the neighbors and gossips had been called. But the law is the law, duty is duty, and a man defrauds his own name if he but once neglects his office. And this was Brigge's office, his calling. The coroner went wherever there was a sudden or unnatural death, wherever there was a body to view.

A body, for his purposes, might be no more than a jawbone and a finger, or some parcels of rancid black meat worried up by the dogs. It might be a young man gored by a bull, his bowels hurled out, or a gummy old crone brought by despair to a rope fastened from the timbers of a barn. Or it might be, as it was in this case, a birth-smothered infant.

Brigge lived with signs and saints; they were everywhere in his life. To his mind nothing in the world was without signification: dreams were portents, phantoms real, and only a fool believed in such a thing as chance. He could not but note the nature of this particular sudden death coming as it did so soon upon his wife's confinement. Gazing at Elizabeth huddled by the fire with her maids and the women, whispers and slow gestures of care and comfort between them, he thought it a very ill omen. He went to the window and lit candles and there under his breath said a prayer in the name of the Father, the Son and the Holy Ghost, as his mother had taught him he should:

> *Whose candles burn clear and bright, a wondrous force and might,*
> *Does in these candles lie, which, if at any time they light,*
> *They sure believe that neither storm nor tempest dare abide,*
> *Nor thunder in the sky be heard, nor any devil spied,*
> *Nor fearful sprites that walk by night, nor hurt by frost and hail.*

John Brigge was of the old faith.

When he had said his prayer and completed his preparations, Brigge admonished Elizabeth's girl Dorcas to be assiduous about her mistress and do everything to be a good comfort to her, and of Mrs. Lacy, the wife of his neighbor, he begged the same. Then he went to his wife and slipped into her palm a little bottle of holy water so she might have consolation in the extremes of her labor. About her neck he hung three small eaglestones brought long ago by ancestors who had once traveled through the groves of Cyprus. Stones within stones, mass within mass. A body inside another body.

Brigge kissed his wife and said some tender things to her, that he did love her and that with Christ's mercy he would find her and their new child waiting on his return. Calling Adam, his clerk, from where the boy was mewed up in his chamber, he went to the stable and got ready the horses. The three men started on their way.

○ ○ ○

WINDS AND RAIN-WINDS raged around Brigge's lonely stone house. The land about was poor, that which was not marsh being nothing but cold moor, moss and stones exposed to hard frosts and biting winds. Little grew at the Winters. Brigge and his household depended on the black oats he sowed in the sloping field below the house and on the sheep and few cows he pastured on the stubble between harvest and spring planting. In years gone by he had had good profit by his wool and woolfells and tallow and grain.

His horse walked on and he took a last look over his estate. The wet snow raked them and foreboding welled up in his heart. Like all men facing uncertainty, he desperately wanted to know the future. He wanted to know how things would stand a year from now, in five years, ten. What was God's plan for him? He looked ceaselessly for signs and struggled with their meanings—a robin's return to a branch, the bud of a wildflower where none had grown before, the appearance of a strange dog with a walled blue eye. Signs might be hidden and hard to discern, and sometimes they are obvious and overlooked for trifles.

As they approached the high pass where the snow was thickest on the ground, the gray-white light began suddenly to fade as though a great shadow had crossed the face of the sun. The gloom continued its advance until it became quite dark. They dismounted, having no choice but to halt, for a blind foot in these breakneck mountains would certainly be fatal. All around them was silence and stillness, and the world began to be an empty, lost place. The horses became fearful and the men touched with trepidation and wonderment.

Scaife whispered that strange occurrences were now reported from all corners of the kingdom. His voice was credulous and fervid. Comets had been perceived in the skies and credible witnesses had seen monsters delivered to women at London, Devises, Newark and Carlisle. There were fluxes, inflammations and infirmities that men had never seen before and doctors could not cure. He and all who were his right religious friends feared all this prophesied nothing good to come, for the world was in confusion and chaos, and men said war would be the nation's fate as it was now in Germany, laid waste by the papist armies of emperor and pope.

As the darkness began again to give way to light, Brigge asked of the infant whose body he would shortly view, inquiring whether the child appeared to have come before its time. The dolt could not say and seemed to think the question a trick, regarding Brigge slyly with a stupid, popping fat blue eye. Brigge inquired of the one the constable had apprehended, taking her to be, as was the usual circumstance in these courses, a young girl who had consorted with a fellow servant, or with her master. He imagined her waiting for him already overcome by remorse of conscience, the Machine of the World collapsed and fallen in around her, her head dissolved to tears.

Scaife answered that this one was no girl but a full woman of thirty or more years who had come out of Ireland and that her name as she gave it was Katherine Shay. Her manner, Scaife continued, was not sorrowful in the least, but prideful and very brazen and uncontrite. What else could be expected from one such as she, he asked, singing the verse of the times, one of the horde of foreigners and idle wanderers and vagrants who plagued the good people of these parts like the locusts that descended on Egypt's corn?

Brigge, his heart sentimental and volatile as that of any man soon to be a father—and more quick to extremes and turns of emotion because this was Elizabeth's first conception to come to full term—listened with abhorrence, wondering what sort of woman this could be who had killed her child and yet did not repent. The coroner filled up with loathing and revulsion for Katherine Shay.

When they were able, they mounted their horses to go through the pass. Brigge's mare grew nervous. The declivities here were very sharp, the paths perpendicular, cracked and without integrity. Stones trickled treacherously away at the side with the sound of faint, descending notes, a frozen musicality. The horse snorted and strained against him.

Scaife looked back over his shoulder and said, "You shall not fall, your worship, if you are but brave."

For this, the coroner gave him the hard words that were his due and commanded the fool to get on. Brigge was not afraid of falling, but the foreboding he had experienced as he left the Winters now gathered into dread. He could not be sure of its causes—his fears for his wife, his horror at Katherine Shay, the storms around him or the black sky above—but the apprehension was strong in him that the summons he had answered this morning was already taking him further than was safe to go. He tried to pray and he thought of the candles in his house and this thought led him into a waking dream. He could see the candles very plainly, burning in the window, Elizabeth behind them, her face all deathly white. Then a huge gust came, the air was exploded and the flames snuffed out. Through the gloom he saw Elizabeth in her white winding sheet, hands crosswise on her breast, with rosemary and rue in her fingers. A bell tolled as Dorcas and the women watched her, she senseless and without motion, as still as the child beside her.

This vision passed before his eyes. There were shadows in the mist and the hairs on his arms and neck stood up.

⊙   ⊙   ⊙

THEY DESCENDED TO the new bridge. There was no settlement on the wastes on either side of the river, nor even a cottage, but they came upon a band of beggars dragging furze bushes and stones to a clearing where they had erected one cabin of scratches and were beginning a second. There were some women—some young, some old—and a scattering of children, pallid and dirty, two or three with miserable, deformed limbs and dropsy bellies. Seeing the coroner, they became still as stones and watched warily, dogs disturbed in stealing scraps.

Ten or a dozen more strangers, several armed with swords and staves and carrying the marks of a recent fight on their necks and faces, came up from the direction of the town. Brigge demanded of the company who they were and what they were about, but they gave him only the usual high, pelting speeches of wanderers and vagrants. The coroner spurred his horse into their midst, knocking one to the ground and others out of the way, and then they were all *your honor this* and *your honor that*, pleading they had nowhere to go and in any case dare not attempt to travel further because the country people hereabouts had offered them violence.

Only one stood his ground, forward and dauntless. He wore dirty black breeches and a torn gray coat. His hair was black and unkempt and his broad, open face streaked with dirt and blood. The coroner demanded to know his name and he said he was called Exley. He and his companions had gone to the town to solicit relief, as he alleged, but the tocsin had been sounded and they were driven off with blows and abuse.

A tall, lame, wasted man with blains and sores covering his head in a great disease stumbled in front of Brigge's horse. He stretched out a bony hand, the long fingers gloved in soot and filth.

"A halfpenny, your honor," the diseased one begged, "to buy some corn."

"You are in unlawful occupation of this land," the coroner said. "You must move on."

"We are Englishmen," Exley said, "and must live somewhere."

The coroner dug his spurs into the horse's flanks and rode over to Adam and Scaife, who surveyed the disreputable company with expressions of contempt.

Brigge led them on. The hour was getting late.

The black moor stretched before them, disappearing into a dark gray wash that might have been sky or sea or the ends of the earth. The snow continued to fall, but here it did not lie. The moor was vast, malevolent and borderless, and it claimed the water for itself, for the freezing black pools into which, in time, dogs and lambs and even men and their horses would innocently stray, slide and drown. The road was mud, stones and water.

Two

THEY CAME INTO THE TOWN OVER CLARKE BRIDGE AND SKELDER Gate where the watch challenged Brigge most uncivilly, without regard for his person or rank. The coroner demanded to know their names and said they should answer for their impertinence. To which they replied that the times were dangerous and they were doing no more than their duty, being commanded to stop all who came into the town, though they be coroners, governors or lords. To add to their insolence they gave their names, shouting them out and repeating them provokingly one after the other.

They continued on their way, passing kindling-sellers and carters bent into the wind and a swineherd herding his red barrow hogs. Brigge stared up at the dark windows of the pretty Church of St. John. The gargoyles grinned back at him, their faces full of sour hilarity; the rainwater in their throats was mocking laughter. Near the woolshops he stopped to buy a small parcel of figs and raisins from a petty chapman come from Hull on his way to Manchester. A present for Elizabeth. Little surprises like this never failed to delight his wife, and his heart lifted momentarily at the thought of her receiving them. They turned up Crown Street toward Gibbet Lane, where the gibbet stood on its solemn stone plinth.

⊙   ⊙   ⊙

AHEAD WERE THE high walls of the House of Correction, built two years ago to mark the coming into power of the Master and governors. It stood with imposing solidity, three stories high and thirty yards long, a simple, regular building of dark stone hewn from the local mountains and dressed by the town's masons. The governors' emblem of bay-laurel was inscribed at the four corners of the façade.

Occupying the upper two stories were the inmates, God's poor and the Devil's: vagrants and rogues and other notorious persons of disordered habits, as well the blind and maimed, the aged and decrepit, the weak widow and young orphan, those past their labor and those before it. It was both symbol and seat of the Saints who had begun the great project to bring light where there was darkness, order where there was chaos, discipline where looseness and vileness flourished. The austere arched entrance through which the coroner passed was crowned by an escutcheon bearing the legend: *And when was sin more plentiful?* It was presented not as speculation, but apodixis: it was now a universal truth that scruple was past and this was the darkest age.

The ground floor, divided by a broad stone staircase, had at the north end a hall for the holding of courts and sessions, and, on the opposing side of the stairs, a smaller chamber in which the Master and governors met to order the town's regulation and work the reformation of its people. This room was bare but for a long, simple joined table and the chairs around it. The walls were unadorned, the ceiling low, and the polished floorboards gleamed in the candlelight.

Brigge took off his gloves and cloak, pinched the breeches from his numbed thighs and went to warm himself by the hearth. The Holy Book stood propped on a stand, opened at the thirteenth chapter of Paul's letter to the Corinthians, as the Master had prescribed it should to remind them that besides justice they were also to be compassionate: *Charity suffereth long, and is kind; charity envieth not; charity vaunteth not itself, is not puffed up.* Charity and justice—these were the governors' business, the chief business and eternal ambition of all good government since the time of Solomon, tipping sometimes one way in the balance, then in the other, but always in good government finding eventual, approximate correspondence. Darkness gathered at the windows.

The constable came in. Doliffe and Brigge were fellow governors but their greeting was stiff with strained politeness.

"We have not seen enough of you these three months past, Mr. Brigge," Doliffe said. "It is almost as if you had banished yourself into exile."

There was good nature in the constable's tone, but it was counterfeit. He was a man of peevish temper and little moment, one who imagined himself unjustly disparaged by all, including the coroner. His imaginings had made him close and reserved, and quick to discover insults where none was intended.

"I live remote from the rest of you," Brigge answered, deploying the same false lightness. "I do apologize."

The constable made a little forced laugh. Brigge closed his eyes in gratitude for the fire. The heat began to warm the backs of his legs and creep up through his buttocks. The winter had been hard and he had ridden little. His thighs were sore and the lower part of his back stiff. The thick smells of damp wool and wet horse and wet leather rose to his nostrils.

He was about to ask of Katherine Shay and the business of the dead child, but Doliffe put in first, "I understand you were stopped by the watch."

"Their manner was most zealous," Brigge said.

"They are required to be zealous," Doliffe answered with a thin smile. "You have not been to town for some space of time and may therefore be unaware of the difficulties we face. In spite of our labors, the people are grown wild and loose in their morals and occupy themselves in broils and disturbances. We have seen rioting and disorder in our streets. Only last market day some women of the baser sort attacked the corn merchants and overturned their carts. A great deal of grain was stolen."

"Corn is scarce," Brigge said, "and dear."

"And then there are the vagrants," Doliffe continued, "swarms of them, threatening to beggar us all. Only a few hours ago a desperate band came and threatened to fire the town before they were driven off by the watch." Brigge thought of Exley and the squatters at the vagrant camp. "I have to tell you, Mr. Brigge," Doliffe went on, "that the neighbors are frightened out of their wits. Already some of the better sort have left. They say we tax them but do not protect them. I wonder: are they wrong? Can we say we have done right by our best inhabitants?"

The constable peered at Brigge in expectation of a response.

"I am sure there is in this, as in all things, room for improvement," the coroner said eventually.

"Indeed," Doliffe said; then added, as though in afterthought, "You should know, Mr. Brigge, that your absence from our meetings has given rise to some comment."

"I hope the reasons for my absence have not been misunderstood. As you know, my wife is with child and her pregnancy has been difficult."

The constable made some broad sounds to convey sympathy. "Some men attract speculation, it is inherent in them," he said. "One man goes about his business completely unremarked while his brother attaches every kind of rumor for doing no more than the same—it cannot be avoided. Some murmur that you have become disaffected with the rigorous and scrutinous work we do here."

"They have no reason to harbor such thoughts," Brigge said. "I have always been, and will always remain, the Master's faithful follower."

"What the governors, and many of the better sort of townspeople too, begin to doubt—forgive me if I speak freely, Mr. Brigge—is your continued devotion to the great project on which we are embarked. Unfortunately, the addiction to sin and delinquency remains as general as ever it was. We thought to cure it by charity. We must now accept that our remedy was insufficient. If we are to save the town, we must be unsparing in the execution of justice. We must be a sore scourge and sharp whip of evildoers, wherever we find them."

The refrain of the times, the foot of the song that all now sang. Brigge knew the words; every man knew them. How honest men lived in fear and their labors went unrewarded while thieves and rogues prospered. How pity and charity had enervated the poor. Sin in all its forms lurked in the imagination: theft, fornication, drunkenness, murder, rape, the immutable disorders of the poor, the multiple threats to life, property, chastity and good religion.

"But I am keeping you from your business, Mr. Coroner," Doliffe said. "You will not find the matter difficult. The woman's guilt is very apparent and will be easily proved."

Brigge thanked the constable curtly for his observations.

"I shall wait for you in the sessions hall," Doliffe said through pursed lips. "The jurymen and witnesses are ready."

Brigge stayed by the fire though the heat had begun to scorch the backs of his thighs. He remembered as a child his mother scolding him for standing so close to the hearth, saying he would catch fire and burn like a torch, like the saints and martyrs of the holy church. Rapt by the flames, he ignored her. Eventually, his mother lost patience and snatched him away. She held him fast by his thin wrists and beat him once or twice with light strokes. "What would have happened to you," she chided him, "had I not taken you from the fire?" She shook her son for an answer. "Would you have the flames consume you?" He had no answer then, and none now. He looked down at the firedogs and tongs and stretched out a hand toward the flames and wondered at the glory of immolation. He recalled the embrace of his mother's arms, his head pulled to her breast. Brigge had always had a sense of the abyss.

He roused himself from his brooding. The witnesses and jurors were waiting, and so was Katherine Shay, who had murdered her child.

Three

THE SESSIONS HALL HAD THE BITTER FRIGIDITY OF BARE STONE
walls in a perpetual winter. The Master and governors had executed much
justice here, examined and corrected a multitude of delinquents. Some
they punished severely; others they showed compassion. Katherine Shay
would be among the punished. Murdering mothers could have no mercy.
That was the law.

The coroner looked over the prisoner. She flickered momentarily but
faced him without sign of fear. There was no beauty in the Irishwoman,
but there was an obvious if jaded carnality. Her body, no longer young,
was strong-shouldered and full enough in the breast and hips. Her hair, all
loose about the ears, was dark with some red in it, and her long face had
been grimed and blushed by the sun and wind. Her clothes had once great
color—red and green and orange-tawny—but now were faded and smelt
of human stains; she appeared *used*. A perfect barn whore, a hedge whore,
the very image of a sinner. A knowing sinner. An undone and lascivious
sinner. To the men who were gathered to witness her destruction, it was a
concoction to excite their imaginations. And among the women there was
a spleen against her, a particular contempt for the unrestraint written into
her body and bearing.

Adam set about the preparation of his parchments and pens but little escaped the boy's notice, and he was especially vigilant of the things between men and women. He noted the momentary hesitation in the coroner as Brigge took in the woman and perceived the lusts lurking within her and responded to them, fleetingly, ineluctably. Adam had coral lips and a cold eye.

At one end of the long oak bench was a bundle of soiled kersey cloth. Inside would be the infant's body. Brigge's fears resurfaced. He could not escape the thought that the coincidence of this life snuffed out and the imminence of Elizabeth's delivery had a meaning intended for him, that this life and the life of his unborn child were connected in a symmetry. Under his breath he prayed to the mother of God to intercede for his wife.

> *Good Mary, Christ's mother,*
> *Mary mild, of thee I mean.*
> *You bore my Lord, you bore my brother,*
> *You bore a lovely child and clean.*

"Sir?"

> *Virgin before childbirth,*
> *Virgin in childbirth,*
> *Virgin after childbirth.*
> *Fount of mercy,*
> *Mother of orphans,*
> *Consolation of the desolate . . .*

"Mr. Brigge?"
The voice was Adam's.
"Will you not begin the inquisition?"
The coroner dragged himself out of his thoughts. They were waiting, all of them. The jurors and the witnesses, impatient to hear the story of this sinner and wretch, of the child conceived in the sinful enjoyment of her woman's wantonness and murdered in the shame of it. The women searchers of Shay's body, good and sufficient matrons with their stiff,

reproving necks and their milky fingers. Doliffe, prim and thin-lipped. Scaife, slavering and foaming like a run-out horse, unable to take his eyes from the Irishwoman. The more Brigge felt their expectation, the less his appetite for the work at hand. He felt suddenly weary. His clothes were still damp. His thighs and back ached. He shifted forward, straightening his shoulders to ease the discomfort.

He turned to the prisoner. She was unsteady on her feet, having exhausted her natural strength in childbirth, Brigge assumed. He motioned to the constable's man to bring up a little plain matted chair. The Irishwoman took the opportunity to sit. She gave no sign of gratitude.

"What is your name?" the coroner asked.

The Irishwoman said nothing. The scratch of Adam's pen was the only sound in the hall. Brigge repeated the question and asked if she understood what was asked of her. She gave no answer and looked away with an air of boredom. Brigge put the question again, making his voice round and frank to convey the power he had over her.

She said at last, "My name is none of your business."

Her accent was unfamiliar and outlandish. The jurymen inclined their heads to consult each other and, as comprehension seeped in, a slow murmur went up.

"I am Mr. John Brigge," the coroner said when he had worked through her words. "I am coroner in these wapentakes and a governor of this town. You must answer me. Is your name Katherine Shay?"

"If you say it is, then it is."

"Never mind what I say—"

"I do not mind what you say."

Brigge had come across defiance before in prisoners, though not often and then usually only after heads had been fuddled with drink: clear heads apprehended terror clearly. But as he studied Katherine Shay, the coroner saw something more than contumacy. He saw she had a perfect understanding of what was required of her, that she play her part. It was no more than was required of any prisoner. The thief, the murderer, the robber—all who go on trial and offer up lie after blatant lie to save their lives are playing their part. The magistrate has as much need of their desperate inventions, their evasions and despairing bluster as he does of the prison, the stocks, the whip, the pillory and the gibbet. A lie acknowledges the law the liar has broken; it is pleasing to the magistrate's ear. Katherine Shay knew what was required of her and withheld it. Prideful, brazen and uncontrite, Scaife had said of her, and for once Brigge could not fault the fool.

"Be careful how you answer me," he said slowly and deliberately. "These proceedings are to determine the truth of this charge of murder. If the jurors find that you have murdered your child, an indictment will be returned against you and you will be kept in safe custody to await the next assizes. Do you understand me? Your life depends on what is proved here tonight."

"I know the truth of the matter and so does our Father in heaven—that is enough for me."

"But not enough for this inquisition," Brigge said sharply, "to which you owe obedience."

"I owe nothing to this inquisition or to you," she said with a careless shrug.

Her words echoed in far corners of the hall as whispering interpreters went to work, repeating and amplifying her provocations.

Perhaps encouraged by the repetition of her defiance, she launched into vaporing and ranting: "I say I owe nothing to any court or any pretended power or magistrate put over me," she shouted. "I say I owe obedience to no one on this earth."

The sessions hall erupted in outrage. Some jeered, some hawked and spat on the ground. Brigge shouted at the prisoner to be quiet, but she would not be shut up. This was defiance as Brigge had not heard it before. Incendiary notions are not uncommon among the ignorant sort of people, but they are generally whispered behind the backs of the hand. Perhaps the woman's mind had been deranged in childbirth. He signaled to Doliffe who came up and bent to his ear.

"Fetch the bridle if you please, Mr. Doliffe," the coroner said.

The constable received his instruction with an expression of earnest approval and went off with a quick step.

The Irishwoman continued to rail and taunt while those in the hall jibed and derided her. Brigge no longer heard what was said. He took the bundle of dirty cloth and began to open it. As he did so, the Irishwoman began to falter and her tormentors too began to fall silent.

◎　　◎　　◎

THE INFANT HAD not been washed and the coarse kersey stuck in places. The coroner picked it carefully away to reveal what appeared to be a full-formed male child. He had known it would be a boy, as his own child would be. Since conception, Elizabeth's right breast had grown bigger than the left, her right pulse quicker, right eye brighter; her urine had a reddish tinge. In her womb was a son and here was a son. To Brigge's providential mind, the symmetry was undeniable.

The prisoner was quiet now, a wary look in her eye. The coroner came up to her and raised the bundle to her eyes. The tumult from the hall had subsided; the silence was complete and expectant.

"Is this your child?" he asked quietly.

The Irishwoman said nothing.

"Surely you who have so much to say on magistracy and obedience can answer a simple question: is this your child?"

Katherine Shay turned her face aside. Brigge gazed down at the tiny body in his arms and became lost in the contemplation of it. The long trunk and helpless short legs; the wrinkled, unfilled bottom; the cord, gray, viscose, obscene and wilted, hanging from the empty belly. There seemed too much skin for the body; only the hands and feet appeared full. These were quite livid. The little finger of the left hand was crooked as though caught in a deliberate gesture of the utmost delicacy. The fine black hair was plastered forward to the skull with dried dark blood and other filth. Brigge could not bring himself to look at the eyes. In the brief life the child had known (minutes? hours?) what had those eyes seen? A mother lying in her bed, blood between her legs, breast rising with hard breaths, eyes fixed on the ceiling. And, determining what was to be done, propping herself up, weak and giddy but with strength enough to wrench the bolster from behind her shoulders. Did Katherine Shay hold the child?

Did she kiss him and cry before she covered the mouth and nose? What expression had the child seen on his mother's face then, before the bolster came down?

"Look at this," the coroner said, holding out the dead infant to its mother. "Have you no pity?"

"Who are you to talk of pity?" the Irishwoman snapped back. "You whip and prison and hang—and you talk to me of pity?"

"These punishments we inflict are prescribed by law and ordained by God."

"When Jesus sent his apostles into the world, did he order them to whip the backs of the poor and stretch their necks in nooses?"

"Enough!" Brigge shouted. "None of this has anything to do with your crime!"

"*Be harmless as doves,* that is what Jesus said!"

The coroner could have struck her; he was light-headed with rage. "Who are you to talk of doves?" he said coldly.

He turned and motioned to Doliffe, who came forward with the bridle. A cage for the head, a stone in weight, black-painted hoops of iron in the shape of a helmet. Brigge looked at the protrusion of spiked metal attached to the inner part of one of the lower bands, the bit that would stop Shay's tongue. He had seen women retch and vomit when the bit was forced into their mouths and the bridle locked in place. He had seen smashed teeth and broken jaws and gashed lips and gums.

The coroner nodded and Doliffe and Scaife set about their work. The prisoner swore at them, in English and in her own language, calling them dogs, rogues and hypocrites. Scaife pinioned her arms while Doliffe took hold of her hair and pulled forward until she was on her knees. Shay fought and screamed, but the men overwhelmed her and soon she was wailing pitifully. Brigge replaced the dead baby on the bench. When he turned back to Shay, the bridle and bit were in place. There was blood on her mouth.

"Breathe through your nose and try to be calm," Brigge told her, "else you will choke and die."

⊙   ⊙   ⊙

THE CORONER CALLED for water to clean the infant. Inviting the jurymen to come forward to view the body, he lifted the right hand to the candlelight to show them there were nails on the fingers. There was no obvious wound or observable bruise. He searched the skull with his fingertips and announced that to his judgment it appeared unbroken.

He next took informations from the matrons and midwives who said on their oaths that the Irishwoman known as Katherine Shay had used very vile provoking language when the constable brought her to them and had offered them violence and threatened to crack their heads. By the constable's order they subdued her and examined her body and found the breasts were hard and tender and, when squeezed, produced the milk that comes in the first days after birth. By these intimate signs and others they had when they examined her further in her privy parts, they were certain she had recently given birth.

As to the dead infant, the child was whole and fair-seeming, and, to their thinking, had not come before its time. It was their belief that Katherine Shay had by some means murdered the child—though by what means did not appear to them—and, no women having been called to assist her at her delivery, her intention must have been to conceal the birth and wickedly do away with the baby.

The coroner asked if Shay had, in their hearing, confessed or said anything that might be taken as an admission of guilt. They conceded she had not, though from their pauses and the looks they gave, it was clear they wished their answers might have been otherwise.

Throughout their evidence Shay sat slumped in the chair, her head lolling forward under the great weight of the iron cage, which she did her best to support with her hands. Blood dribbled from the corners of her mouth to her chin and dripped to her lap and the floor. She whimpered from time to time.

The coroner next examined Quirke, keeper of the Painted Hand, the tippling-house near Bull Green where the dead child had been discovered. It was a place of very ill repute, suspected of bawdry and notorious for the thieves who haunted it.

"When Shay came to lodge at your house, did you see that she was pregnant?" Brigge asked.

"To tell the truth, your honor, I did not pay close attention to her, except that she seemed very weary and carried a flasket before her and could have been pregnant for all I know," Quirke answered.

"How did you come upon the body?" Brigge asked. His gaze was trained not on the witness but on the crudely swaddled corpse.

"It was not I who discovered the child," Quirke said, "but my serving girl Susana Horton who, while about her work, came upon the body hidden in a cupboard among some old clothes."

"She is here, this Susana?"

"No, your honor. She is gone to Burnsall."

Brigge looked up sharply. "Did you not tell the girl that she would be required here to give her evidence?"

"I did not know to tell her, your honor," Quirke said, "never having had before the like occurrence in my house."

"Why has Susana gone to Burnsall?"

"To help her sister there, your honor, whose husband suffers from a shaking palsy."

The coroner dismissed the man and called Doliffe forward to give his information. The constable took his oath on the Holy Evangelist, his high, light voice straining to convey the special sincerity he had for scripture, truth and the responsibilities of his office. He said on oath that the first he knew of the matter was when Quirke came to him with the body and told him of the Irishwoman who had left her lodgings at the Painted Hand. After he inquired of some townsmen and received intelligences from them, the constable set out on the road to Rochdale and, about five miles from the town, following her tracks in the snow, found Shay hiding under a hedge, and there apprehended her on suspicion of infanticide, brought her back prisoner and sent his man to fetch the coroner. Although his evidence could not have been more straightforward, Doliffe delivered it with pedantry, picking his words with exaggerated care and, like a scholar, correcting Brigge on trivial points of detail.

"Did you speak with the serving girl Susana Horton?"

"I spoke to her briefly."

"Did you tell her she would be called to give evidence at this inquisition?"

The constable shot him an indignant look. "I did not consider her evidence to be necessary, the prisoner's guilt being so plain."

"The necessity of her evidence is for me to decide," Brigge said, dismissing the constable. He took some moments to consider the matter. At last he announced he would adjourn the proceedings until Susana Horton was brought back from Burnsall, when the jurors and witnesses would again be required to give their attendance.

Doliffe strode forward and leaned toward the coroner. His voice was low and angry. "What do you mean by this, sir?"

"I mean to see justice done," Brigge answered, "as best I am able."

"Then send this tinker's drab to be hanged," Doliffe said. "You have heard what the women searchers had to say, what Quirke said. You heard my evidence. The jury will send Shay for trial. They need no more convincing."

"No doubt in time she will be hanged," Brigge said, "but that time is not come yet, nor will it until Susana Horton is produced before me. If you would be so kind as to send to Burnsall for her, I would be most obliged."

Doliffe turned and left the sessions hall, watched in silence by the jurymen and the witnesses.

The coroner made orders to have Shay detained in the jail and for the release of her child's body for burial in the grave that had already been made for it outside the church grounds.

⊙ ⊙ ⊙

WHEN THE HALL WAS cleared, the coroner ordered Scaife to remove the bridle and fetch some drinking water. Shay bent forward and vomited some foul stuff which a dog, being by, it lapped up. Brigge kicked the animal and it ran off yelping.

"Hear me, mistress. This is not a simple homicide for which your life might be spared," Brigge explained. "Your crime falls under the statute which was brought in to prevent the murder of bastard children. If you are innocent, you must say so or you will be hanged."

"I did not murder my child," Shay said thickly, dabbing fingertips to her bloody mouth.

Again, Brigge had to work at the strange inflections in her words. When he had them understood, he said, "You acknowledge the child is yours?"

"I did not murder my child and I shall not suffer for something I have not done."

Scaife entered with a cup of water, which Shay accepted with trembling hands. When she had taken her refreshment, the coroner ordered her escorted upstairs to be held with the other prisoners. In due course the coroner would reconvene the inquest jury to hear Susana Horton's evidence. The jurors would find that Katherine Shay had done away with her child. She would then be received into custody until she was produced for trial at the next assizes. If she survived her time as prisoner, she would be led to the bar and the charge put to her. She would make her plea, the witnesses would be heard, the trial jury would convict her and the judge condemn her. Katherine Shay would die on the gallows. There could be no doubt as to the outcome.

Brigge found Adam waiting outside the House of Correction. He put his arm across the boy's narrow shoulders and walked with him toward the Lion, where they usually lodged when in town. Two jurymen passed them and muttered under their breath as they went. The Irishwoman was guilty, they said, and justice had been mocked and abused again as it was daily by those in authority who cared not a fig for the wronged.

"Did you see the blue ribbons in their hats?" Adam said as they went on. Brigge turned back to look. "There were others in the hall—men and women—also wearing them."

"A new fashion, perhaps," Brigge suggested.

"Will you need me tonight?" Adams said. "I would like to visit my friends in the town."

"Which friends are these?"

Adam mumbled the names of some youths. They meant nothing to Brigge. Adam was not inclined to be forthcoming. Brigge became aware of the stiffness in the boy's shoulder and removed his hand.

"Do not stay out late," Brigge said. "We must start back for the Winters at first light."

They walked on in silence, Brigge snatching glances of the boy as they went. The coroner saw him then as he had seen him twelve years before, when Adam had come to the Winters an orphaned scholar from the free school, a reticent intruder in the world. Drilled by his teachers in deference and by the hard life he had lived in caution, he was like a puppy that did not know if it was to be fed or kicked.

They came to the Lion. Brigge wished Adam a pleasant time with his friends. He himself had business elsewhere.

Four

THE FIRST STAIRCASE LED TO THE ANGEL AND, OFF A SMALL
landing, to the Canary, the Star and Columbine chambers. They were all
large rooms, each decorated in the motif of its name, with comfortable beds
of down, upholstered chairs and Turkey-worked cushions and carpets.

Brigge came to the Dolphin, the most luxurious of the Swan's apart-
ments. A servant brought him to the fire and offered him refreshment,
explaining that the Master was in conference with a visitor. Brigge asked
for bread and cheese, and settled down to wait in one of the armchairs on
either side of the mullioned window. Embellished on the walls were
handsome pintados of dolphins, galleons and legends of the sea. There
were sweet herbs to scent the air. From an adjoining room came the
lulling murmur of men's voices. Brigge imagined Elizabeth in labor,
pretty Dorcas at her side, Mrs. Lacy and the neighbors all busy about
her, the midwife whispering encouragements, plying her with pennyroyal
and rue. At the far end of the room was a bed with bed-steps up to it, its
posts intricately fretted, the canopy and valance colored in jacinth, mul-
berry and jade, and embroidered with mermaids and figures of Poseidon
and Amphitrite, and Triton and his shells. In the sumptuousness of his
surroundings, Brigge could imagine sweet things. He saw Elizabeth
lying beside their baby son. He would love this child, of that he had no

doubt. But would he provide for him? The fees the coroner claimed brought small gain: a mark for every inquest held on view of a body slain. A mark also in cases of *felo-de-se;* nothing for deaths by misadventure or visitation of God. This year, with God's grace, his land would flourish. This year he would buy marl and lime, and when the snows cleared he would see his fields properly graved for planting. He would hire a looker to watch his sheep for the rot and the turn and to guard against dogs and thieves.

A glowing coal suddenly tumbled from the fire to the floor. Brigge leaped to his feet but the manservant was quicker, a good servant indeed, on the lookout always for the safety of his master's property. He snatched up the tongs, dropped the coal in the hearth and, stooping, inspected the scorch marks on the floor.

Brigge sat back in the chair. His eyes grew heavy.

☺   ☺   ☺

HIS DREAMS TOOK their own course. They led him to a rich city he had never seen before. He stood outside the walls, and a procession of the great men of the place came through the gate to meet him. The greatest among them came forward and, while the others of the procession watched, held up a key for Brigge and with tearful entreaties begged him to accept it, which Brigge denied to do. This great man then threw the key to the ground, bowed gravely, took out his knife and cut his own wrists and, having done so, sat down in the dirt to bleed. The procession clapped courteously. Brigge stepped over the cadaver and, ignoring the key, entered at the gate. In the market square he found a long table set out with roasted capons and boar's heads, souse and apples, plums and cheese, and great quantities of beer and wine. But when Brigge sat down at the head of the table and invited those about to partake in the feast, he saw that none of the great men of the city had come with him to the meal. Instead came forward lepers and beggars and strumpets and the very worst-conditioned sort of people. A woman came to sit next to Brigge.

"Eat," the woman said. "Eat."

She tore at the loaves with bleeding fingers and offered Brigge to eat.

He gazed at her stubbed fingers and at the meal of bloody bread she held
out for him to take.

◦   ◦   ◦

BRIGGE BECAME AWARE of the Master standing before him. He got to
his feet, drowsy and dazed, his senses disordered.

"John, John!" the Master was saying. He cleaved the coroner to him
and kissed him. "It is so long since I have seen you. I am sorry to have
kept you waiting."

The Master repeated the apology twice more and begged Brigge's forgiveness, though this was all unnecessary. He had won the good will of
many in the town with the courtesy he used to speak to every man. He was,
for one of his years, unusually ceremonious. He indicated his visitor—Dr.
Favour. The vicar was tall, broad-shouldered, pale in the face and strong
and straight-backed. His hair was the color of dark amber, and his mouth
also reddish for being scarred with harelip. Brigge was disappointed to
find the vicar here, for he wanted his friend to himself. He and Brigge
saluted each other like hollow men, their insincerity equal.

Favour asked about the inquisition. "An Irish vagrant, I understand?"

"It seems so, from her speech at least," Brigge replied. "She has said
nothing about herself, not even to confirm her name."

"Has she confessed her crime?"

"She has not."

"But there is other evidence against her?"

"There is a great deal against her," Brigge said.

"Yes, I have heard the evidence against her was strong," the vicar said.

Favour gave him a straight look. Vagrants did these things. The Irish
did these things. Brutality was expected. How could it not be so? They
were ignorant of the Word. They had no Luther, Calvin or Melanchthon
to guide them to salvation. Katherine Shay was a vagrant, a foreigner. She
lived as the beasts live, without enlightenment. She murdered her child.
There could be no doubt about it.

"The Irishwoman is a papist, I take it?" Favour asked.

The implication hung in the air with the question. The coroner had shown partiality to a fellow Romanist. Brigge thought for a moment the Master might intervene in his behalf, but he did not.

"I did not ask," Brigge said.

Favour allowed a short silence to mark his surprise.

"Did you examine the prisoner as to what knowledge she has touching the strangers who have been lately seen in these parts?"

"Which strangers are these?" Brigge asked.

"You have not heard, sir, that there are horsemen who go by night, armed with cutlasses and muskets?"

"I have heard rumors of these, nothing more."

"They are no rumors, Mr. Coroner, but verified as true reports. You did not think to question the prisoner about them?"

"In what particular?" Brigge asked.

"Whether they be Frenchmen or Spaniards, sir," Favour answered coldly, "or soldiers come from Ireland, or traitors from within the kingdom."

"I had no reason to think she might have information concerning horsemen of any kind," Brigge said, his voice stretched as his patience. "My concern was with the dead child she is alleged to have murdered."

"Yet for all your concern you were apparently unable to conclude the inquisition?"

"An important witness was unavailable," the coroner said curtly.

The Master said, "I am sure Mr. Brigge will conclude proceedings with all possible speed as soon as he is able. I myself will speak with the constable and have him closely question the prisoner to discover what she knows of any horsemen."

"The lives and freedom of those who walk in the truth depend on it," Favour said.

The vicar took his leave and went out of the room.

"What madness is this?" Brigge said as soon as Favour was gone. He looked to the Master, expecting him perhaps to roll his eye or give a weary shrug, a politician obliged for the sake of quiet to indulge the powerful in their rantings but now free to express his true opinion. But the Master's reply was solemn and without the easy affability Brigge was used to in his old friend.

"You have been remote and cut off from us, John," he said. "There are things you do not know."

The Master smiled to soften the harshness of what he had just said and led Brigge by arm to the table where servants were already setting out plates of mutton, pork and eggs, and carbonados and a shield of brawn daubed with mustard. Brigge insisted that all he wanted was bread and cheese. His host waved away his protestations.

"You look tired, John," he said as they took their seats.

Brigge had thought the same of the Master, how he had aged in the months since he had seen him. Though his smile was still ready, the exhaustion was apparent in the eyes: the left was quite normal, but the other seemed to belong to another, older, more discouraged man. His shoulders were rounded, his hair thinning at the front.

"I was beginning to wonder if you would ever come to town again," the Master said. "You received my letters?"

"I should have responded," Brigge said. "I am sorry."

The Master's voice took on a more serious tone: "I wondered if I had offended you."

"No."

"As Master I am forever giving offense. I seem to disappoint so many."

Brigge took some mutton and drank his beer; it was as clear and fine in color as old Alsatian wine.

"I know there are those who harbor suspicions of me," the Master was saying. "They say I am impatient, that I am ambitious, that I am contriving to concentrate all authority into my own hands. I am sure you have heard these things said."

"I have heard some talk of it."

The Master seemed dispirited by Brigge's admission though he had solicited it. He exhaled heavily and held his hands out.

"I am Master, first among the governors. I do as my office requires. I have no ambition for anything other than the good government of the town and the reformation of its people. Those who allege otherwise forge pretexts for faction and sedition." He smiled wanly before continuing, "If I have offended you, John, you know how sincerely I would regret it. I hope you will not keep yourself distant from us again for so long. Tell me, how is Elizabeth? The child is due soon?"

Brigge told him of Elizabeth's condition and how he had left her this morning. They ate and talked of their homes and wives. The Master had no children. His wife had never conceived. Doctors and physicians had plied her with remedies for her condition but with no success.

"She suffers vehemently with pains every month before her purgation," the Master confided. "She believes herself to be barren, and in believing makes herself so. Gladness is fertilizing, and too much care has the opposite effect."

"This land is hard," Brigge said. "It is not fertilizing."

"Yet Elizabeth conceived, with God's grace."

With God's grace and the intervention of a friend of Mrs. Lacy's who made a poultice for Elizabeth of strong herbs and butter and earth, and directed Brigge to press the stinking pad on Elizabeth's naked belly and to say seven Hail Marys and three Our Fathers in honor of God and the Holy Trinity, and then would Elizabeth conceive. Brigge said nothing of this to the Master, who would condemn it as magic and blasphemy and Romish superstition. And yet it succeeded; Elizabeth became pregnant and there was no miscarrying.

The Master stared at the pintados and decorations. "I will have no children now," he said.

Until their talk of wives and conceptions Brigge felt he had been watching a performance of friendship. The Master had spoken with respect and courtesy enough but with nothing like their former free familiarity. The sudden sincerity with which he spoke of his childlessness gave Brigge hopes that he would drop this enforced ceremony. But then the servants came in again to bring them fricassees and quelquechoses. Like Caesar, the Master ever kept a good board. The food was excellent, but the opportunity for intimacy was lost.

"We must talk," the Master said when the servants left them.

Brigge knew their discourse would not be of secret fears and hopes. He had long before now seen in his host the unmistakable signs of a hot friend cooling.

Five

WHAT MAKES A MAN A LEADER? NO ONE WHO KNEW NATHANIEL
Challoner as a young man, least of all John Brigge, foresaw the extraordinary career of his middle years. As a young man, he was no great scholar but
was pleasant and sociable enough among his friends, and seemed without
great ambition or thought of how to advance himself beyond the ordinary.
Certainly, Brigge had no inkling of the prodigious qualities others later came
to admire in him. When as youths he and Challoner rode out together over
the moors, when they climbed the fells and swam in the rivers, Brigge
thought he was watching someone little different than himself.

But then the flower began its spectacular bloom. Once Challoner
entered Middle Temple and was called to the bar, his rise was swift,
assisted by his oratory and his patrons at court. Many predicted he would
advance to lord keeper or lord chancellor, that high office was his for the
asking. Yet at the very height of his renown in London, he suddenly gave
up his pursuit of honor to return to the town of his birth, where Lord Savile's harsh rule was notorious throughout the country.

The young lawyer who came to visit the Winters on his homecoming
was a magnificent sight. Tall and straight, with dark hair and dark eyes, he
was dressed in a grave black suit of the best broadcloth, with white bands
and cuffs. He was much loved by the women in the house. The kitchen

maids fussed about him, and Brigge's mother enjoyed the opportunity to talk of religion with so heartfelt and learned a listener. Challoner always listened respectfully, and for a time Brigge's mother had hopes of his conversion. Brigge did not. It was not that he doubted his friend's sincerity, but he knew how Challoner hated to make an enemy. With passions running high about so many things—the town's government, the king and parliament, heresy and good doctrine, law and disorder, war and invasion—men were accustomed to hearing opinions delivered like volleys of musket fire. All the world was set to argue, men to fall about each other's ears at the slightest provocation. Men took their stand at the drop of a hat and bellowed they could do no other; opponents were enemies, and argument, conducted with one hand on the hilt of a sword, was the surest way to know the truth: the feeling for dispute had asserted itself over the instinct for settlement.

But Challoner knew how to listen, this was his gift. Brigge's mother was not alone in having hopes of him. In those days, before he entered into power, every person with whom he held conversation came away with their own expectations; Brigge sometimes looked at his friend and wondered who he was. Yet Challoner was loyal. When Brigge's mother was on her deathbed and no one dared come to the house of so notorious a recusant, Challoner came, and he came not in secret but said openly that he was going to see old Mrs. Brigge. The ancient woman, death in her face, was lifted up and brought to the fire, the heat a comfort to that poor little old body. "Beware of rising too high," she whispered to Challoner. "Be content with what God has lent you." It was as though all along she had seen more deeply into his friend's soul than Brigge had guessed. She died two nights later, by the same fireside, drawing a long breath and holding it while Brigge and those in the room held theirs until her spirit departed. Challoner helped carry the pall.

Soon after his mother's death Brigge received an invitation from Challoner to meet him with some men of the town: Doliffe, Antrobus, Fourness, Lister, Wade, Binnes, Straw and others—they were twelve in number, all persons of reputation, wealth and standing. Challoner rose to address them. He denounced Lord Savile for a corrupt monopolist and rack-renter whose promotion of greed and corruption had divided the people, set rich against poor, masters against servants, fathers against their children. He declared that here there was punishment but no justice, wealth but no charity. Though his audience were rich men, they were soon swimming out of their senses, swarming to his speeches. He had learned to perfection the lawyer's good art of leading others into his own principles and wants; he spoke with the sharpness of the logician, the gravity of the philosopher, the gesture of the actor.

There was nothing wrong with riches and honor, Challoner held. By them men were more enabled to do good and it was right that wealth should be the reward of the godly and not of the wicked. But to pursue private wealth and neglect the common state was to seek in vain peace and happiness for oneself. For all men inhabited one body—the body of the commonwealth—and the health of the body stood in this, that one part answered to another: a man's hand helped his head, his eye helped his foot, and his foot his hand. The health of the body would be safe only if the higher members considered the lower and the lower answered in the same way to the higher. If they were not as Paul commanded the Romans to be—*every one members one of another*—they and the town would come to inevitable despair and ruin.

Challoner promised that if they joined with him they would overthrow Savile from his power. Then together they would make such a strong godly reformation that sin and idleness would be rooted out. Piety would breed industry, and industry procure plenty. Then there would be good commerce, good morals and good government. They could not create heaven on earth, but they could build a city on a hill, as the great John Calvin had done in Geneva, a light for others lost in darkness, where the body would become whole and healthy again. This would be their great project.

When, afterward, Brigge told him privately that he could not in conscience join with him, that he was not—as his friend knew too well—one of the godly reforming sort, Challoner asked him simply, "Will you object, John, when justice, charity and order reign?" It was Challoner's gift that he united men like Brigge and Doliffe. There was something for everyone in what he promised.

It was four more years before Challoner, through his influence at court and with the agitation of the townspeople, wrested power from Savile and secured the letters patent that became the foundation of their government. There were parades in the market square and on Bull Green, with effigies of Savile burned and bunting and banners proclaiming this glorious new Revolution of the Saints. The people went about in a delirium, waving sprays and sometimes whole branches of bay-laurel to mark their triumph. All hailed the new Master, Nathaniel Challoner, all hailed this handsome lawyer who had brought Savile's rule to an end. They garlanded him with laurel and put a branch into his hand as though he were Caesar, and when he got up to address them, the crowd went into a frenzy so that he could not be heard above their roaring. Brigge believed they would have made him king had it been in their power. Challoner, still clutching his laurel branch, looked helplessly at Brigge, then pulled his old friend to him and embraced him for all the town to see.

"This day would mean nothing to me, John," he said, "were you not here by my side." There were no orator's tricks that Brigge could see, no contrivance in his ceremony. Brigge was moved beyond measure, his heart enlarged by Challoner's words, his whole being made tender. He loved him then as he had always loved him. They were David and Jonathan, Orestes and Pylades, friends who would die for friendship's sake.

ʘ   ʘ   ʘ

THE MASTER PUSHED away his plate and leaned back in his chair, his belly full.

"It is a pity you felt unable to complete the inquisition tonight, John," he said, drumming his fingers on the table with an air of distraction and impatience. "It creates the unfortunate impression"—he paused to let Brigge know he was seeking the most discreet way to continue—"that you are remiss in the execution of your office."

"Remiss?" Brigge said, his voice taut. "In what way?"

"They complain about you, John," Challoner said, the restraint in his voice giving way to the impatience. "Doliffe came to see me immediately after the proceedings, bringing three jurymen with him."

"Doliffe can say what he likes, the jurymen too."

"Are you mad? The people of this town are worked up into a fever of fears. For all you scoff, men have seen these horsemen and other suspicious strangers."

Brigge could not help but let out a skeptic cry. The Master fixed him with a hard look.

"Do you think England so safe?" he said. "Do you imagine we have neither enemy over sea nor in our bowels, or that these would not delight in the extinguishing of our liberties?"

"I am certain they do," Brigge said.

"Then why do you treat these matters with such lightness?"

"I am sorry," Brigge said, apologizing to extract himself from an argument he could only lose. "As you say, I have been cut off from the conversation of men for too long."

"John," Challoner began, his voice taking on tones of high earnestness, "the dangers the kingdom faces come not only from without, nor only from armies and spies. The condition of the country grows ever more lamentable. The last harvest failed and the harvest before that."

"I know the harvests as well as you, Nathaniel," Brigge said with some asperity. "I live by them."

"The people have murrain in their cattle," Challoner continued. "Their swine are infected. Clothiers have no work for their spinners and weavers, their markets have collapsed. When calamity threatens, men seek enemies to blame. Everyone should be very attentive to what is said about them."

"What do they say about me?"

"Some question your faithfulness to the work we are engaged in here," Challoner said.

"Tell me what you want me to do, Nathaniel," Brigge said.

"No, John! No!" Challoner cried out. "You are not some servant to be ordered about, a soldier to be commanded. You are a governor of this town. What do you think we must do to promote prosperity and good morals, to keep order, protect property? What is your answer?"

"I have none," Brigge said.

"Tell me what you would do," the Master said, his anger barely suppressed. "Tell me how would you deal with the disorders and crimes we see committed every day? Are people not entitled to be safe? Can they not expect their lives and their goods to be secure?"

"I have no quarrel with you, Nathaniel," Brigge said, "or with what you do."

"Then why are you not here? Why do you isolate yourself at the Winters and sit in judgment on what we do?"

"I do not sit in judgment. I have said nothing. I say nothing."

The Master glared at him. "I do not have your privilege, John," he said tersely. "I cannot remove myself as you do. I remain here, at the heart of things, and must act as I see best." The Master left the table and went to the window to look out into the street. "These blue ribbons people are wearing in their hats and coats—do you know what they signify?"

"No."

"If you or I were to ask the wearer the meaning of his ribbon, he would swear it was nothing more than a fancy. But it is no secret that it is the badge preferred by Savile's partisans. A third part of the population sport the ribbon, perhaps half, chiefly the poorer sort who once cried that Savile was their oppressor but now are won back to him so that it is he who appears the liberator and we the tyrants. They want a strong man to lead them, even if he is cruel. This is the third year of our government. It may be the last. If we cannot rule, Savile will come back."

It did not seem possible to Brigge. So complete was the Master's victory that Savile was thought gone for ever, sealed up in his house by his own volition. No one saw the great lord but his most intimate servants; there had been no reports of him.

Challoner dropped into an armchair and rubbed his eyes. "Tomorrow morning," he began wearily, "there will be a court of sessions. I expect your attendance."

"Elizabeth is about to give birth, she may already have given birth. I must return to her as soon as I can."

"To see your son," Challoner said.

The two words—*your son*—sounded strange to Brigge's ears. "My son," he said. On his lips the words also sounded strange, strange and exciting.

Challoner was silent for a moment. "Nevertheless," he said at last, "you would be well advised to attend."

Brigge got to his feet and went to the door. "My place is with my wife," he said.

"John!" the Master called after him. "John, you are suspected." Brigge opened the door. "Did you not hear me? You are suspected! Charity constrains me to be blunt with you, which I think a most precious thing among friends."

Brigge turned on his heels. "With one word you could dispel the suspicions," he shouted. "If you chose to say it."

"Can I say it? In all honesty? Can I say that my friend Mr. Brigge is a godly, loyal subject? Tell me I can say it, John, and I will proclaim it everywhere I go. Nothing would give me greater pleasure."

"What have I ever done to show that I am disloyal?"

"Show? Show?" the Master said with bitter sarcasm. "The showing is not important, John. Outward conformity is not enough. What we must have is your heart," he said, jabbing a finger to his own breast. "You are in danger from your enemies," Challoner said, coming up to the door, "and you will be more vulnerable if you are absent. Help me and I will help you. Do your duty and I swear I will do everything in my power to protect you and your family."

The Master looked closely at him. "You know you have no choice," he said.

"There are always choices," Brigge answered.

Challoner embraced him. "I hope you do not live to regret the one you make," he said. "God keep you from adversity."

⊙   ⊙   ⊙

AT THE CLOTH HALL there were guards with pikes and muskets, and at the corner of King Street he came on the watch, who stopped him and asked him his name and what business he had there. Brigge told them to go to, that they knew who he was.

"Indeed, sir, we know you very well," one of the pikemen replied.

Another strong fellow that sported a blue ribbon in his hat put a meaty hand to Brigge's chest.

"Let me alone," Brigge said, reaching for his sword, "or you will soon regret what you do."

"I wish no more than to discuss a matter of theology," the man said. "Will you not do me the courtesy? Papists hold a wafer put into their mouths by a priest to be the body of our Savior, to be His very flesh. Is that not so?" Brigge brushed the man's hand away. "Yet we all know what becomes of that which we have eaten and taken down," the man said; he turned to his companions to laugh with them before facing Brigge again. "I hope you treat your shit with great reverence, it being so sacred."

"Given your care for it," Brigge said, "I will naturally save some for you when next I have occasion."

He pushed past the watch, being jostled as he went, and heard insults and abuse come after him as he made his way onward. He passed the House of Correction and, looking up at the windows, wondered how Katherine Shay fared. *Be harmless as doves,* Jesus commanded his apostles to be. Brigge knew the quotation well: *Behold, I send you forth as sheep in the midst of wolves: be ye therefore wise as serpents, and harmless as doves.* It was said that when St. Francis heard the tenth chapter of Matthew's gospel it was with unspeakable joy. The words did not bring joy to Brigge, but troubled his conscience. No man now pretended that harmlessness was a virtue. The times were martial.

Six

THE BED WAS COLD AND NARROW, THE MATTRESS MADE OF
straw and the coarse, harden sheets were faintly damp. There was no sign
of Adam, though the hour was late.

Brigge went over his talk with the Master. He had always taken care to
be discreet about his religion. Since becoming a governor he had made outward conformity with the established church, attending divine service and
taking communion three times a year as directed by law. If he found it hard
to put up a pretense of enthusiasm, if he did not go gadding to sermons, still
no one could point to any act or saying of his that made him a Catholic. But
now acts and show were no longer enough. They wanted his heart. Of those
who knew what was truly in his heart, Elizabeth would die before betraying
him, and his confessor, who had been prey for half a lifetime, would be torn
limb from limb rather than run as a dog before the hunters.

Anxiety and exhaustion battled within him. His thoughts were random
and led one to another until there came to his mind an inquisition he had
held at Tong on a woman who had died in childbirth. The midwife had
been ignorant and unskillful, and several of the gossips gave hard evidence
against her, how, after many hours of labor, the dull-witted wretch put one
foot up on the bed, planted the other on the floor, reached in and pulled the
child from its mother with such violence that the sound was like the report
of a gunshot. Brigge imagined it now as clearly as though he had been

standing at the bedside; he saw the horrible contortions on the midwife's face as she strained and wrenched, he heard the awful snap, and when he looked down at the woman in this hideous labor he saw it was Elizabeth.

Brigge let out a cry and turned on his side, wracking his memory for sweeter thoughts of his wife. The thought of her belly. As Elizabeth had grown, he wanted more of her. By the sixth month, when she was very heavy and the veins in her breasts were visible and the nipples darkened, he found himself in a state of almost perpetual desire. She responded to his heat with excitement, fecundity and passion going together. Brigge would keep his eyes open when she had her due and see her turn rigid in her limbs, hear her cry out. In those moments he felt that, if only in this, he had done well by Elizabeth, that he had, after so many failures, at last made her happy. He had not been a good husband; he had sinned. He had sinned. But when she was in his arms, naked and swollen and sweating, the world became for her a place of joy and boundless sympathy of souls, and he knew she was happy because she felt herself loved by him.

He recalled one occasion, about the time of her quickening, when they lay in each other's arms. She asked, "Do you remember our wedding night?" And so for her, because it pleased her so plainly, Brigge recalled aloud the deep feather bed he had from his mother, and the bolsters by bequest from his beloved sister, now dead. He recalled for her the floor of the chamber, a carpet of rushes she had gathered from the marsh, scented and strewn with white jasmine and honeysuckle and colored with primula and violets. He had never seen or smelled anything so beautiful as the carpet Elizabeth made that day. He recalled them put to bed and her being naked before him. Brigge had never seen her fully unclothed before. He would carry to his grave the image of Elizabeth lying facedown on the bed and he at work on her with strength he had not known he possessed, and when she turned her head, her eyes saw nothing. "I cannot move," she said, her breath faint and her force all gone.

☉   ☉   ☉

I AM CARNAL, Paul told the Romans, *sold under sin. The law of sin is in my members.* Brigge had sinned.

Love God, his mother had taught him to pray:

> *Love God,*
> *Fear God.*
> *Falling down, despair not.*

Brigge had fallen. He had fallen so often he sometimes could not tell whether he was standing or prone. He fell because he was weak. Doliffe and Favour and their kind did not fall. They were men of weight—weighted by authority, commandment and expectation—and a heavy man dare not fall. They lived in terror that once on the ground they would never rise again; the hotter sort have horror perpetually in their conscience. Brigge fell, again and again. But he believed there would be mercy.

> *Man without mercy, of mercy shall miss;*
> *And he shall have mercy, that merciful is.*

Did Doliffe and Favour have stars by which to fix their way? How else could they be so certain? How else could they judge the sins of men so readily? If they had stars, what had he? Jumbled points of light, a swirl in the heavens.

Eventually, Brigge slipped into a light, unhappy sleep, and in his troubled dreams he fell again. Now it was Katherine Shay who sat next to him at the great table with the lepers, beggars and whores. She had before her bread, milk and also the key to the city. Brigge took the bread she proffered. She gave him milk too and he took it. But when she offered him the key he had left outside the walls, he scorned to receive it from her, saying such things were vanities and trifles to snare man. She threw her head back and laughed and her eyes glinted with desire.

For that which I do I allow not: for what I would, that do I not; but what I hate, that do I.

Brigge did not understand what he did. He needed there to be mercy. He woke before dawn. He was still alone in the bed.

Seven

BRIGGE HAD HOPED HE WOULD NOT BE DETAINED LONG, BUT his heart sank when he saw Scaife herd the prisoners and petitioners into the sessions hall. There were some forty or fifty, the usual miserable company, shuffling and coughing and glancing fearfully about. He looked for Adam but could not find the boy.

Fourness, the oldest and most venerable of the governors, came in convoyed, as was usual with him, by splendid youths of the better sort, among whom he enjoyed the reputation of a hero for his selfless fight against Savile's misgovernment. On seeing Brigge the old man at once broke into a smile and shuffled over, taking the coroner's arm and kissing him and asking him how he did. "Come with me," he said, taking Brigge aside and dismissing the youths with a wave of the hand. He walked stiffly and his fingers were so deformed with arthritis they appeared as claws. He eased himself into a chair and used a hand to unbend his knee and straighten his leg.

"You have returned not a moment too soon, John," he said, casting a glance at the constable, who was keeping a narrow interest in their conversation. "In your absence the Master has inclined his ear close to the mouths of incautious men, and I fear the words he has heard on their lips have sent him into unnecessary alarms. He now appears to believe the greater part of the town has turned against our project."

"Perhaps he has reason," Brigge said, indicating the blue ribbons among the witnesses and spectators.

"There will always be men who favor a Draco," Fourness said. "But this is no reason to court and flatter them. Rather it is better to refute their prejudice for severity and insist that men deal justly with each other without they have to deny their neighbors charity and go about threatening to hang as they please."

"Mr. Brigge! I had news you were in town."

They looked up to see Dr. Antrobus approach. The doctor was so spare he scarcely seemed there at all. He was not well liked or trusted by his fellow governors; even Fourness, noted as a generous Christian gentleman who was gracious to every man until shown good reason to comport himself differently, was unceremonious with him. Seeing the slyness in his manner, the ambitions in his eyes, Brigge could think of Antrobus only as a creeping lust for power.

"Your wife is well, I trust?"

Strange, Brigge thought, how Antrobus could load a simple question with hints of menace and conspiracy. His tone was always facetious, even when he intended to be solicitous. It was his habit to bring his face close to those he addressed as though to compensate for the meagerness of his presence. Brigge shifted uneasily.

"I cannot say," Brigge answered. "I left the Winters yesterday and have received no word since."

"Did you not tell the Master of your predicament? Surely he would have excused your attendance had he known." It was an invitation to prate and complain; Brigge pretended not to hear. Turning to Fourness, the doctor continued, "Have you informed Mr. Brigge how things have developed since he was last here?"

"We were discussing the matter just now," Fourness replied coolly; turning to Brigge, he said, "John, you must speak with the Master. He holds you in great esteem and would certainly listen."

"What would you have me say?"

"Remind him of the solid principles of our project. Mr. Doliffe is a man of integrity and sufficiency, and Dr. Favour a most pious, religious and indefatigable Christian. Both see sin first and most, which is right but must always be tempered with forgiveness."

"Speaking with the Master will do nothing," Antrobus said. "The reason he listens to Doliffe is because he is already inclined to the constable's methods."

"I flatter myself I know the Master, sir," Brigge said sharply, "and he is and has ever been a man for justice."

Antrobus smiled thinly; he said, "This is most reassuring."

The hall fell silent as the Master entered, leading the governors in a solemn procession to the bench—Doliffe, Straw, Admergill, Wade, Lister and the other great men of the town.

"I should take my place," Brigge said.

Antrobus cocked his head as though sifting his words for hidden meaning. He said, "We should all take our places while we may." Brigge was about to do so when the doctor said with a pawky smile, "If I can be of assistance—to you or your wife—please do not hesitate to ask." Brigge thanked the doctor courteously and went to his place.

Dr. Favour got up to make his sermon.

o   o   o

"*IF THOU DO THAT which is evil, be afraid,*" Favour began, stretching tremulous hands out before him; he enjoyed to the full his reputation as a strict and passionate divine. "*For he beareth not the sword in vain: for he is the minister of God, a revenger to execute wrath upon him that doeth evil.*"

The voice was marred by his disfigured mouth but had all the nasal vehemence of the Elect and so was heard. "When Moses executed justice, was he not merciless?" he went on. "This is no ordinary time. It is a time of judgment when we preach no gospel but the sharp law of vengeance. We exhort those in authority therefore to return to Moses' law and deal strictly with evildoers and villains in all their guises."

Amen.

"Let them sear fornicators with a hot iron on the cheek so that honest and chaste Christians might be discerned from whores and whoremongers."

Amen. Brigge searched the faces around him. It was plain that many in the hall had a special affection for the vicar. The only peace their tormented souls knew, peace of a kind, fleeting and unperfect, was to hear that their torments were not theirs alone, but universal and ineluctable, connate with man's condition, and in this Favour did not disappoint them.

"Let them kill adulterers, for adultery is the foul disease of marriage and society itself," Favour continued, growing more heated as he went. "Did not Luther say that he who broke his marriage had already severed himself from life and was to be regarded as a dead human being? And in Geneva the great Calvin had adulterers tied with stones and drowned in the Rhône. Who dares say this is harsh? If a man who steals a horse is hanged, why should the man who steals another's wife go free?"

Favour paused to look from face to face. "And if it is right to kill these, what of the horde of papistical malignants in our midst? What of these Catholics and recusants? Why should these heretical papists with their insatiate avarice and thirst for blood, why should these conjuring priests and scheming traitors—why should these live?"

Amen. It was then Brigge noticed Adam among the crowd, listening attentively to the sermon though the boy had never shown himself inclined to the words or company of the hotter sort but rather shunned them as fanatics.

"And what of these masterless men that plague us? These rogues and beggars, these vagrants who live as the brutes do, who consort together with the instincts of dogs. They are villains and the sons of villains. They live by theft and plunder. They have disfigured the face of God. They are the base excrements of the commonwealth. Do they not deserve death?"

Amen. Adam glanced at the bench and met Brigge's eyes. The coroner sent his clerk a questioning look: where had he been? The boy turned his gaze from his master back to Favour.

"And yet these vagrants live," the vicar went on, growing yet more impassioned. "Authority is indulgent and tender, the governors of our town are bound by the lax laws of the commonwealth. They are not free to execute Moses' justice. At this most fearful time, let our governors act to the full measure of the law, insufficient though it may be! Let them look about! Search out the fornicator! Search out the adulterer, the vagrant, the thief and the papist! Let them not hesitate to wield the sword of justice as mercilessly as our present laws allow!"

When Favour finished, many on the bench were in tears, marveling at the clear truths he had laid before them. The Master made great show of nodding vigorously and commenting on Favour's ingenious sermon. Staring at the coroner, he said loudly, "Amen."

The Master let his gaze fall on Brigge and linger there.

"Amen," Brigge murmured.

John Marsh of the town, weaver, whose wife was dead and who is now without work so he is not able to maintain his three children. His fourth time before the governors seeking relief. Ordered given one shilling by the Overseers of the Poor but told he shall have no more.

A child of nine years, suspected to be a bastard, having lived with his grandmother who maintained he was her son and who was now dead, and with no one left to care for him. Ordered sent to the House of Correction to be put on work.

Alice Cartner of Sowerby, spinster, found dancing and far gone in drink and gave foul insulting language to the watch and derided and scorned their authority. Ordered put in the stocks and bridled.

A Scotchman and a woman from Cumberland found sleeping in a barn and consorting together like beasts to the great consternation of he who chanced upon them. Unable to give evidence of where they were married or by whom. Ordered stripped and whipped until both their bodies are bloody, then burnt through the gristle of the right ear and put out of the town.

Charles Denton of Ovenden, labourer, stole two chickens from Mr. Sharpe worth 6d and threatened to burn his house to the ground. Ordered whipped and sent to the House of Correction.

The last prisoner was a girl of sixteen with pretty, fair hair. She was thin and delicate, with a pallor. "Green-sickness," Antrobus whispered to Brigge with a smirk. "The girl is plainly suffering from love-melancholy."

Margery Farrer of Rastrick, spinster, whose father was grave-maker in the town and died of a dropsy two years ago. Now maidservant to Mrs. Hodge. During divine service found in a barn committing the detestable sin of fornication with someone who ran away. Refused to reveal his name.

Doliffe pressed her on the one whose name she protected, but the girl only sobbed. Brigge thought of her being kissed in the barn, of her back being caressed and the words her lover breathed to her. He hoped the words were tender, that the lover was a good doer, that Margery Farrer had at least some pleasure before the pain she would shortly endure.

Doliffe leaned to the Master and said she should have fifty lashes.

"A good number," Antrobus said behind his hand, "if they wish to put her in one of the graves her father made."

Brigge stared at the girl and thought of her receiving the lash. The governors had never been slow to punish, but there seemed no diminution of thefts, fornication, begging and drunkenness. Still offenders came before them, week after week, sessions after sessions, an endless torrent. They were punished severely for an example to the rest, but the rest did not seem to take heed. And when the rest were apprehended in their turn, they were whipped, branded, cucked, stocked, pilloried, bridled, sent to the House of Correction and put on labor. Some were sent to the judges of assize and hanged, others burned. But still it went on, the crime and the punishment.

"Fifty lashes to be laid directly after these sessions," the Master pronounced. "To be whipped again, fifty lashes every market day until she names the man."

There were gasps from those in the hall and also from the bench.

Brigge suddenly stood up, pulling his sword from its scabbard. Before he had time to think, he threw the sword clanking to the floor in front of the girl with the anger and force of a soldier launching a spear. She looked up at him in terror and shrank into Scaife's arms for protection. The constable's man pushed her roughly forward and soon there was coarse laughter from the baser sort. The clatters on the stone seemed to echo around the hall for a great space of time. The Master and governors and the crowd turned to Brigge.

"Mr. Brigge?" the Master said at last. The silence continued for some moments, no whisper or cough to break it. "I think you have forgot yourself."

He nodded to Scaife, who took up Brigge's sword and handed it back. Brigge took his seat again. Beside him Antrobus yawned. The judgment was duly delivered. Margery Farrer would have fifty strokes and fifty more every market day until she named the man with whom she had sinned.

After the sessions Brigge found himself the center of a circle of men, all pressing in on him with curiosity or admiration in their looks. He shifted uneasily under their stares, never at ease with men's expectations of him. Fourness came forward to congratulate Brigge on the courage of his gesture.

"Fifty lashes," he scoffed. "Why not a hundred? Why not a thousand? You were right to protest."

Brigge saw admiration in the eyes of the handsome youths that accompanied the old man when they looked at him, and two or three expressed their esteem in such exaggerated high terms that the coroner began to feel more affronted than flattered.

Antrobus too came up. "I always took you for a man who liked to keep his foot in the stirrup," he said, pretending to marvel at the coroner's audacity.

Brigge was not conscious to himself that he had protested; he was not sure what he had done, or why. He knew, as wise and cunning men did, that the safest way for men in troubled times was to say nothing.

Eight

IN THE ROOM RESERVED FOR THE CONDUCT OF THE TOWN'S
business, they gathered at the long table. The Master got to his feet and
looked the governors over. Whenever he was about to come into his sin-
cerest manner, he would tighten the muscles around his mouth and push
out his chin to make himself appear more forceful.

"Our situation worsens by the day," he announced gravely. "The recent
disorders have undermined the confidence of the better sort. Many are
abandoning the town, complaining of the taxes and assessments we levy on
them. If they desert us, the town shall be utterly impoverished, unable ever
to recover itself. We must make prudent and necessary regulations to prevent any further flight."

"What do you propose?" Fourness asked, suspicion gathering in his voice.

The Master paused before continuing. "We must reduce the levels of
assessments, and reduce them substantially, and we must do so at once."

There was some murmuring among the governors. "By how much?"
Fourness asked.

"By three parts in five," Doliffe answered for the Master, not apologizing for the measure or the sad necessity of it, but delivering what he
said harshly. There were expressions of approval and astonishment in
equal measure.

"Impossible!" Fourness declared. "We have growing numbers of poor—we should be unable to pay out doles to maintain them."

"We cannot ask those of modest means, who labor diligently for their families, to beggar themselves so the poor might live well," Doliffe said.

"We are to let the poor starve then?" Fourness said. "Such miserable parsimony would be a depravity, it would be the greatest corruption of the foundations of our project."

"There are other corruptions and worse depravities, and you would do well to remember it, sir," Doliffe said in brutal rejoinder.

The table fell silent. Fourness was venerable, crippled and white-haired, having declined greatly in health during the imprisonments he suffered under Savile, and no man, not even Challoner himself, could rival him for credit and respect among the people of the town, both the better and poorer sorts. For Doliffe to treat him with such contempt shocked the governors, even those among the constable's friends. The old governor's face flushed with affront and his eyes blazed, but he did not respond to Doliffe's goading. Brigge looked to the Master, who had always been careful to preserve unity among the governors, trimming skillfully so as to offend no man, to rebuke the constable for his lack of charity.

"Something must be done," was all the Master said.

"Our Poor Law was well designed to relieve God's honest poor and set them on work," Doliffe said, warming to his argument. "But through abuse it is now the mother of idleness. The law should be: he that will not work, let him not eat."

The governors began to argue among themselves. At last the Master called them to order. "Gentlemen, we have more business to attend to. If you please." He waited for silence before going on. "We must show our determination to stamp out the present disorders. To this end the constable, Mr. Doliffe, will reorganize the watch and search all manner of inns, alehouses and taverns and other places of ill repute to discover what rogues, vagabonds and thieves there are. Such persons will be brought before us at sessions and duly punished. Foreigners will have their passes strictly examined and those who cannot give good account of themselves will be expelled from the town.

"From this day forth in this town, there will be no toleration for any crime, error or sin, however slight. Those whose offenses we have too often looked at through the fingers, pretending they did not exist or were nothing but the common sports of Englishmen, such as fornicators, swearers and drunkards, will be punished. Those guilty of larcenies, murders, rapes and the like will taste the bitter cup of justice to its full. These measures are most necessary for the greater number of the guilty have commonly escaped justice, and those few who do suffer for their crimes often do so far from here because we are required to send the worst offenders to the castle for trial at assizes, not having ourselves the power to hang." The Master waited a moment, then added: "At least until now."

There was an outpouring of questions and exclamations. They had now authority to hang? How had this come about?

The Master explained, "I have petitioned for a special commission of oyer and terminer so that we might have authority to hang those delinquents whose death we deem necessary for the maintenance of our security. The people should be able to see justice executed."

"Who will be the commissioners that shall have this power?" Lister asked.

"Mr. Doliffe, Dr. Favour and I," the Master replied. He looked over the assembly, perceiving the consternation and unease. "We must not be afraid to be bold," he said. His voice, though he attempted to make it ring with determination, sounded flat.

At the finish of the meeting the governors gathered in little knots in the courtyard by the entrance. Brigge approached Fourness to say he was sorry for the terms in which the constable had spoken to him, but the old governor went off alone and without a word, scorning the youths that usually followed him. The coroner went to search for Adam but did not find him.

⊙   ⊙   ⊙

DOWN CROWN STREET and past the market cross, past the woolshops, beyond the trestle tables where are the bacons, cheeses and eggs. Past the capons, cocks and other fowls. And further, beyond the eels, trout, grayling and chub and the stink of fish. On, further, toward the shambles smell, not sharp like the fish, but deep, secret and laden. On to the shambles itself, through the viscera of the market, the panting contents of steaming cavities and all the carnal evidences of the solid world. Brigge went on, continuing to the cornmarket end where the maypole once was and where poor people now thronged to buy handfuls of last year's musty corn by tuppence and the groat. A woman was complaining at the dearth, saying the corn being offered was old and stale, and, jabbing her finger at the badger, rebuked him for setting his prices so high.

"The prices are fixed by the governors," the badger replied with a shrug. "If this corn is not good enough, you must wait for the new."

"The new will not come till harvest," the woman cried. "Are we to wait half a year to feed our families?"

Brigge came up against a man who would not move out of his way. The coroner rebuked the fellow, who turned and swore an oath at him.

"This one is a governor," the man's companion said, putting a hand out to restrain the other. "Leave him, or you will suffer for it."

"What do I care that he is one of those rogues? Let him push me again and we shall see what will become of this mighty governor."

"Let him alone," his friend said, trying to bustle him out of the way.

The one Brigge had rebuked spat on the ground. "Soon Lord Savile will throw them out by their ears," he said at last, before consenting to be led away.

Brigge came to the market square, arriving as Scaife was boring the Scotchman with a heated iron. The crowd roared its delight, grateful for the sating of its most insistent appetite—punishment. The Scotchman's consort came after. She did not faint away but mastered her terror and stood her ground and set her jaw. One of Scaife's assistants held her head fast. With one hand Scaife took the tip of her ear and brought up the iron's glowing tip in the other. At its touch the woman howled and staggered backward. The constable's man threw down his hot iron and stood panting beside the mangled pair, worn out from the efforts of his flogging and boring.

It was here, among the throng, that Brigge at last found Adam. "Where have you been?" he demanded.

"I was with my friends, as I said I would be," Adam replied.

The boy, though naturally given to closeness, had always been obedient. Brigge was perplexed at this new evasiveness; nor did he have appetite to question him further, now being so preoccupied with thoughts of Elizabeth.

"Is it true that we shall see hangings in the town?" Adam asked.

"Who has told you this?"

"The whole town is talking about it."

"Is that so? And what does the town say?"

"That something must be done."

"Do you share this opinion?" Brigge asked.

Adam paused before answering. "The town's argument has force."

"*Something must be done* is hardly an argument," Brigge said, his voice quick, his tone hard. "These are the words of rash men who cannot otherwise defend their schemes."

"These are the words of Mr. Challoner, the Master," Adam reminded him.

The people parted as Doliffe brought Margery Farrer forward to receive her punishment. A silence fell as the constable stripped the girl to the waist. Many, the women as well as the men, pretended not to look, but peeped at her little white breasts. Scaife went back and forth, pretending to see to the preparations, so that he could have a look at her, and he did not stop in this until the crowd's sniggers became so loud they shamed his master the constable.

Doliffe, his voice ringing out with severity, read aloud the sentence on Margery Farrer passed by the governors of the town sitting in lawful sessions as magistrates of the law. He cut off the girl's fine fair hair, drawing blood on the scalp with his blunt scissors, and when he was done, he held up the shorn mass to the baying crowd.

Brigge heard a voice at his ear, smooth and guileful. "The Master says he wants only to suppress the present disorders," Antrobus whispered, "but the carnival of retribution he means to unleash is only a mask for his motives. He intends with Doliffe and Favour to erect a tyranny over us."

The sly doctor waited to hear what answer Brigge would make, and when he made none, continued with greater insistence in his tone, "Do you mean to tell me, Mr. Brigge, that you will be happy to see this triumvirate of ferocity, ambition and cunning concentrate all power into its hands?"

"The men you speak of have labored tirelessly in the service of the town and its people," Brigge said, "without profit to themselves."

"I do not believe that in your heart you look upon their enterprise so favorably."

"Who are you to know what is in my heart, Dr. Antrobus?" Brigge said, shooting him a glance.

"Your friend the Master did great service to the town in helping to oust Savile," the doctor said. "But he is no longer the man he once was, he no longer believes what he once believed. Mark me, he will take Savile's place. Who then will be safe when he has overawed the town? Will you be safe, Mr. Brigge?"

"I have no reason to fear sanction," Brigge said shortly.

"Only saints have no fear of sanction," Antrobus said with a harsh laugh. "For myself, I go in fear of retribution every day."

The coroner pushed forward through the press, leaving the doctor behind. He came upon Adam among the people following Doliffe as the constable led Margery Farrer to be tied to the cart's tail. He called him to leave off and come with him to get their horses, that it was time to return to the Winters. But Adam was in a frenzy with the rest, shouting in the girl's ears and tormenting her with mockery, calling her a hot-arsed bitch and a dirty tattered slut, a whore that would burn in hell for her evil life. Adam did not see the coroner even when Brigge came right up to him.

Brigge looked at the boy in amazement of his passion for this sordid entertainment.

"It pleases you to see this?" he asked.

"The girl has sinned. The law is that she must be punished," Adam replied simply.

Brigge did not try to argue with him: youth is not tender. If it is to be made so, it is by wounds and experience, not argument.

They heard the first stripe laid on, heard the girl cry out as though lanced with a knife. The crowd surged as the horse started forward. Jeering, the people followed the cart, yelling at Scaife to strike the whore harder. Those nearest spat at the girl. A woman stepped up and invited her to drink before emptying a can of stale piss over her bleeding head. Brigge danced back to avoid the yellow splashes but could not avoid the smell. Scaife snapped his whip again, breaking the skin across Margery Farrer's thin shoulders. After two more stripes, the girl was broken. She fell to her knees and made as if to shelter under the cart, but her hands were fast before her and bound tight and so she was merely dragged along. Her legs, knees and feet were instantly torn, the flesh grated away by the sharp stones. She went out of all consciousness, to the disappointment of the raving mob that followed her with their taunts and scoffs. The drops of blood on the cobbles and stones were like those left by a bitch in season. The market square emptied. The sounds of the lash and the jeers faded in the distance. The rain came on, washing away the evidence of Margery Farrer's sinful heat. They saw Doliffe looking stern and triumphant as a conqueror.

"Have you sent to Burnsall for the serving girl?" Brigge asked.

"There is no necessity to hear the girl," the constable said. "You have sufficient evidences. I can assure you the jurymen are content to send the Irishwoman to trial and will return a true bill against her."

"If you have not already sent to Burnsall for Susana Horton, do so at once or I shall be forced to report the matter." The constable's face clouded with anger. "When she is brought back, send word to me at once. I would like to complete the inquisition on the dead child as soon as possible."

Brigge wished the constable good day and went with Adam to get their horses. They passed the jail and the House of Correction, where the governors diverted some of the torrent of sinners and evildoers who came before them. Perhaps the necks they would shortly stretch from the gibbet would at last succeed in stopping up this raging fast flow of delinquency. Something had to be done.

☉   ☉   ☉

AT THE NEW bridge there were now four hovels of sticks and reeds and clay daub. Brigge thought he was witnessing the foundation of a city of paupers, but then did not every great city, even mighty Rome, begin this way, in mud and wattle? If the meek shall inherit the earth ought he to despise their first claim upon the ground?

They had built a small fire under a precarious shelter, more remarkable for its abundance of smoke than for its glow and heat. They had no animals, not even a goose or a chicken. There were some bags of meal and coarse bread, but no meat or fat that he could see. Looking beyond the camp to the thin wood fringing the moor, Brigge saw a woman pulling gray bark from a sapling and stuffing it in her mouth to chew. Beside her a filthy infant sat on the muddy ground, drenched by the rain. The children who gathered around them smelled like wet dogs.

As he and Adam approached, the diseased man who yesterday had asked for alms hobbled over and doffed his cap.

"Good morning, your honor," he said cheerfully. He appeared to have neither eyebrows nor eyelashes. The coroner was fascinated by the wound in the man's leg. The left calf was almost torn away. The knee was scarred and seamed with hard red welts, but the lower part of the leg was scurvy with running tetters and scabs. Brigge had never seen so horrific an injury on a living man.

"What is your name?"

"Thomas Starman, your honor. May I be of assistance to your worship?"

"How did you come by this injury?"

"I had it when I was a soldier, your honor."

He seemed an unlikely soldier, even without the wound. There seemed about him a lightheartedness and wit that was at once, Brigge thought, a mark of gentleness and of intelligence.

"How did you come to these parts?" Brigge asked.

"We took the road south to seek harvest work in Suffolk or Essex as we found it. That work finished, we started north again."

"With what purpose?"

"With no other purpose than to find shelter, and so came to these fields, thinking to disturb no man."

"You know that in so doing you are in breach of the law?"

"What terror does the law's whip hold for them that would starve?"

Someone came out of the wood toward the camp. Brigge recognized Exley, the vagrants' leader. He carried an old fowling piece. Two dead pigeons twined together hung over his right shoulder. Noticing Brigge, Exley did not falter in his step but walked boldly to the fire, neither acknowledging the coroner nor attempting to hide from him.

"What have you there, Exley?" Brigge called out.

"Can you not see?" Exley answered without looking at the coroner but placing his fowling piece on the ground and tossing the birds to the women.

"He has been hunting game in the woods," Adam said. "We should inform the constable."

Exley heard what the boy said and flicked his eyes to Brigge. His manner remained what it was: resolute, angry and dark.

"Take this as a warning, Exley," Brigge called to him. "If I come upon you hunting in these woods again, I will have you brought before the sessions." He looked over the encampment, at the men sitting and standing idly about. "Are any of the men here experienced in the care of sheep?" he asked Starman.

Adam turned to the coroner, disbelieving his ears.

"Does your honor have need of a shepherd or looker? There is someone, a young fellow, a very willing worker, who would happily care for your honor's flock."

"Which one is he?"

"He is not here now but will be back soon."

"Send him to my house at the Winters," Brigge said, "on the other side of the mountain."

He remembered the raisins and figs he had bought in the town and told Adam to give them to the children.

"You should move on when you are able," he shouted to Exley as he went. "You shall never live well here."

Nine

BRIGGE HEARD THE SCREAMS ABOVE THE WIND. SARA AND ISABEL, the old kitchen maids, came running out in tears and agitation. Leaving the horses to Adam, the coroner hurried inside.

He found Elizabeth in her bed, the midwife and her helpers in a press around her. In her agony she tore at the sheets. She writhed and heaved and would have thrown herself to the floor had the women not prevented it. The clean white linen prepared in the weeks before her confinement lay in bloody soiled heaps by the bedside.

The midwife tried to bustle him out, but Brigge rounded on her with hard words and went to his wife. Her face was flushed and contorted, her hair flat with sweat. Her eyes were filled with fear and this, more than anything else he saw, brought Brigge to the point of tears. He searched among the tangled sheets and found the little bottle of holy water Father Edward had blessed.

"Drink," he said. "Drink this, my love."

She could not take the water down, but Brigge was satisfied that at least it had touched her lips. He took her hand and held it.

Mrs. Lacy, his neighbor's wife, came up and guided him gently from the bed.

"When did she come into her labor?" Brigge asked.

"Soon after midnight."

"How is the child? Is the head down?"

"All is as it should be, John," Mrs. Lacy said as soothingly as she was able. "I myself have had many dangerous confinements and yet all was well in the end. Let the midwife do her office."

Elizabeth let out a pitiful howl and sank with a gasp while the women stroked and mopped her face. Noticing the ring on Elizabeth's finger and the bracelet on her wrist, Brigge demanded why they had not been taken off. "Removing them eases the passages from the womb," he said angrily.

Mrs. Lacy nodded, directing that the ring and bracelet be taken off. Brigge glanced to the midwife. He had doubts of her competence. "They should have been removed at the first," he said.

The midwife made to take the eaglestones from around Elizabeth's neck.

"No," Brigge said, taking hold of the woman's wrist and holding it fast. "Not these."

Mrs. Lacy intervened herself between the two. "Leave them," she told the midwife quietly, "they will help her."

The midwife eyed Brigge suspiciously. These papists and their superstitions. Brigge could read her thoughts.

On his way out of the room Brigge paused at the chest in the corner. Opening it, he saw the mantles and swaddling clothes Elizabeth had gathered for her lying-in. There was something methodical and determined about her preparations, as though they proceeded from deeply instinctive causes. The strict impress of nature, he supposed; he could not but be reminded of the cat he had kept as a child, the way the restless animal had sought the dark and a place for its nest, and he thought it would never be satisfied but then, suddenly, it made its choice and from that day until the litter came hardly stirred from its chosen site. When Elizabeth had at last laid in all she needed, after much fretting and many changes of mind, she stood by the window and looked out over the two sloping fields. They had been recently harvested and were stubbled and empty but for trees without leaves and twists of coarse grass blasted by the wind.

"Please God, we will have cause to rejoice in next year's crop," she said. She fell silent for some moments, then continued, "I have done what

I can, John. I have completed all I know how to do. All that remains is to make my winding sheet."

Women with life in their wombs walk with death itself. Coroners knew it, midwives and surgeons knew it, maids and neighbors knew it, and so did husbands and wives. She smelt of sleep and tears. Brigge wanted time brought forward so he might be spared the agony of uncertain fate: a child, healthy and whole, plump and laughing, its eyes curious and frank, its mouth fringed with milk. Elizabeth recovered in her spirits, restored to the woman she had been before. A crop carpeting the long slopes stretching out from the house as far as the little beck that marked the boundary of his land, endless ears of corn fat enough to please a pharaoh. Sheep with lambs and long wool and no sign of the rot or the turn. He would gladly give up twelve months on earth to know that this was what lay in store for him and his family.

There was a scream that only women in labor make. It was from deep inside, searing and animal. The women surrounded Elizabeth and tried to soothe her.

Brigge put his hand to the swaddling clothes and mantles. Underneath he saw the winding sheet Elizabeth had sewn. He felt Mrs. Lacy's hand on his elbow.

o   o   o

HE STOOD BY THE fire in the kitchen, his hands trembling as he stretched them toward the flames. Dorcas brought oatcakes and cheese.

"I am sorry," she said. Brigge seemed not to hear her. She waited a moment, then said, "Will you not speak to me, John?"

He looked up at her as though she were a stranger. "I have no words that are right to say," he answered at last.

She put a hand over his and came forward as though to embrace him but stopped when she saw the look on his face. "I wanted nothing more than to be of comfort to you," she said to explain her intentions.

"You have been more than a comfort to me," he said, "which is why you must be less to me now."

She bit her lip at his coldness. Sara and Isabel came in and she withdrew her hand. Brigge did not know if the old kitchen maids had seen anything; they seemed hardly to notice Dorcas at all so concerned were they with their master's condition. They fussed about him and fried him eggs for his bacon and bade him eat. Dorcas waited a moment for an opportunity to be alone with him again, but, finding no invitation in his manner, abandoned hopes of it and slipped quietly out of the room. Brigge found he had appetite to take what was put before him.

◎   ◎   ◎

AFTER AN HOUR Brigge sent Sara to have news of his wife, but the maid came back with the same report, that the child was not yet come.

Though it was late, none of the household would go to their beds, not even the boy James Jagger who had lately come to them and had not yet twelve years. The kitchen maids put him to work fetching coals and wood for the fire while they busied themselves at chores of their own devising. Brigge's taciturnity stifled their usual prating and they went about with subdued steps. He sat by the fire and pondered the meaning of his dream of the great feast with the lepers and the whores, and the key he denied to receive before him on the table. Some held a dream to be a dream and nothing more, but so strange a vision, he felt, had to contain a meaning. His failure to fathom it troubled Brigge; he had sore need of understanding.

Dorcas came in to ask for her supper. Adam joined the table, which occasioned some surprise, for of late his habits were rarely sociable. The boy shifted in his seat. Brigge heard him clear his throat.

"I have something for you," he announced to Dorcas. She turned to him with a smile, expecting no doubt a ribbon or some other little token. Adam said, "I know it will lift your heart and inspire your spirits."

Dorcas kept the smile on her face, but she was alert to the gravity of Adam's manner and speech. They had been as playful and gentle together as the most loving brother and sister.

"What?" she asked, frowning merrily.

Adam produced a book from his pocket. The frown on Dorcas's face deepened in perplexity. She read aloud. "Mr. Tyndale's *The Obedience of a Christian Man.*" Brigge looked up sharply. Dorcas seemed hardly to know what to say. "Why, thank you, Adam," she murmured, her tone doubtful, "how kind."

"Where did you get this?" Brigge asked, taking up the book and riffling its pages.

"From my friends in the town," Adam replied, "people of good religion who meet together as occasion permits to discuss how they may live better lives and be better men."

"Mr. Tyndale is noted a most strict professor of religion," Brigge said.

"The true word of God is strict," Adam said. "It must be so for, as Paul says, it is written for our learning, not for our deceiving."

Brigge looked uncomprehendingly at his clerk. "Since when have you been interested in this?" he asked.

"Do you rebuke me for seeking to live my life in accordance with God's laws?"

"I was not aware I had rebuked you for anything, Adam," Brigge said.

"I think if you look truly into your heart you will find that was your meaning."

Brigge did not respond. He replaced the book on the table.

Adam turned to Dorcas. "Mr. Tyndale discourses on all manner of things: how God is to be served; how to know hypocrites." He paused before continuing. "He also writes much of husbands and wives."

Silence fell over the table. The kitchen maids sent each other flustered glances. Adam pushed the book toward Dorcas and said shyly, "I have marked the passages on marriage and the duties attendant on that happy state. I hope you find them of interest."

Adam stood up, smiled gently at her and left the kitchen. Dorcas lowered her gaze; her face was flushed and hot.

Brigge saw the boy Jagger asleep on the floor. He took him up in his arms. The boy groaned with the innocent petulance of the disturbed sleeper but did not wake. Brigge went to put the boy to bed. When he came back to the kitchen, he found Dorcas still in her seat. "I had no idea Adam was leaning towards the hotter sort in matters of religion," he said. "But then, I suppose, it is the fashion of the times."

"It is the spirit of the times," Dorcas corrected him.

"He means to marry you."

"He has said nothing to me on the subject."

"Not directly, perhaps," Brigge said. "Will you read Mr. Tyndale's book?"

"I doubt it will be to my liking," she answered.

"You think not?" Brigge said facetiously. He leafed through the pages. *"Lusts and appetites are damnable,"* he read aloud. *"To follow lusts is not freedom, but captivity and bondage."* He held out the page to Dorcas so that she might see. "Mr. Tyndale writes very well and to the point, do you not think?" Dorcas turned away. "I think you will find much that is instructive and beneficial within these pages," he said.

"Please, John," she said, "if we cannot forgive ourselves, all we can do is hope to forget. Perhaps that way you will not hate me."

They gazed at each other for a moment. "I am sorry," Brigge said.

Dorcas got up and left him.

Brigge heard Elizabeth scream. He strained to listen, hoping, praying to hear a child's cry. None came. He took the book to the fireside and began to read, marveling at the ferocity of the words, the heat of the language, the condemnations and damnings. What had drawn Adam to such vehemence? What imaginings did they create in his mind, what dreams did they make the boy dream? It was not unusual for youth to be severe, to cry out for discipline and rant against the failings of their elders. Brigge hoped Adam would outgrow these unyielding strictures, that he would remember to forgive; forgive in hopes to be forgiven, that he would learn to be weak. Perhaps the passion he had conceived for Dorcas would teach him. His lusts, the very lusts the book condemned, would teach him, in time they would teach him. One day he will fall as all men fall, and with his face on the ground he will see others in the like condition and he will say: So, this is the truth: I am one of these, no more, no less.

○　　○　　○

DORCAS CAME TO THEM when she was thirteen, brought by her aunt, who could no longer care for her and who wanted a place for her where she might be brought up in the true faith. The child was slight and pretty, with straw-colored hair and brown eyes. She was open and spirited, bringing noise and life to every room she entered. Elizabeth conceived a pure love for the girl, as a sister, as a daughter. Adam, three years older than Dorcas, delighted in her company. She it was who drew the quiet boy out of himself, who made him laugh at the world and at himself, who teased him and cared for him, and contended with him and railed at him and his habits. Brigge knew the boy loved her, but he supposed it an innocent love, and for this, for not seeing what all others saw only too clearly, Elizabeth mocked him gently.

Dorcas was with Elizabeth when she suffered her fourth miscarriage, her conception coming forth as the women were drawing water from the beck. Hearing her cry out, Brigge came running from the close where he had put his horse and found Elizabeth sitting on the bank, her back straight, her legs splayed out, blood on the grass, the tipped leather bucket beside her. She cried with a grief that Brigge could hardly bear.

"Take it away," she cried, "take it away."

While Dorcas helped Elizabeth to the house, Brigge wrapped the fetus in his handkerchief, averting his gaze so he did not have to look on it. As coroner, he had seen such things before, and much worse besides, but he could not look on his own lost child. In his hand it felt warm and hard and wet. There was such doleful heaviness in his heart he thought he might faint. He turned his eyes to the blue sky above and let the breeze refresh him. He went to the barn and took a spade and made a little grave by some trees a little way off from the house.

It was Brigge's role in their union to find reason for hope and delight, Elizabeth being much given to discouragement. She had suffered the earlier losses with a brave heart, but now she felt her failure to be unforgivable. Brigge could bring her no solace. She turned away from him, from his arms and kisses. One evening when he was scouring his ditches, Dorcas brought him beer and bread and sat beside him while he ate. He was grateful for her lively company. Brigge was not surprised that he should be stirred by the nearness of Dorcas to him. Men and women were thus. Men and women had always been so. Brigge kissed her and, out of sight of the house, they lay together.

Brigge was sorry for his sin. He was sorry and he was not sorry.

Ten

IT WAS NOT BRIGGE'S HABIT TO SUFFER A FIRE TO BE KEPT IN at night, even in dead of winter, for fear of accident, and the maids had let it go out. He woke, cold and stiff. Pitiful cries and shrieking came from Elizabeth and he hurried to her room. The midwife, determined to prevent his entry, called the other women to assist her, and they kept their weight against the door even as he pushed and damned them with oaths and curses. Only when Mrs. Lacy came out to plead with him, saying the commotion was upsetting Elizabeth and was keeping them from assisting her, did he give up his struggle.

The kitchen maids attempted to calm him as they had when he was a child, but Brigge's agitation was such that their well-intentioned words were like goads to him. He stormed about and swore at the world. Elizabeth's screams continued. Brigge left off his angry pacing and looked at the two old women huddled silently together, shivering with fear of their master's mood and their mistress's torment.

Then he decided. He had been loath to have Antrobus come to the Winters, for he misliked and mistrusted the doctor. He found Adam in his room. The boy was on his knees in prayer.

"Forgive this interruption," Brigge said. "I want you to go to Mr. Antrobus and ask the doctor to return with you here at once to attend to my wife. Will you go, Adam?"

"Of course I shall go."

"Then go now. Go as fast as you can. Tell Antrobus there is not a moment to be lost."

They hurried together to the stables and made ready Brigge's mare, it being the stronger and quicker of the horses. Brigge watched Adam make his way down the path between the fields, cross the beck and ride on at speed toward the mountain. He did not know if Antrobus would arrive in time or if he would be able to do anything to help, or do anything at all. But the doctor was now his only hope.

○   ○   ○

BRIGGE RETURNED TO the parlor and to Elizabeth's screams. From time to time Mrs. Lacy came to him and Brigge questioned her. Was there no sign yet of the child? What did the midwife say? What obstruction was there? What complication? He waited with growing desperation for Adam to return with Antrobus. He doubted he would see them tonight. The hard season made the journey to and from town difficult to undertake in a single day. If Adam and the doctor attempted to return to the Winters today, darkness would certainly catch them on the mountain to the great peril of their lives. He should have sent for Antrobus immediately on his return. Why had he not?

It was perhaps less to do with his opinion of Antrobus than his fear of intercession. Brigge preferred to let things be. We meddle at our peril, in everything. What were the governors if not pragmatical, meddlesome, stirring persons? Doctors meddled in men's bodies, the governors meddled in men's lives. They meddled in men's breeches, in women's skirts. Margery Farrer had been whipped by their meddling, and would be whipped again; the Scotchman and his consort had their ears mutilated and their backs flayed. The governors had punished hundreds in the like manner because they had their breeches down and their skirts up when they should not, because they drank in tippling houses where there was no license, because they swore and cursed when others were listening, because they preferred to sleep or smoke or fondle their lovers when they should be at divine service or about their work. The governors regulated and ordered because the lives they saw all about them were dissolute, wanton, profligate, failing. They wanted to reform and cure, as doctors did. What success could they expect? What success could they show? The spirits of men and women were capricious and chaotic. Was the meddling of doctors less futile? They diagnosed freely—dropsies, distempers, agues, fluxes, jolly rants and falling sicknesses and fits of the Mother, apoplexies, rheums, palsies, shaking-palsies, dead-palsies and a thousand other names they gave to diseases and afflictions. They prescribed their pastilles, vomits and decoctions. They bled, they sweated and they voided. They poked stools and held urine in bottles up to the light. *Beware of doctors,* Cato said. They bring death by medicine. Left to itself, the body was its own best doctor. The noble Petrarch's body had cured itself when the physicians attending him had declared all was lost. *I die by the help of too many physicians,* Alexander the Great lamented at his end. We meddle at our peril. In all things.

He pushed aside the food the maids offered him. He could not settle, he could not be still. His head ached and his eyes were dry and heavy. In the afternoon, overcome with fears and apprehensions, he went to the storeroom above his wife's chamber and lay down amid the bacons and grain sacks on a palette bed there. Though he felt enervated of all force, he knew he would not sleep. He prayed to the Blessed Virgin to see his wife and child safe, and he prayed to St. Michael to let him sleep and so preserve him from madness. Perhaps when he woke, it would be all over.

He murmured a lulling lament:

> *A falcon has borne my mate away.*
> *He bore her up, he bore her down,*
> *He bore her into an orchard brown.*
> *In that orchard there was a hall,*
> *That was hanged with purple and pall.*
> *And in that hall there was a bed:*
> *It was hanged with gold so red.*
> *And in that bed there lay a knight,*
> *His wounds bleeding day and night.*
> *By that bed there knelt a may,*

And she wept both night and day.
And by that bed there stood a stone,
"Corpus Christi" written thereon.

He whispered it three times. He began the first line a fourth time, then closed his eyes.

⊙   ⊙   ⊙

HE DREAMED AGAIN of the key. It lay before him on the table. The harlots and the lepers left their meal and gathered at his side. Katherine Shay was foremost among them, her paps out of her dress and her hair loose about her shoulders. She pressed in on him, as did the rest, the men and the women alike, saying, *Take the key, take it.* Yielding to their encouragement, he reached for it slowly and, lifting it up, he asked of Shay what was he to do with it. She would say nothing, but pushed him forward with her hands toward the city walls and to the gate that was closed, where the rich citizens were marshaled like soldiers to oppose him, very warlike and fierce, armed with pikes, axes, swords and muskets. The coroner hesitated to go but none would take a step forward without he went first. He said, "Where do we go?"

He woke with a start. Dorcas stood above him. "I am come to fetch you, John," she said. "Elizabeth has called for you." Brigge swung his legs to the floor. His head was clouded with sleep. "She is very weak. I fear if she closes her eyes she will never open them again. She wants only to see you and hear your voice."

Brigge hurried along the passage to the stairs. The wind was driving so hard that he did not hear the horsemen approaching. The little boy James Jagger came running out, shouting that Adam and the doctor were here.

⊙   ⊙   ⊙

ANTROBUS CLEARED the chamber but for the midwife and Mrs. Lacy. He was brisk and accepted no demurrer. He gave Elizabeth a swift examination and allowed Brigge a brief moment with his wife. The pain had all but overwhelmed her senses, but her eyes flickered on seeing him.

"The child has come by the arm and shoulder," Antrobus explained, setting out his brutal instruments of black iron.

Brigge nodded a mute understanding of the unspoken reckoning. The doctor directed Mrs. Lacy to lift the sheet.

"Go, John," the doctor said. The voice carried notes of consideration, unusual in Antrobus. "Rest if you can and leave me to my work. It will not be easy, I shall not try to deceive you, but it is not hopeless."

There was no opportunity to kiss Elizabeth or say anything to comfort her, Antrobus and the helper being so busy about her. Brigge went out of the room. The door closed behind him with an ominous finality.

Dorcas was waiting. Brigge embraced her knowing that it was in full view of the maids who waited at the far end of the passage. "It will be well now," he said, putting his hands on her shoulders and holding her before him. "By God's mercy Elizabeth and the child will be saved."

Adam came into the passage. The boy paused on seeing Brigge with his arms around Dorcas. Brigge hailed him warmly and went to embrace him. "You must have ridden hard, both on the way to town and back, to have covered such ground so quickly," he said.

"I went as fast as I was able," Adam said. "I hope we have come in time."

The boy glanced at Dorcas, searching her face for some message or clue as to her feelings for him. He said, "Have you had an opportunity to read any of Mr. Tyndale's book?" His voice was unconfident and slightly tremulous.

"Not yet," Dorcas said. "There has been so much to do."

"Of course," Adam said.

Dorcas excused herself. Adam and Brigge stood together in the passage. They were silent until at last Adam said, "I would like to speak to you, sir, privately if you would grant me that privilege." Brigge nodded slowly but said nothing. Adam continued, "I know this is a most distressing time for you and I would not ask except that it is a matter of great importance to me."

"Of course you must ask," Brigge said.

o   o   o

Ronan Bennett

THEY WENT TOGETHER to the parlor.

"I am your servant," Adam said, "as is Dorcas."

Brigge ran a finger across his eyebrow; his heart felt heavy.

Adam went on, "I hope, sir, I do not go beyond the bounds of courtesy or regard when I say that I think of you as my father as much as I do my master. You have always treated me as lovingly as a son. I do not know what my life might have been had you not taken me into your home. I hardly know how to give thanks to you and my mistress for the kindness and generous regard you have shown me." The boy began to wring his hands, his voice was thick. "I want you to know that I will ever be your true and loyal servant, that I shall render to you any service, small or great, that I am able to perform." Tears had come into his eyes and he seemed at a loss as to how to go on.

"You want to ask me something, Adam?" Brigge coaxed him. The boy nodded. "Then why do you not ask?"

Adam began to weep. Brigge went to him and pulled him to his feet. "There is no need of tears, Adam," he said.

"I am sorry," Adam said.

"Why should you be sorry, child?"

"Because the thing I seek, if God grants it, will lead to my going from here where I have been kept safe and happy."

"What is the thing you seek?"

Adam hesitated a moment. "I want to ask your permission that I might marry Dorcas," he said.

Brigge looked him over. Adam was twenty-four years old. He had not yet filled out as a man. Brigge kissed him and said, "You may ask Dorcas."

Adam sought his hands and held them and murmured his thanks. Brigge sent him from the room. He had no sooner gone than there was a commotion in the kitchen. Brigge hurried out, fearing the worst.

Antrobus stood by the table, the midwife next to him. "You have a son," the doctor said. The doctor smiled broadly, a man pleased for another man, one he has helped.

The midwife held out the swaddled child for him to hold and said the words Brigge had never thought he would hear: "Father, see there is your child. God give you much joy with him, or take him speedily to his bliss."

Brigge became aware that his arms seemed to be holding only air; he sensed no weight. As he gazed at the swollen eyes and silky wisps of reddish-fair hair smeared with traces of blood, it was not easy to know if the thing he held was dead or alive. The head seemed misshaped, long in proportion to its breadth, and bore the violent marks of forceps.

"Elizabeth?"

"She sleeps," Antrobus said. "She is very weak."

"Will she live?"

"She may live, she may not."

Brigge held the weightless bundle and prayed his thanks to God. The midwife took the infant again. The wet nurse had been fetched, a good milk-giver according to Mrs. Lacy, who knew her. The two old kitchen maids chattered noisily and declared all would be well with God's gentle grace. The house began to fill with the noises of relief and brittle laughter. Dorcas gave him a smile. Her eyes were red-rimmed. She came to look over Brigge's shoulder at the infant.

"Oh, he is so beautiful," she said, and began to cry.

ᴒ   ᴒ   ᴒ

IN THE CHAMBER Elizabeth lay motionless and for a moment Brigge saw his wife as she might be as a corpse. He bent down to listen for breath and, discovering it, he took her hand in his. Antrobus came softly in. "Your wife is very enfeebled," the doctor said. "You should not despair of her, but neither should you entertain false hope. If infection and fever set in, as after violent births they often do, she will hardly have the strength to recover herself. I have left decoctions and medicines and instructions in their use."

"Will my son live?"

"In truth, I am amazed he survived to be born alive. I have spoken to the wet nurse. She is of good character and free of disease and appears to have an abundance of good milk. The last child she suckled was also male, so she is suitable. Let us hope your son takes to her teat."

"I can hardly express my gratitude to you," Brigge said.

He found the eaglestones still about Elizabeth's neck and removed them as gently as he could. They were warm from the heat of her body. His mother had given him the stones on his marriage. She had worn them when he was born. He put them to his ear and shook them and heard their rattle. Aetites, stones within stones, bodies within bodies. They had done what had been asked of them. He kissed the hand he held, laid it down and covered it.

They left the room, now made perfectly dark and safe as the womb so neither sunlight nor moonbeam would imperil her.

Antrobus closed the door to the parlor. Even in so simple an act his relish for intrigue was plain. His ministering done, he became again the plotter. His movements were furtive, his eyes filled with calculation; a perpetual dishonesty glowed dimly there.

"Fourness is arrested," he said.

"On what cause?" Brigge said, astonished at this information.

"Challoner and Doliffe will not reveal it. They have committed Fourness to strait confinement in the jail where he may have neither pen nor paper, nor receive visitors, not even his sons and daughters."

"When did this happen?"

"Soon after you left the town. Fourness went to the Swan and dined there with Lister and Wade. When he left them to go home, he was apprehended in the street by Doliffe and the watch."

"What do they intend for him?"

"Why, to hang him."

Brigge snorted in disbelief. "They will need proofs first, evidence that he has committed some crime."

"They will discover what is necessary, and now they have their commission of oyer and terminer, they have authority to hang whom they please. They will brook no opponent to their ambitions."

Brigge considered what he had been told. His wits were so addled by all that had transpired that he could find no logic or reason in the doctor's relation.

Antrobus leaned forward and spoke deliberately. "You are in danger, Brigge," he said. "I am in danger. We are all in danger." Brigge shook his head. None of this made sense. "Do you think your friendship with

Challoner will protect you from your enemies?" Antrobus asked with a laugh. "No. The Master has been put into a great fright. He sees he is losing the affection of the people and fears that Savile will return and put him out of his power. He believes that by throwing in his lot with Favour and Doliffe he can save himself, and he may succeed. But the price these ranting dogs have exacted from him is that he turn himself into God's warrior on earth and make the town into a citadel of hypocrisy, which they call righteousness.

"And now he is in this new combination, the Master must be careful whom he calls friend. It would not do to be intimate with one tainted, say, with popery." Antrobus paused and smiled knowingly. "The people of these parts are very exercised by religion—they have always been among the hotter sort and Favour maintains their heat with admirable dedication—and it would be to the great scandal of his name should the Master be discovered to harbor papists among his circle."

Antrobus waited to see what Brigge would say. When the coroner said nothing, he continued, "You do not believe me? You think I exaggerate?"

"I cannot say, I do not know."

"Brigge, as we speak, they are preparing to indict you."

Brigge stared at him in disbelief. There was no facetiousness about the doctor now.

"It is true," Antrobus said quietly. "I am sorry."

"Of what am I accused?"

"I have not been able to discover the nature of the accusation," Antrobus said, "but I assure you it is true."

"Why?" Brigge said.

"Doliffe has been whispering in the Master's ear that you harbor ambitions to overthrow him and elevate yourself to Master."

"I have no such ambition!" Brigge scoffed.

"Every man who has power fears to lose it. The Master is very in love with power and he is afraid. He is afraid of the man who will displace him. He is afraid of you."

Brigge laughed scornfully. "He has no reason to be afraid of me."

"Your only chance is to strike first."

"Strike?" Brigge said, his incredulity growing. "Strike whom? How? To what end?"

"If you do not, they will destroy you."

"No blow I struck would do any harm. I have not the weight. I have no standing, no faction. My fortune is narrow, my estate unsettled, almost ruined, and I am, as you say, a notorious suspected papist."

"Yet you have the reputation of an honest man. You are honorable and capable, conscientious in your dealings with every man. There are those who would follow you if you gave them cause."

"Who would follow me?"

"I, for one. Lister, Wade. Fourness—if he lives. There are others, friends at court who would speak on our behalf. Listen to me. All justice is dead, all pity and mercy, and faith and honor, the very things we came together to promote. You are a just man, Brigge. Will you, for the sake of quietness, do so much violence to your conscience that you will let these fanatics rule?"

"I will have no further part of this conversation," Brigge said. "This is an absurd, extravagant fancy."

"Then you are a fool."

Brigge, his manner curt, excused himself and left the doctor to his own conspiracy.

o   o   o

LATER IN THE MORNING Brigge saw Antrobus off at the stable.

"It is said that to confide in a man is to make yourself into his slave," Antrobus said. "I have, by speaking so freely, given you an advantage over me."

Brigge owed no loyalty to the plotter and schemer before him; he had no debt to that man. But he owed everything to the doctor who had answered his call. "I am aware of no such advantage," he said.

The rain and sleet, which had eased in the early part of the morning, began to fall heavily again. Brigge waited until Antrobus was on the path leading into the mountain before he went inside to the kitchen, where he found the wet nurse with his son. The women looked up on his entry and fell silent. He sensed they were keeping hard news from him.

"How does the child fare?" he asked, looking from one to the other.

The kitchen maids answered that the child would not suck. They were quick to assure him this was not unusual, especially after so arduous a delivery. They said that as a baby Brigge himself had been very slow to feed, yet look at him now. His son was not suckling. But he would. He would soon suck.

Brigge found Dorcas sitting with Elizabeth. The girl was in her own thoughts. Brigge asked twice if anything was wrong, but she denied it. She showed him the potions and pastilles the doctor had left behind and repeated what he had told her as to their use. She asked to be excused.

"Tell me what is wrong," Brigge said gently.

"Adam says you gave him permission to speak with me."

"I could hardly deny him."

They said nothing for some time.

At length, Brigge asked, "Have you given him your answer?"

"No," she replied. "I said I would consider his offer."

"He is"—Brigge sought the words—"a fine young man."

She glanced at him sharply, then turned and left him with his wife.

Brigge sat with Elizabeth and the hours passed. He did not let go of her hand. It was large and strong and calloused. He remembered one freezing winter night when the water poured off the mountain in a sudden deluge and pushed over a wall where the sheep were folded and would have carried them away and drowned them. Brigge and the men toiled in the darkness, lashed by the winds, colliding and tumbling in the mud, desperate to save the flock. Elizabeth labored with the rest, straining to lift stones the men could hardly carry, hauling them and rolling them back into place. She dashed about from corner to corner, wherever a breach threatened, soaked through, muddy and frozen, until the wall was remade. The flock was saved; Brigge did not lose a single animal in the flood. When at last they got to bed that night, Elizabeth put her hand to Brigge's naked belly and stroked him. He felt its harshness, its scour, as it took hold to coax him. There was no delicacy in her touch or movement and Brigge did not become aroused. He thought he heard her crying and his shame grew inside him.

Brigge was sleeping when he became sensible of being watched. Bringing himself to, he saw that Elizabeth's eyes were open. He did not know how long she had been awake.

Her voice was weak. "How does our son?"

"He is well," he whispered in Elizabeth's ear. She smiled and the muscles in her face relaxed. "I would like to call him Samuel, my father's name."

Elizabeth moved her head to show she consented, then closed her eyes.

Eleven

AT FIRST THEY MARVELED AT THE FURIES. BUT AS THE BITTER rain lashed in torrents and the wind threatened to lift the roof, their amazement soon turned to trepidation. Even within the Winters' stone walls, as thick as a man's arm is long, they had to shout to make themselves heard. They were cold, for all that they wrapped themselves up and huddled by the fire. Nothing was ever full dry, not the kindling or coals, not their clothes nor their bedclothes. The bread was moldy.

The wet nurse was vexed and tearful. Brigge watched her lift a swollen pap to Samuel's mouth and squeeze some milk to his lips.

"He will not suck, sir," she said in despair.

"Do not lose heart," Brigge said. "He will suck."

They brought Samuel to his mother. Elizabeth, propped up in her bed, took him in her arms and whispered soothingly. The infant was angry and distressed, and nothing Elizabeth could do would settle him. After some short space of time they removed him from her, for she was still much enfeebled from her labor.

During a lull in the storms Brigge rode out to inspect his flooded fields and sodden flock. Spring planting was not far off, lambing was near, but he would sow nothing and have no flock at all if the rain did not ease and the sun did not soon shine to help him farm.

On his return he found Dorcas waiting for him by the backside of the house. "The constable's man has come again to fetch you to town," she said.

Brigge's heart skipped a beat. "Did he say on what business?" he asked.

Dorcas shook her head. Brigge thought of Fourness detained in the jail and Antrobus's warning. Was it possible the Master was plotting his destruction? He could hardly believe it. But these were strange days and strange things were happening. He nodded and made to go past Dorcas, but she put a hand out to detain him.

"John," she said quietly. "Have you nothing to say to me?"

"On what matter?" Brigge asked.

"I think you know the matter very well."

"Dorcas," Brigge said, making his voice kind and soft, "I have by my actions forfeited all entitlement to say anything to you touching this matter. You are free to say yes to Adam, and you are free to say no."

Dorcas turned away, hurts in her eyes. "It feels to me that you are, in a way, letting me go," she said.

"I do not have that power over you," he said. He looked at Dorcas. Pity welled up inside him, but he did not know how he could be kind to her.

He entered the kitchen to meet the constable's man, quite believing he might be apprehended and brought to the Master in chains. Instead, Scaife informed him that some prisoners in the jail had died and the coroner's presence was required so that the bodies might be viewed by him as the law demanded.

"Is Katherine Shay among the dead?" Brigge asked. Scaife claimed not to know. Brigge also asked whether the serving girl Susana Horton had been brought from Burnsall. Again Scaife said he did not know.

"You are the constable's man, are you not, the one Mr. Doliffe would send on such an errand?" Scaife shrugged impudently like a scornful apprentice. "Has Mr. Doliffe asked you to go to Burnsall to carry Susana to the town?"

Scaife, having so slow a mind he was ever fearful that what men said to him were tricks to get him to admit to that which would be to his disadvantage, blinked before the coroner in a high confusion while weighing the risks of his answer.

"It is a simple question," Brigge said.

"No, sir," Scaife conceded with reluctance.

Brigge dismissed him and told Adam to make himself ready for the journey. The boy appeared downcast. As they left the house, he sent Dorcas longing glances, which she did not return.

o   o   o

THE VAGRANTS AT the new bridge came out from their shelters, and the crippled one called Starman came leading a boy and called to Brigge that here was the one he had put forward to be his shepherd, but the coroner passed without he cast them even a look.

At Skelder Gate the watch challenged him but without show of especial insolency and permitted him to enter unmolested. Brigge rode to the House of Correction, and Taylor, the keeper, came in to offer him refreshment. Taylor, a man of extraordinary bulk and slow movement, looked so disheveled and pressed that Brigge asked if he was well. The keeper confessed he had not slept, that he and those with him had been kept very busy throughout the night.

"When the inmates finished their labor," Taylor explained, "we ordered them to their rooms, the men to go with the men, the women with the women, as we do every night. But they, having been incited, defied us and refused."

"You say they were incited?"

"They were, your honor, and not for the first time."

"Who has incited them?"

"The Irish tinker that is called Shay, sir. They should never have unbridled her."

Brigge experienced an unmistakable feeling of relief—fleeting and disturbing—on hearing that Shay was still alive.

"She has taken advantage of the great numbers of inmates we have been lately forced to keep but cannot control," Taylor continued. "We are full to overflowing, though still the governors send us more to keep every day."

"How has she incited them?"

"She tells them they are unjustly kept prisoner."

"I can see that would hold a certain appeal for her congregation," Brigge said.

"She calls the governors rogues and puritan dogs and dissembling puritan knaves and hypocrites," Taylor said. "I have heard her with my own ears say this and worse—that rich men have gotten all into their hands and would starve the poor, but what could rich men do against poor men, if poor men rise and hold together, for there are more poor than rich. Last night when Shay spoke to them, within the hour they were in a rebellion against us. At first I was greatly amazed by reason that some are notorious felons but for the most part the rest are feeble persons, in mind and body, many of them lame or old and infirm and dull-witted, habituated to instruction, and if there is any difficulty, the whip soon reminds them of their obedience."

"How are they now?"

"They appear quiet, but I cannot say how long they will remain so."

"I will speak to the Irishwoman," Brigge said.

⊙   ⊙   ⊙

IN THE INMATES' room there was little light. The coroner could make out the shapes of the looms and spinning wheels and other things belonging to the weaving and making of cloth, and perceived the prisoners were gathered at the far end of the long room. As he approached, he heard the murmur of Katherine Shay's particular voice, lulling and hoarse and soft.

The Irishwoman fell silent when Brigge came up. "Here comes a governor, we must honor him," she said. "Have you come to bridle and whip us again?"

Her mouth was still swollen and bruised from her bridling; her lower lip was fat and had recently been bleeding.

"No," Brigge said. "I have not."

"You have the appearance of an honest man, Mr. Coroner," she said, looking him up and down. "If you say you have not, for myself I will say that I believe you. Perhaps you have come like St. Germanus to free poor prisoners from their captivity? I was relating to my companions and friends"—she swept a hand to encompass the miserable assembly that made up her audience—"of the time St. Germanus came to a town and passed before a jail crowded with innocent prisoners awaiting torture and death on the orders of the town's rich governors. Do you know the story, Mr. Coroner?"

Brigge knew the saints and knew the miracles they worked. But the inmates knew nothing of St. Germanus and they pleaded with her to continue her relation.

"When the prisoners heard that Germanus was outside, they shouted for him to save them, raising a great clamor. Germanus went to the governors, but the cowards and dogs refused to see him and the guards hid from him. St. Germanus was not afraid of blood and dirt. He did not pass on the other side of the road and hide his eyes when he saw suffering. Instead he asked God for the help men would not give him. He walked up to the jail and threw himself on the ground and began to pray."

Her voice became low and trancing, a fanatical hedgerow preacher. Brigge found himself, like the inmates, impatient to hear her tell what happened next, though he knew the unfolding of the story.

"Germanus prayed, calling on God to see that justice was done. Suddenly, the gates of the prison, though they were secured by chains and bars, flew open, and the iron bolts leaped back. The prisoners staggered out from their dark dungeons into the light, and as they came into freedom, the fetters that bound them fell away. The jail became empty and harmless, and Germanus led the prisoners through the town to celebrate the victory of kindness. No man came to oppose them. Germanus had restored them to the light and they would let no man force them back into darkness."

"Where does St. Germanus live?" an old woman asked.

Shay rounded on her. "What do you mean, where does he live, you old fool?"

The woman hesitated. "If we send word," she ventured, "will he come here to free us?"

Katherine Shay's face reddened with anger. "I am surrounded by oafs and rattlebrains. St. Germanus is dead, you dullard!" she shouted. Seeing the look of despondency in the faces of her listeners only sharpened her rage. "Did you not listen to what I said? Was it not plain? Germanus was no more than the tool—it was God who worked the miracle."

She gave them time to comprehend what she said, but when she saw the bafflement in their eyes, she said loudly and deliberately, "When God decides to intervene again for the sake of the poor and oppressed, he will find another to do what Germanus performed."

"When will he decide?" another of the inmates asked.

"How should I know this?" Shay shouted in exasperation. "All I know is that when Jesus came he did not go to the rich, but went instead to comfort the poor and take the part of the downtrodden and despised. God loves kindness and to end cruelty he will work all manner of miracles."

"Let us hope he shows you more kindness than you showed the child you murdered," Brigge said. "I have questions to ask of you, mistress. Come with me."

A murmur went up, some of the inmates very agitated at the thought of her going from them, but she calmed and said she would go with the coroner for she could see he was no Pharisee.

He led her from the room into a passage, where a guard stood by a closed door. "Who do you keep prisoner there?" Brigge asked.

"Mr. Fourness," the guard answered.

"Open the door," Brigge ordered.

"I cannot," the guard said. "I have not the key."

Brigge went forward to speak to Fourness through the door, but the guard stood in his way very determinedly. "I have strict orders that the prisoner is to have no conference with any man, save at the constable's command."

Brigge glared at the man but saw he would not be overawed. He took Shay by the arm and led her forward to the keeper's own quarters.

"You have been inciting the inmates to insolency and rebellion," he said.

"I have done no more than show them the truth."

"Do you say you know the truth?"

"I know the truth is not secret."

"Tell it to me then."

"Your kind is not prepared for the truth."

"What is my kind?" Brigge asked.

"You that have, you that rule."

"Did you not say I was honest?"

"Hypocrisy struggles within you," she said. "Those that have and rule must also have hypocrisy in their hearts, and hypocrisy blinds the hypocrite so he cannot see the truth."

"You say we are all hypocrites?"

"I say you are hypocrites and parasites and the future will prove it so."

"Do you also claim to know the future?" Brigge asked.

"I know enough of it," she said.

"You are too boastful," Brigge said. "To know the future is nothing special. I know your future for it is not secret."

"Do you think so?"

"Your future is that you will hang," Brigge said.

"You admit you hang the innocent?"

"Do you say you are innocent of the child's murder?"

"I know nothing of any murder."

"A child's corpse was found in the room where you lodged. The women who searched your body found it in the condition of one who had lately given birth. You can see, can you not, how this points to your guilt?"

For the first time Brigge perceived some agitation in the Irishwoman. He persisted, "If you are innocent, tell me and I will do all I can to help you." Shay made no answer; she looked away, then back again. Brigge thought he saw tears coming in the corners of her eyes. "If the child died and it was not any of your doing, you must tell me," he said coaxingly.

Shay bit her lip.

"Do you confess you gave birth?" he said.

"I do confess it," she mumbled.

Brigge nodded slowly, making himself understanding and patient, confident he was at last about to get to the bottom of the matter. "Tell me what happened. How did the child die? Did you fall asleep, perhaps, and lie on him? Many mothers in their exhaustion innocently kill their babies thus." Shay sniffed and wiped her eyes. She shook her head. "Tell me," Brigge said, "is this what happened?"

"No," she answered quietly.

"Did you drop the child unintentionally?"

"No."

"Was the child born dead?"

"I do not know."

"How can you not know?"

"Because it is not my child."

"Do not try my patience, mistress, or play me for a fool," Brigge shouted at her.

"Why so angry, John?" she said. "Why so vehement?"

Brigge bridled at the sound of his Christian name in her mouth. He saw her for the trickster and temptress she was. He would not deny that she had perception, but it was a wicked perception, the whore's perception, the triumphant perception of the woman who knew too well man's motives.

"I am no poor deluded beggar like those you incite," he said coldly, "and you are no seer. You are the murderer of your child. I will be present to see you convicted of your crime and I will be present to see you hang for it. I look forward to both with pleasure."

Wanting no more to do with her, he called the keeper and had her returned to the inmates' room. As he led Shay out, Taylor informed the coroner that his jury was now assembled and waited for him below.

Twelve

DOLIFFE WAS WAITING AT THE FOOT OF THE STAIRS. HE HAD
the air of a man who had urgent business elsewhere and for whom the
present matter was a nagging, inconsequential nuisance. He did not greet
or acknowledge the coroner but turned at once to enter the room used for
the keeping of kindling and coals, and often also for the corpses of inmates
who were carried off by fevers and infections. The bodies lay on the floor,
a disorder of torn rags and blue flesh smeared and powdered by coal dust
and dirt. Their death smell was in the air but was not yet offensively high
owing to the great cold of the chamber.

"This will not delay you long," Doliffe said. "We need do no more
than record findings of death by visitation of God."

Brigge was trying to conjecture the sex of those muddled on the floor.
Two women and a man? Two men and a woman? That one that was so frail
and malnourished, was that a child?

"You have heard how the Irishwoman has stirred the inmates to disturbance?" the constable asked Brigge. "Had you completed your inquisition at the first we should have been able to hang her and so saved the
keeper and the town the great inconvenience she has since caused."

"Why have you not sent for Susana Horton?" Brigge asked, his tone
direct, without hints of courtesy or apology.

"By reason, sir, of vital work on which I am presently engaged on the town's affairs," Doliffe answered.

"This vital work compasses the apprehending and imprisonment of Mr. Fourness?"

"Indeed," Doliffe said, meeting Brigge's directness with an equal bluntness.

"On what cause is Mr. Fourness detained?"

"His offense, sir, is so odious and despicable I will not say what it is."

"Is he in league with the French or the Spanish," Brigge said, unable to prevent himself from sarcastic jibes. "Perhaps he is one of the strange horsemen that ride at night."

The constable regarded him coldly. "These are matters of urgency and weight," he said. "I am surprised you see fit to turn them into jests."

"Someone will have to reveal what Fourness's crime is at some near time," Brigge said. "No man can be held without he be brought to the bar and have charges put to him that he may answer."

"His arraignment will be time enough for men to hear the horrid things Fourness has done," Doliffe said. "I myself will say nothing of it for such foul deeds should not be spoken of without it being necessary."

"This is a most convenient way for you to proceed."

"What do you mean, sir?"

"No one is more esteemed in the town for honesty, charity and wisdom than Fourness. Or for the suffering he endured for his opposing of Lord Savile. You know that anything you lay to his charge will inflame the people's passions, for they know him to be innocent."

"They know nothing of the sort," Doliffe answered with a frigid look. "And when they learn of his offense, I assure you, Mr. Brigge, what reputation Fourness had will vanish at a stroke."

The constable's vehemence unsettled Brigge and made him think he had uncertain ground for his argument, that in speaking for Fourness he had gone beyond his proper business. He turned back to the corpses on the floor that were his business.

The jurymen entered.

"What are the names of these prisoners?" the coroner asked when they had settled.

He would do no more than record the names of the dead and tell the jury to find they had died by visitation of God. There was little purpose in prolonging the proceedings, unless it was so Brigge might himself catch his death by the contagion of the place.

Taylor pointed out the dead and gave their names.

Isaac Mann . . .

Christopher Sharp . . .

Margery Farrer.

On hearing the last name Brigge pushed the jurymen aside and went to see for himself. It was true. Margery Farrer, the girl who had gone to the barn instead of divine service, who had listened to her lover's entreaties instead of Favour's raving, accepted his caresses and not the host in her mouth. Now she was dead. Brigge peered at the corpse. It was wrapped loosely in a coarse blanket of undyed cloth.

"How did she die?" Brigge asked Taylor.

"Of fever, like the rest," Doliffe answered for the keeper.

"Help me with her," Brigge said, snapping his fingers at Taylor and Scaife.

Instructing Taylor and Scaife to take the arms while he managed the feet, Brigge began to lift Margery Farrer's corpse clear of the tangle in which it lay.

"Make room there," Brigge said.

The jurymen parted so they could put the girl down. The blanket had come away to reveal her nakedness. Brigge turned her over and saw that her back had been flayed so there was hardly an inch of skin between her arse and her neck.

"How many times was she whipped?" he asked.

"She was chastised three times, given fifty lashes each market day until she would reveal the name of the man who sinned with her," Doliffe answered. "You will recall that was our judgment."

He gazed at the body a while, then turned to the jurymen. "As you see, a perfectly perceptible instance of death by visitation of God," he said.

The jurors did not know whether he intended an ironical sense and they shifted uneasily on their feet. Brigge said, "Do you not agree?"

They looked at each other in bewilderment, none speaking or answering the coroner. "Well?" Brigge shouted at them. "Have you not eyes? Can you not see?" He turned to the keeper. "Fetch some candles, Taylor. The poor light obscures their vision."

"The light is perfectly good," Doliffe said, making it plain he considered the coroner's performance to be tedious. "No candles are necessary."

Brigge looked over the jury. "You have heard Mr. Doliffe," he said. "The light is good. So, having viewed the bodies before us, we can see by the signs on them that they came to their deaths by visitation of God and by no other means. Is that not so?"

One juror, more forward than the rest, or perhaps simply more tractable, mumbled his concurrence and others took up his lead.

"Draw up the inquisition and have these clear-sighted gentlemen put their signatures or marks to it," Brigge told Adam, then hurried after the constable, who seemed eager to be gone.

"Mr. Doliffe," he called. The constable turned to face him. "I will return in five days to continue the inquisition on the dead child of Katherine Shay. That will give you ample time to have Susana Horton fetched back. If she is not here, it will be necessary for me to inform the high sheriff of your dereliction."

Doliffe looked at him with open contempt. "Inform as you please," he said.

☉   ☉   ☉

HE WENT DIRECTLY to Ward's End, to the house of Dr. Antrobus, which was neatly built of brick, but finding him not at home carried on to Mr. Wade's house in Blackledge. There he found Wade together with his fellow governors Lister and Antrobus.

"What offense has Doliffe laid against Fourness?" Brigge asked.

"Every man is guilty of something," Antrobus replied. "All that is ever needed to convert guilt to destruction is another man's malice."

"Nevertheless," Brigge said quickly, irritated by the doctor's foolish drollery, "they must have accused him of some crime."

"For all we know, they have," Antrobus said. "But they will not tell us, and since they allow Fourness no visitors, he has been unable to inform his friends of the reason for his imprisonment."

"I will speak to the Master tonight," Brigge said.

"To what purpose?" Antrobus asked.

"Doliffe has done Fourness a great wrong," Brigge said. "I hope I shall make the Master see this."

Antrobus laughed bitterly. "It was the Master himself who ordered Fourness arrested and carried to jail," he said. "It is nothing to do with any offense, it has nothing to do with right or wrong. It is to rid himself of an enemy and overawe the rest." Antrobus leaned toward Brigge, very earnest and passionate. "It is said love is blind, but even the most silly lovesick girl can see plainly enough when her false lover fondles another woman," he said. "Challoner has turned against you, Brigge. He has fallen into the arms of Doliffe and Favour. Why do you deceive yourself?"

"I will speak to the Master as soon as I have opportunity," Brigge said.

"When you do," Wade put in with sarcasm, "be so good as to ask of him what charges he intends to lay against me."

"And me," Lister added.

"We are all threatened," Antrobus said. "Unless we strike, we will be struck down." The doctor paused before continuing. "We are together four governors. There are others—Admergill and Ramsden to name but two—who would come with us if they believed you to be part of this combination. Then we would be six. And there are others in the town, honorable men, who are in dissatisfaction at the Master's abandonment of all principle and justice, though they have not yet found the courage to oppose him openly."

"Do not waste your words with the Master," Lister said. "I will send for those men who would support us so you may have conference with them."

"By force of numbers we will overthrow Challoner, elect a new Master and set about the continuance of our project as it was originally designed," Antrobus said.

Brigge considered what they said. Taking his hat and coat, he went to the door. "We are Englishmen who live under a constitution, not Romans in the forum," he said. "The Master has not tyrannical power and we are not assassins."

Thirteen

WHEN THE MASTER APPEARED AT LAST, AFTER BRIGGE HAD been waiting more than three hours at his apartment, Challoner had the same air Doliffe had, of a man hard-pressed by business and interviews and the expectations of the world, but where the constable exulted in the opportunity to comport himself as a great man, Challoner had a weary and troubled look. He eased himself slowly into one of the armchairs by the window. His hair was unwashed and unkempt and there were spots of blood on the white linen of his collar where he had cut himself in his shaving.

He had in his hands a roll of examinations and informations, which he untied, and put on eyeglasses to read.

"Please," he said to the coroner, keeping his attention on his reading. "How can I help you?"

Brigge said nothing but watched the Master pore over the documents. At last Challoner, alerted by the silence, looked up.

"You wished to speak with me?"

"Yes, Nathaniel," Brigge said, "and I had hopes you might listen."

After a moment's consideration Challoner put aside the papers and removed his spectacles.

"I understand you have a son," he said.

"I have named him Samuel."

"Your father's name," the Master said. "You are very fortunate." He peered at the coroner as though only then taking proper notice of him. "And you, John, are you well?"

"I am well enough," Brigge replied, "and in any case in a better condition than Mr. Fourness presently finds himself."

The Master exhaled noisily to show his displeasure at Brigge's raising of this matter. "For that," he said tersely, "Fourness has only himself to blame."

"Nathaniel, I have to tell you that this arrest has caused great anxiety in the town. They allege Fourness has been thrown in jail for no other cause than that Doliffe and Favour want him ousted from his office of governor. They say, Nathaniel," Brigge went on, "that you have forgot what justice means or you would not suffer to see Fourness so abused."

"Do you say that because Fourness is a governor he should not have to answer for his wickedness?" the Master said with a vehemence that startled Brigge. "Magistrates, constables, coroners, overseers, governors—we must all show ourselves the keenest prosecutors of justice. We must be like Moses—the harshest tormentor imaginable of every delinquent and offender whether it be the robber who lurks in the highway or the fornicator in the hedge. How can the City on the Hill be the beacon for those who grope in the darkness if its governors themselves are licentious and wicked and would commit the most horrible of crimes?"

"We could also be like the Mongol or the Turk and have those who displease us impaled on stakes." Brigge's levity incensed the Master and his face darkened. Seeing this, the coroner made himself more serious, and when he spoke again, it was with greater passivity and earnestness. "Moses' law was very sharp," he said, "too sharp for Englishmen."

"The law must be sharp or it is no law worth the having," the Master said. "Englishmen are too tolerating. All around are outrageous seas of ignorance and darkness. They threaten to overflow the commonwealth, yet many still account them no sin at all, but rather a pastime, a dalliance. They are not rebuked, but winked at; not punished, but laughed at. From these sins proceed other crimes. Turn a blind eye to one and no evil will be seen anywhere."

The Master spoke hotly, but then he put out his hands in a gesture intending to give the impression of one doing all in his power to overcome provocation for the sake of a great good as yet unapprehended by the provoker. "John, I no longer flatter myself that you hold me in any degree of esteem," he continued more quietly. "I will not speak of the injury and sadness I feel at our former love and regard for each other being now so desiccated. But even if you think me the most wretched creature on earth, I hope you will in your heart acknowledge that the project I have promoted with as much diligence as my poor capacities and parts enable me is still most worthy and of the utmost necessity."

"No man has been more active in the promotion of order and reformation," Brigge said.

"Am I wrong to oppose the overthrowing of good and raising up of evil, the beggaring of the better sort, the decay of good morals? Am I wrong to devote my energies to the rooting out of disorder and licentiousness, to the correction and improvement of the baser sort, those whose lives are disordered, to the enlightening of their minds, the purifying of their souls? What is so contemptible about desiring to see things stand better? Why do you hold me in such plain contempt?"

"I do not."

"I think you do!" the Master exclaimed. "How have we come to this, John? Why do you oppose me? Antrobus, I understand. The doctor is vain, ambitious and pragmatical. He imagines himself Master but knows himself to be so mistrusted and disliked that he must have one to run before him, scattering his enemies, gathering friends, winning the battles from which he plots to profit. Wade is a mere trifle, a nothing, a dim-witted fellow and easily led. As for Lister, do not say his name in my presence, for he is an odious and reprehensible man, as all the world will soon discover."

Brigge had long ago noted the tendency to reward even a query of the Master and his allies with displeasant glances and stares, as though merely to *ask* were a declaration of enmity and opposition. There was a logic to it, he understood as he listened to the Master, a proclivity of power: for a follower to follow required faith in the leader; if the leader was right, those who questioned were wrong, and those who questioned persistently were more than wrong—they must be enemies. Although the habits of interrogation were strong in Brigge—the coroner was used to probing men with things to hide, he was used to searching organs and bones with tales to tell—he had responded to these unspoken reprimands by holding his tongue. He could sometimes wrest answers from dead men, but not from Challoner when he was Master.

"Why do you oppose me?" the Master said again. "Why?"

"I do not oppose you."

"Neither do you support me."

"I balk at the severity of our rule. I cannot help myself. I search my conscience and ask myself if such strictness is necessary."

"What would you do? Indulge weakness? License sin? Disregard the flood of vice and evil? Tell me what would you do!"

"I cannot," Brigge answered wearily. "I know only that the City on the Hill you are resolved to build, with Favour its chief architect and Doliffe the mason, these sour spirits and inventors of trouble, these busy-heads and dogmatics—the city they build will be a cold place, Nathaniel, full of spies, terror and mischief, as Fourness could give evidence of were he here."

"Fourness is a foul, corrupt man," the Master said harshly. "He has committed the most heinous, contemptible of crimes. Not once, not twice, but countless times."

"What crime has he committed? Why will no one say what it is?"

The Master reached for his papers and selected a parchment. "I myself took this deposition from Fourness's own valet," the Master said. "He accuses Fourness of unspeakable crimes against nature as well as other detestable acts infamous to, and unworthy of, any Christian man." He held out the parchment to Brigge. "You may read for yourself, John, if you have stomach for what you will discover recorded there."

⊙   ⊙   ⊙

BRIGGE SAW IT WAS a legal deposition: *The information of Daniel Emsall, servant to Mr. Joseph Fourness gent., taken on his oath before Mr. Nathaniel*

Challoner esq., governor and justice of peace. He searched it with a practiced eye and found at once what he was looking for. He looked up at the Master.

"It is true, John," the Master said gravely. Brigge turned back to the parchment but, his head swimming, all he perceived was a miasma of words. "The valet describes how he witnessed Fourness at divers times commit lewd acts with certain youths and men, severally and together, who came to his house."

"The prattling gossip of a servant," Brigge said after he had recovered from his initial astonishment. "Such a man might say anything if he had a mind for wickedness."

"It is not just the valet," the Master said. "Four of those with whom Fourness committed these foul deeds have been arrested and confessed to their crimes. There are other witnesses who say that Fourness corrupted youths of ten and twelve years. Lister is likewise implicated and shall shortly be arrested. Fourness is a sodomite and corruptor of children, and he will hang for it. Heed what I say, John. Doliffe and I now have authority to put on trial and judge whosoever is suspected of crimes and disorders."

"Do you threaten me, Nathaniel?"

"I desire only to prevent you hurtling to your own destruction," Challoner said. Brigge put his head in his hands, his mind a swirl of confusions. "John," Challoner said tenderly, "there is no need for bitterness between us. Can you not see how Fourness and Antrobus would use you? Forget them and resume your place by my side. Help me with our great project."

"You do not need me, Nathaniel," Brigge said.

"To the contrary, I have the greatest need of you," Challoner insisted, his voice sincere and pleading. "Savile is plotting to return. His agents in the town report every rumor, and the rumor they report to their lord is that John Brigge, the Master's most trusted friend, is discontented and foments revolt."

"It is not true."

"They report that John Brigge and other governors are in a combination together to overthrow the Master."

"I have combined with no one."

"Not with Antrobus, to whom you owe much since the birth of your son?"

Brigge hesitated. "No," he said.

"You have had no imparlance then with the doctor about the town's government?"

"I have combined with no one."

"Good," Challoner said; he added, "As one who loves you and wishes to keep you from harm, I advise you to stay away from Antrobus and his friends."

As the coroner was about to take his leave, Challoner said, "How does your son fare?"

"The birth was difficult for both mother and child," Brigge replied. "Elizabeth is every day more restored, and Samuel, with God's grace, will prosper and grow in strength."

"May God watch over and protect them," Challoner said. "I will come to visit you as soon as I have opportunity, if I may."

"I would be honored to receive you, Nathaniel."

At the door Brigge paused a moment. "Do you know of any reason why Doliffe might be reluctant to have Susana Horton fetched back to the town?"

"None whatever," the Master answered sharply. "Why do you ask?"

"The constable is famed for his diligence, yet in this matter he seems disinclined to do his office."

"That I doubt—he is, as you say, most diligent. Nevertheless, I will speak with him," Challoner said. "The sooner the inquisition is settled, the better." Challoner smiled and clasped Brigge to him and kissed him. "Take care how you go, John, and remember I am your most loving friend."

Brigge went to the Lion. Adam was asleep in their room. Brigge got into bed beside him and considered what he should do. Doliffe's reluctance to fetch Susana Horton was plainly suspicious, though Brigge could not think what were the constable's motives in keeping her from the inquisition. He thought of going to Burnsall himself to find her but was reluctant to suffer further separation from Elizabeth and Samuel, being desperate to know how they did.

○   ○   ○

HE WOKE WITH a start, his heart beating fast. He wiped the sweat from his face. He was hot and his bones ached. He felt enveloped by confusion and fear. He tried to tell himself that it was nothing but the black chasm of the night, that in the morning light things would appear better. He tried to pray, but he could not make himself unafraid. This is man's true state, he thought, to know fear. This is what being human means, above all else. We are bundles of fear and need. The rest is a mere distraction, a way to deceive ourselves out of our terrors, which we sometimes hide and sometimes forget, but we remain afraid. We are all afraid.

He became aware that Adam was awake beside him. "Is something wrong?" the boy asked.

"No," Brigge said. "Go back to sleep."

Adam was silent for a moment, then said, "Dorcas avoids me. She will not give me her answer." Brigge said nothing. "Would you speak to her for me?"

Brigge was sweating profusely; his mouth was dry and his eyes hurt. "Go to sleep, Adam."

He felt Adam turn his head on the pillow. The boy lay still in his sadness.

"Adam," Brigge said softly, "Dorcas will make her own decision in time."

"She would listen to what you had to say."

"I think you have too high an opinion of my influence over her."

Adam was silent for some moments. "I would like to see my friends before we leave for the Winters," he said.

"These friends, are they the men of good religion you spoke of, the ones who want to be better?"

"Your tone is mocking," Adam said curtly, "though I can see no reason for it to be so."

"What are you doing gadding with these hotheads and fanatics, Adam? You never wanted their company before, why do you seek it now?"

"Do you not see what is happening in the land? Sin piled upon sin, error upon error. Crimes and thefts multiply daily so that no man is now safe, neither his life nor his property. Everything is uncertain, nothing is solid. The foundations of good government are crumbling before our eyes."

"Strange," Brigge said. "I thought my eyes still good and yet have seen none of this."

"Your eyes cannot be so good as you think."

"When I was a child, there were also men who prophesied calamity and preached harshness and rigor. Every age, it seems, is the most dangerous there has ever been."

"This age is particular. Darkness threatens to overwhelm us as it never has before."

Brigge sighed wearily and mopped the sweat from his brow. "Your friends will have little regard for papists," he said. When Adam made no response, Brigge continued, "Have they asked you about me?"

"Out of regard for you and my mistress," Adam said, "I have said nothing."

Brigge took care what he said next. For all that he loved and trusted the boy, he did not want to let his clerk think he had a power over his master. "The days ahead may be unsettled," he began slowly, "and dangerous. I fear that men have become so afraid they are ready to turn on each other like wolves. Some may turn on me."

"I have said nothing," Adam said firmly, "and will say nothing."

Brigge nodded his thanks. They lay in silence and eventually Brigge heard Adam's breathing deepen and slow. He himself did not sleep. He rose before it was light.

"I am going to Burnsall to find Susana Horton," he told Adam as he pulled on his boots. The effort left him weak; the fever was taking hold. He rallied himself as best he could and pulled on his coat and hat. "There is something the girl knows that Doliffe does not want heard," he said.

"What?" Adam asked.

"I do not know," Brigge conceded, "but I am certain there is something." On his way out he looked at Adam. "I will speak to Dorcas," he said.

Adam's face burst out in a grin. He reached for Brigge's hand and kissed it.

In the parlor below Brigge drank a posset of herbs, wine, hot milk and hot sugar and ate a penny loaf for his breakfast. Immediately he was outside, he swooned and vomited and did not stop until he had voided his stomach. His shirt was wet and cold with sweat. He waited some small space of time to recover himself, then went to pay the ostler and set off through the town. The watch offered him no insult and was content to let him pass. There was neither rain nor sleet, but a piercing raw wind. The frozen mud of the way blinked in the last of the moonlight.

Fourteen

THE CORONER RODE HARD AND ARRIVED BEFORE MIDDAY AT Skipton, where he rested an hour at an inn in the lee of the castle and revived himself there with small beer and bread. His fever was neither less nor more, and with hopes of the attack being not very severe, he set out again, taking the road to the north. He came to a great moor which he traversed by means of the bridleway. The rain fell heavily; there was not one tree for shelter.

As he went, he considered again the purpose of his journey, asking himself if he were not mad, if he should not, with this tertian fever coming over him, return to the Winters to be with Elizabeth and his new son. But the more he thought about it, the more certain he was there was something amiss in what he had heard at the inquisition. Quirke the alehouse-keeper had said that Susana Horton went to Burnsall to her sister whose husband suffered from a shaking palsy. He recalled Quirke's manner in the giving of his evidence. It had been furtive and sly. How had the alehouse-keeper allowed his serving girl to go to her sister? Could she not have waited one day more for the coroner to come? And why had the constable consented to the said Susana's going? This was the question Brigge wanted to answer above all others. For Doliffe to consent to the girl's going was a dereliction of his duty. Brigge could think of no explanation save that Doliffe did not want the girl heard, though for what reason he could not guess. If he could find out the cause, perhaps he might turn the tables on the man who was conspiring to destroy him, and for this reason he went doggedly on.

At a place where there were miners burrowing the hills for lead, he stopped to be sure of his good direction and there again took beer for his refreshment before continuing on his way and, coming to a broad river, followed it a mile or so and entered at last into Burnsall just as the sky grew dark.

He went to an alehouse at the east end of the great stone bridge and sent for the constable, whose name he discovered to be Beattie, to come to see him there. Brigge took some salt bacon, bread and peas and, by the warmth of the fire, began to think he might yet fight off the fever, that by morning he would be well again, for though he was tired, he felt his strength returning. After an hour there was no sign of the constable, nor of the man he had sent for him. Brigge began to be impatient. The keeper said it was strange, for only that afternoon he had seen the constable drive his cows over the bridge. Brigge questioned the man about Susana Horton, whose sister was married to a man with a shaking palsy. The keeper frowned and pursed his lips and said he knew no Susana, nor one in Burnsall with such a disease. The tipplers in the house said they likewise had no knowledge of any Susana.

When he could stay awake no longer, Brigge went to his room, leaving instruction he was to be woken the moment Beattie came. He found it suspicious that the constable could not be found, but fell into a deep sleep before he could ponder what this meant.

He woke late in the morning feeling thick in his head and heavy in his limbs, the fever still in his blood and bones. He roused himself and went to find the keeper and was short with him when he asked why the constable had not come.

"He did come, your honor," the keeper protested.

"Why did you not wake me?"

"We could not, sir," the keeper said. "For as much as we tried, we were unable to stir you."

Brigge felt abashed. "Where is the constable now?" he demanded.

The alehouse keeper summoned his boy and told him to lead Brigge to the constable.

They found Beattie in a pasture on the far side of the river, carrying hay to his kine. The man put down his load and came to greet the coroner, saying he was sorry for the lateness of his coming last night but that he had gone to visit his brother who lived in Appletreewick. He asked in what way he could help the coroner. Brigge told him. The constable said that he had never heard of Susana Horton, or her sister, or her husband who had the shaking palsy. He asked if Brigge was certain it was to Burnsall the said Susana had gone. Brigge eyed him suspiciously.

"Do you know Mr. Doliffe?" he asked.

"No, your honor," the constable replied, looking perplexed. "I know no man by that name."

"Do you know Quirke, the keeper of the Painted Hand?"

Again the constable denied he did. He appeared to Brigge to be the sort anxious to please his betters and wanting to be thought well of by them, a humble and honest man, by outward show at least. He said that if he might assist the coroner in any other way, Brigge had only to ask. Brigge shook his head.

"I can only think, sir," Beattie said, "that you have been misinformed as to this Susana's whereabouts."

Brigge rubbed his tired eyes. "I think it likely you are right," he said. He thanked the constable and returned to the alehouse where he paid his reckoning. Though he had not breakfasted, he would not wait to eat but, wanting to be home as soon as possible, set out on his way.

At the very least Quirke had lied in his evidence. But what did that mean for his suspicions of Doliffe? Was Doliffe in collusion with him? And if so, to what end? And what of Katherine Shay? A child was found dead in the room where she had lodged. Shay was discovered to have recently given birth. A birth. A murder. A murderer. How could so simple a matter spin a single complication? Yet Brigge was certain that it did. He would have to find Susana Horton. Where was she? How could he begin to search for her without that Doliffe would discover his intentions and attempt to frustrate them?

o   o   o

BRIGGE'S HEAD SWAM in the contemplation of these questions so that after a time he was not certain where he was. He stopped his mare and looked about. He found he could not remember if he had passed through Skipton or not. All about was blasted moor and black heath with mountains beyond, a pure, benighted wilderness. It started to snow, gentle, fat, wet flakes. There was thunder in the distance. He drew his cloak about him and nudged his horse forward.

A sudden mist came in, and the horse had difficulty picking out a track. Eventually, he found a causey-stone path which he followed until it became submerged in moss and heather and tufts of spiked grass. It seemed to him he was the only man living in the world. Nothing moved before him.

Then, of a sudden, he heard noises in the wind, muffled footfalls, it seemed, behind him, hard breaths, someone charging. Taking out his sword, he turned against his assailant. A shadow sprang at him, or seemed to. There was a flapping, a beating like a sheet struck by the wind, and then silence and emptiness once more. Brigge dug his spurs into the horse's flank and went forward at a gallop, whipping his mount hard, making her go on. But she was soon run out. The mist swirled, clearing for moments only to come in again thicker than before. There was no path before them now, only treacherous soft ground. Brigge cursed his mare, but however much he whipped and jabbed at her, she remained stubborn. Unable to advance, he stayed fixed in his place, in this place, with the wet snow blown about and the clouds crashing on the mountains. Then, as abruptly as it came in, the mist lifted.

o   o   o

THE CORONER SAW he was near a crossroads with a dark forest beyond it. As he drew near, he saw some people gathered there, some playing at a game of bowls on a patch of green, others dancing to a fiddler. A strange place to make such entertainment and such a cold, wet time for it. They had the look of men and girls of the baser sort: butchers' and clothiers' apprentices, laborers, weavers, and light, loose women. When they saw him, they removed their caps and hailed him with careful greetings of *your honor*, and even *my lord*. Brigge examined their expressions for hints of scoffing or sarcastic senses, but it was always hard with the common sort of ignorant people to discern the sentiment behind such words; ridicule was their weapon against those set in authority over them and had to be secret or disguised if it was not to bring a whipping. They offered up a jug of ale with tentative hands and appeasing hearts. When Brigge accepted it, they relaxed into the gilded smiles of false fellowship and said the coroner was to drink and he was welcome to it and whatever else they had. The drink was harsh and had a filthy smell, very cadaverous and revolting. Brigge wiped his mouth with the back of his hand and returned the stinking pot. As he did so, he became sensible that the smell belonged not to the ale.

Lifting his gaze, he saw suspended from a tree, twenty feet high in an iron cage, the scarecrow remains of a man bound in chains—the object of this merry excursion. The tattered clothes were rotting on decayed and shrunken limbs. The crows had been at work on the exposed flesh of the feet and hands, but the face and shaven skull had been pitch-tarred, the longer to be preserved for a terror.

"Who is this man?" Brigge said.

The revelers answered that he was Moore, the highwayman from Mirfield.

Moore the highwayman. The coroner had seen him at the castle when the assize came on and he was tried on seven indictments with his father and brother. They had robbed seven clothiers traveling from Manchester to Hull, taking what coin there was and some packs of cloth, as well as boots, cloaks, gloves and hats for themselves. Their enterprise was not very successful. Their broken nags could not outrun the hue and cry and they were apprehended at Pontefract. Brigge recalled that when he stood at the bar for his trial, Moore looked a pathetic creature, slight and pale and stoop-shouldered and not more than five feet high. He had long lank hair and a wracking cough he fought to subdue but could not. The judge condemned him and, because Moore and not his father was suspected for the ringleader, ordered for an additional punishment that he be taken from the scaffold, where he would swing with the other two, to be hanged in chains at the place where he committed his crimes. Moore wept at this violent retribution, and his mother begged the judge to have the body that she might bury her son fittingly. But she was refused and so the family's shame was perpetuated. All for the dread and better instruction of the populace.

While Brigge stared at the caged cadaver, the fiddler whipped a jolly leaping jig and one of the women pointed to the convict's half-covered groin, now empty of what once was there and had made him a man.

"He was not well provided," she shouted with a coarse jesting laugh.

"He may have been so before the crows arrived," one of her friends replied. "They say the birds will first peck the sweetest parts." There was more raucous laughter.

Brigge wheeled his horse about. The animal snorted and the revelers tripped carefully about her flailing hooves. "The law has hanged this man," he shouted angrily, "not to make brutes of those who gaze on his bones, but to make Christians of them."

They gaped at him, big-eyed and fearful, and backed away with small steps they wished could be larger ones.

"Go!" Brigge shouted. "Get to your homes! Be gone!"

With barely a murmur, and as one body, the revelers obeyed. Brigge was about to nudge his horse with his toes and start forward when a woman's voice, old and cracked, called him by his name. He looked about, startled, and saw a black figure huddled motionless beneath the iron cage, so small that Brigge had not devised it until now.

Brigge drew up to her. "Who are you who calls me?"

"It is Goody Moore who calls to you, Mr. Brigge. The mother of the poor child hanging in chains there."

"Your son was no child, but a notorious thief who preyed on merchants and travelers here."

"He was my child, whatever he did."

"That I must grant you," Brigge said out of pity for her. "Why are you here on such a terrible day?"

"Why, sir, I am here every day and will come every day until I may bury my son with his father and brother."

She held something up for the coroner to see. A broken staff? A gray-white stick caked in black earth? Brigge looked up at the chained felon. It was not easy to perceive what bones were there and what were not. A missing forearm perhaps? The lower part of a leg with its last rotten meat?

"Do you have the key to this terrible cage, sir?" Brigge stared at her, not quite understanding. "I must have his bones to bury him," she said. "How else will he meet Christ on Judgment Day? He must have a grave to rise from, if he is to live again."

"I have no key," Brigge told her, turning his horse about.

The old woman took time to consider this. She seemed quite downcast for a time. She said at last, "You were not in the right in what you said to the heartless wretches you sent away."

He pulled up and turned in the saddle to look at her. "In what was I wrong?" he asked.

"You said the law hanged my son to make Christians of them."

"Your son's punishment was terrible, but he merited no less."

"I am his mother and cannot say anything to that. But this I know: the law will never make Christians of men by hanging other men."

"Good day to you, Goody Moore," Brigge said, urging his mare forward and leaving the highwayman's mother waiting for more of her son's bones to drop from the cage.

The light was fading, the clouds gathered blacker and blacker. The coroner murmured to himself, *This one night, this one night, Every night and all . . .*

When you from hence away are past,
Every night and all;
To Whinny-moor you come at last
And Christ receive your soul.

Thunder rumbled and lightning flashed through the gloom. Brigge had never known lightning and snow together.

This one night, this one night,
Every night and all;
From Whinny-moor when you may pass,
Every night and all;
To Bridge of Dread you come at last;
And Christ receive your soul.

The wind was unforgiving cold; his hands and feet were desperate numb. Brigge craved a bed and rest. He wanted only to sleep. In a place where there was no habitation anywhere near, he found Katherine Shay with some inmates of the House of Correction standing together, their hair and clothes whipped by the wind.

"What do you do here, Shay?" Brigge demanded, perplexed that she should be free from her prison.

"Come," she said, putting out her hand to help him down from his horse. "You have no need of a mount now."

She led him to be among her strange friends. One offered him a staff and bade him take it, which he did. Then Starman the cripple, who was also part of their company, put a silver penny in Brigge's right hand and a gold crown in the left.

"You have all you need," Shay said. "Now you may go on your way."

Brigge looked uncertainly about. "Where do I go?" he asked.

"You will find the way," she said, and kissed him.

A freezing mist came down, thick as milk, enveloping them in pure whiteness and silence. When he looked again, he saw that Shay and her friends had gone. Brigge thought he could hear someone crying and, walking some way, he came on Elizabeth sitting cross-legged in the snow. Before her lay Samuel, cold and inert. Husband sat beside wife and joined in her grieving. Then he lay down to sleep beside his dead son.

◎   ◎   ◎

THE THIEVES BUNDLED him roughly, taking him by the legs and shoulders. Brigge struggled against them and called for Elizabeth and Samuel. He felt himself hoisted upward, heard their groaning as they pushed and pulled. One cursed him; another complained at the weight of their burden. He smelled the sweat and dung of horse. Brigge flopped forward. He felt coarse hair prick his cheek. Hands came up to steady him.

"I will take him," one of the thieves said.

Brigge gazed at this assailant and saw it was Starman. "Have you come to take back the silver penny and gold crown you gave me?" Brigge asked. He saw Starman turn to his companion. He heard their laughter. A hand smacked the horse to set it walking.

Fifteen

HE THRASHED ABOUT, A MAN WRACKED, HEATED AND TOR-
mented from without and within, by the air in the room and by his body's
own fever. His limbs ached, his bones were full of pain. So great was the
torment of his belly and of the vapors ascending to his head that at times
he was not conscious to himself and swooned out of all perception. And
then, at last coming back into himself, he was stricken and overwhelmed
with thirst, horror and heat. He called out for Elizabeth and Samuel. He
called on the Holy Mother of God, full of tender love, fount of mercy and
gentleness. Immediately, his intellectuals became again unclear and imperfect, and he did not know where he was or what he was saying or if he
spoke at all or if he was alone or surrounded in the midst of an infinity of
persons.

ο   ο   ο

A COOL HAND touched his brow.

"Elizabeth?" he said, peering at the form above him. There were mists
and films over his eyes, and the shapes he conceived made no sense to his
brain. He fumbled for the hand to clasp it. "It is you," he said. She seemed
dispirited by his words. "Samuel?" he said suddenly, recalling the vision he
had had of his son lifeless in the snow. "Does Samuel live?"

"He does not feed easily and vomits much of what he takes down. We pray every hour that he might live."

Brigge closed his eyes. Why was he being punished? Was his sin so great that God would take his child from him? He had not confessed. He had compounded his offense by denial and now he was being punished. He felt his head being lifted and a cup put to his lips: a warm drink of bitter herbs and, though sweetened with honey, harsh and pungent.

He shook his head when he could take no more, then took her hand and kissed it. His lips sensed a fine film of sweat and dirt. "I have something I must confess to you," he said.

"Say nothing. You have nothing to confess."

"I must be honest," he insisted. "My conscience is overwhelmed. I must confess."

Elizabeth looked uncertainly about her, over her shoulder to the door. "Do not speak of this," she said, her voice a soft, imploring whisper. "There is no need."

"I must," he insisted. "You gave me no cause and yet I betrayed you. I have sinned, Elizabeth, and I am sorry."

Elizabeth made no answer; her head was bowed and Brigge realized she had begun to sob. He struggled to sit up so he might comfort her, but she resisted him when he tried to pull her to him. He gazed into her bright eyes. Her skin was fresh and clear. Brigge was amazed by the youthfulness of his wife. He was sorry for his sin, he was truly sorry. He smelled the smells she carried in her hair and hands and clothes, of wood smoke and soil, and cheese and yeast, and sheep and grain, the things of the house and the land around it. Tears came into his eyes.

"Elizabeth," he whispered, "I love you more than life itself."

She was rocking slowly back and forth. She said, "I must leave this house and not come back."

"What do you mean, you must leave this house?" His eyes searched hers. "Elizabeth!"

"It is more than I can bear to stay." She leaned forward and kissed his brow. She sat a moment in silence, then got to her feet. "I must go to Elizabeth to tell her you have come into your senses. She has been sitting here with you since you were brought home and only an hour ago, at the urging of all of us in the house, went to rest."

Brigge, amazed and confused, pushed himself up, blinking to clear the deception from his eyes.

Dorcas squeezed his hand and smiled down at him. "Our hearts are never in our own keeping," she said, "though we must try to make them so. It is time for me to go."

Brigge was about to speak when they both became aware of someone at the door. Turning, they saw Adam there. The boy stood fixed to the spot, agape at what he saw. Then he turned and went. Brigge and Dorcas exchanged a look.

"Did he see?" Dorcas said, high alarm in her voice.

She hurried from the room. Brigge, exhausted from the effort of his concentration, was out of all consciousness before she reached the door. Ghosts rose up to take him back to the darkness and havoc where they lived, and the perceptions of this world were lost to him.

In the world where he was taken, he saw again the throng of people at the crossroads. The loathsome stink of Moore's decay rose up in his nostrils as sharply as if he were transported back beneath the cage where the old woman waited. She had asked him for a key to liberate her from her wait, from her suffering. In one dream he had been offered a key. In a waking dream he had been asked for one. This much was plain truth to him. But of the rest? He imagined Katherine Shay before his eyes, taking him down from his horse. And Starman putting coins into his hands, and whores and lepers offering him a staff. What did these things signify? What was God asking of him?

○   ○   ○

AFTER FOUR DAYS Brigge's fever broke. He lay quietly in the bed. He felt weak but quite calm. Elizabeth was beside him. This time he knew it to be no dream, no delusion. He was in this world and his wife was sitting next to the bed. She peered at him, not saying anything, not knowing if he were well or mad. Then he smiled and the anxiety in her face melted away. Her eyes were dancing with happiness. She embraced him and kissed him.

He asked for Samuel and saw Elizabeth look to the far side of the bed where Isabel was. The old kitchen maid went out of the room and returned almost at once with the wet nurse, who handed over the swaddled infant. Elizabeth bent down to show Brigge his son. Brigge shifted to see better. The child was fair-skinned and his eyes were blue. His lips were full.

"Look how he now thrives," Elizabeth said, putting a finger to Samuel's cheek.

At that instant Samuel squealed and his face became red with anger. The women laughed and Elizabeth handed him back to the wet nurse, who put him to her pap. Samuel's cheeks worked like bellows.

"I thought he did not suck," Brigge said.

The wet nurse laughed. "He will suck me dry, I think."

They watched him feed. Elizabeth was crying and laughing.

Brigge searched for a top and a bottom, for a shape to the days he had lost, but could make no sense of them. "How did I find my way home?" he asked. "I have no memory of how I returned."

"You were carried by a friend," Elizabeth said.

"What friend?"

"A good friend, most kind and loving and loyal. At first when we saw him come down from the mountain with your horse, we thought him a robber or thief, for he is in truth very sordid and monstrous to look at," Elizabeth said. "We ran up—Dorcas, Adam, Isabel, Sara, even little James—ready to fall on him and beat him, demanding to know what he had done with the one whose horse it was. But on our approach we saw the horse carried a cargo and the cargo, when we inspected it, was you."

"What is the name of this friend?" Brigge asked, though he already knew.

◎   ◎   ◎

AFTER HE HAD taken some food and drink and refreshed himself, Brigge went out to the barn, where Starman had kept himself since carrying the coroner to the Winters. The filthy pustules which covered his forehead and cheeks had spread to his nostrils and mouth so that the lips and gums were encrusted with scabs and open sores. His hair was dull and bald in patches like a mangy dog's. Elizabeth had given him an old fustian doublet of Brigge's, and a pair of blue breeches, old shoes, and a shift made of canvas and the cap he now doffed. He stood with his head humbly bowed before the coroner.

"I understand it was you who found me and brought me home," Brigge said.

"Yes, your honor."

Brigge took out his purse and held out a coin for the vagrant to take. "Take it," Brigge said when Starman made no move to accept what he was offered.

"I would rather earn it, your honor," Starman said.

"You have more than earned it," Brigge said.

"I did nothing more than any man who came across one in danger of his life would do," he said. "I merit no reward for any deed I did then, but if your honor was pleased to give me employment, then I would accept what he thought fair."

"What employment do you seek?" Brigge asked.

"Your honor said he had need of a shepherd."

"You said you would bring a boy to tend to my sheep."

"Would your honor be pleased to have me care for your flock?"

"You?" Brigge said, glancing at Starman's ruined leg. "You are hardly able to walk."

"I am able to get about well enough, your honor. Not as quickly as other men, I grant you, but I never fail to arrive at the place I set out for. I am also experienced in sheep."

Brigge surveyed the long, thin, wracked body, the pocked face and the hairless ridges above the eyes. "Did you by chance give me some things to keep?" Brigge asked.

"Some things, sir?"

"One who was with you gave me a staff to walk with."

"I do not think so," Starman said cautiously.

"You did not put into this hand a coin?" Brigge said. "A silver penny in this hand and a gold crown in the other?" It was a nonsensical conceit,

Brigge knew, but his vision had been so vivid he was impelled to question Starman.

"Would that I had these things to give, your honor," Starman said. The coroner looked the strange man over; even now, though much wasted in body, he gave an impression of some strength and fortitude, and he perceived Starman's mind and parts to be sharp. He had great need of a looker and shepherd.

"You say you are capable of the work?" Brigge asked.

"Before I was struck down with my present infirmities, I was known for my great strength and endurance. These qualities, though reduced, I still possess. I would be your honor's most faithful servant."

"There is a cabin in the mountain behind the house which you may have use of," Brigge said. "For your wages, you shall have sixpence a day together with some bacon and salted mutton besides your shelter."

Starman accepted the terms, thanking the coroner neither effusively nor with false pride but directly, and the two men took each other by the hand to seal their bargain, Brigge hesitating before consenting to the diseased man's touch. He thought of St. Francis, whose recoil from the lepers so shamed the saint he went back to kiss their feet and ever after was loved for his selfless care of the sick. But Brigge was not Francis, and the age of saints and miracles was past.

As he came back into the house, Brigge found Dorcas waiting for him.

"I have spoken with Adam," she said, looking about in case they were overheard.

A feeling of disquiet entered Brigge's heart as the recollection of Adam at the door of his room when he was in his fever came back to him.

"He was suspicious of what he saw," Dorcas said, "but I told him he was deceived if he thought he had witnessed any impropriety."

"Did he believe you?"

"I hope I have convinced him."

Neither spoke for some moments. "He has asked me to speak to you," Brigge said at last.

"How can you talk to me of this?" she said.

"Adam would make a good, kind and loving husband."

"No!" Dorcas cried. "No." She put her hands to her ears and shook her head and ran off.

Later, Brigge and Starman sat together to watch a heavy ewe separate herself from the flock. Agitated in the way of ewes when their time is come, she licked her lips and scraped and trod the ground and turned in restless circles. The birth came forth very quick, the creature slipping out. The mother stood up, breaking the membrane, and began to lick and talk to its lamb, it sneezing with the first air it took into its lungs. The first lamb of the season had been born safely. The other sheep came to look.

o   o   o

HAD IT NOT BEEN for Dorcas, Brigge would have gone to bed in a state of great contentment. The convulsions in the town, the arrest of Fourness, the conspiracies of Doliffe and Antrobus—all these seemed remote to him. He had come safely home. Elizabeth was restored and well again, and little Samuel was growing stronger by the day. Brigge's horrid premonitions, his fears of the symmetry set up by the death of Katherine Shay's child had been proved wrong. The Lord had protected him. Dorcas, too, would recover her good humor and gaiety. In time she would forget her infatuation for him. She would marry Adam and have children. He licked Elizabeth's nipple. Milk came forth, light and sweet, and she covered her breasts with her hands and laughed as he moved over her.

Brigge remembered the great revel at Bull Green. That was when he first saw her, among the great crowd of young men and women. There were maymarions who went in women's clothes, and the rest were in white waistcoats and sheets, carrying white banners with crosses, holding garlands and flowers and branches. Pipers and fiddlers played, and drummers too. There was noise and sweat and laughter, with faces flushed with heat and chase and promises of the dark. All the world was giddy and some were drunk and mad and bumped and pummeled one another until they were parted by their friends. Brigge, eyes not seeing clearly, head laughing, stomach uncertain, feet tripping, stumbling, gave himself up to the swirls and convulsions. He bumped into someone he could not see and put his hand out to steady himself and felt softness and she laughed to her friends and said this is a bold one. Brigge would have moved on, but she stopped him and fumbled at the front of his breeches and said to the one standing next to her that she would measure him before she would lie with him, for it was not every man that could please her. Had Brigge been bolder, as bold as he wanted to be, he would have gone after her when she went on her way with her friends, leaving him with lewd eye tricks and backward glances and smiles. Instead he was left in an amazement of sex. He was trembling, fearful, under the strangest fascination. He did not know how to stand and around him was a stream of glistening faces. It was then he saw her. There were white flowers in her hair and sweat on her brow. The color in her cheeks was high. Her face was not beautiful, but full of life. She was in the company of her friends, dancing with them, laughing and calling out. She had seen what had happened and, smiling, she took Brigge by the arm and said that he should not make anything of it since it was just a woman reveling on May Day night. Beside them a man had his hands under a woman's clothes so high they could see her thighs. Later in the night Brigge pressed her against a tree and kissed her. By then he was drink-boldened and brave, and he had also by then sensed he had an advantage over her because she already seemed almost to be in love with him. He was not wrong. This was Elizabeth, who loved him from the first, whose nature was loyal and full of laughing lust.

All was well. All would be well.

Sixteen

ON LADY DAY MORNING THE HOUSEHOLD ROSE TO A STRANGE
quiet. After weeks of storms the wind had given way to calm and the bitter
rain had ceased. The skies were hard and blue. At first none dared believe
the peaceableness of weather would endure even until noon, but they went
to bed that night in stillness and woke again to the same condition. The air
became so mild Brigge went about outside in his shirt.

The women seized their opportunity. There was much to do. They
bustled, going about as though on skates, their hurrying and colliding
almost dizzying Brigge. They stripped the beds and gathered clothes in
great bundles for the wash, pounding them mercilessly with their wooden
bats. They swept the house and washed the floors and put aside the tubs of
fat for the candlemaker when he would come. James Jagger they sent to
the hens to collect the feathers they would cure for bolsters and pillows.
Elizabeth and Dorcas worked among their churns and tubs and molding
boards and made butter and cheese and baked bread. There was a great
lightness of spirit in the house so that even Adam, still waiting to have
Dorcas answer him, was distracted from his miseries.

Samuel was at the center of everything. As they hurried by where he
was—in his cradle, in the wet nurse's lap, by the door of the kitchen from
where he could see the cows and hens—they stopped to admire and coo at
him. He had begun to smile and to hunch his shoulders to protect himself

against the tickles passing hands gave him. He fed well, the wet nurse was content, and Elizabeth and Brigge marveled with pride at all he did.

Hired men came to grave the ground. Brigge cut the earth in a right line, the others pulled the soil over with their hacks. The ground had been much softened by the recent heavy rain, making the work easier and quicker to perform. They declared the omens to be good, that they had worked smaller fields with soil much poorer and seen them produce thirty bushels of oats and barley apiece, that with lime and marl this ground would have richness enough for years to come and Brigge's new son would farm it for as long as he had inclination.

At the end of the day Brigge and Elizabeth together walked the furrows, examining the work, checking the depth and care of the cut.

"The men have labored well," Elizabeth said, satisfied with the graving. The sky was darkening and a breeze had picked up. "I have sent word to Father Edward," she went on, "so that he might come to baptize Samuel."

A priest coming to the house would carry hazard with him, but Brigge knew Elizabeth would not be deterred. He nodded and said Father Edward must come. She looked to her husband. "You are quiet, John," she said, taking his hand. "Does something trouble you?" she asked.

"Nothing," he said. "I shall renounce my position as a governor of the town," he said. Elizabeth gave him an anxious look. "It is the safest course," he said, then at once regretted his choice of words.

"Safe, how?" she asked, alarm in her voice. "Are you in some danger?"

"No," he answered firmly. "But things have become heated. There are ambitious men in the government of the town and they are already at each other's throats. Unless good sense prevails, they will shortly tear themselves to pieces. I have no desire to be part of this."

"Have you told Nathaniel of your decision?"

"I have sent him a letter with Lacy, who went into the town yesterday," he said. "I also intend to write to the high sheriff to renounce my coronership."

"Why?" Elizabeth asked. "There can be no danger in being coroner?"

"None," Brigge answered. He put his arm around her.

"What about the Irishwoman?" Elizabeth asked. Brigge had told her of his suspicions and unease in this matter.

"She is almost certainly guilty of what she is accused," he replied. "And if she is not, others will find her innocency better than I."

"Are you sure, John, that this is what you want?"

"I want nothing more than I have here," he said.

All that mattered was what he possessed. He desired nothing more, not riches, not honor. Man, woman, child, home. If he could not build a wall to keep his family safe from the intrigues of the world, then he might by retiring from the world be forgotten by men, overlooked when the time came for them to reckon accounts.

○   ○   ○

MR. LACY, HAVING been to the town about his affairs and on his way home again, came to the Winters. Lacy assumed familiarity with Brigge by reason of his own family's notorious recusancy, but the coroner had little liking for his neighbor, their religion notwithstanding, thinking him a vain, boastful man.

"I delivered your packet to Challoner," Lacy said.

"Did he say anything?"

"Nothing. He seemed rather distressed at what he read," Lacy answered, taking a letter from his coat and handing it to Brigge. "This packet is from Dr. Antrobus."

Brigge did not open the letter at once. Elizabeth came in with hot spiced cakes and beer for their visitor, whom she greeted hospitably, she being more sociable than her husband.

"The condition of the town grows more unhappy by the day," Lacy told them as he ate. "Grain is short and dear, and the temper of the poor is much inflamed by the reductions in their doles and the hard punishments they now endure for things they say before would have brought nothing more than a rebuke." Lacy swallowed his pot of beer and crammed his mouth with more cakes. "Mr. Fourness remains in prison," he went on. "They say he will be brought to the bar when the special assize comes on. Doliffe boasts openly he will see the old man hanged and promises the like fate will befall a score of prisoners now in the jail."

At last Brigge broke the letter's seal.

"The watch report mysterious warlike horsemen," Lacy continued, wiping crumbs from his lips, "whom some say are come from Ireland, and others priests and Jesuits." Lacy left off his munching for a moment and sent Elizabeth a knowing glance. "If only there were such conspiracies— then might we be delivered from this madness," he said. "There are such heats and animosities the whole town has lost its head in the searching out of strangers. Did you hear of the vagrant taken by the watch at Gibbet Hill?"

Elizabeth said she had not and she filled up Lacy's pot. Brigge listened with half an ear as he unfolded the letter.

"He would not say who he was and so was set upon and beaten to his death," Lacy related with relish. "Only after he was dead did they learn from his companions that the man who would not answer was as mute as a fish and had been so since birth."

Brigge read the single line Antrobus had written: *Where is John Brigge?*

Lacy looked to see what the coroner would say about what he had read.

"An inquiry of my wife and son," Brigge said.

"Ah," Lacy said, draining his pot. He went on, "The country suffers new calamities with every day that passes. The meaner clothiers continue to manufacture their kerseys and dozens by the week but cannot sell them for the cloth merchants are ruined and have not the money to buy. Plague is reported from divers places throughout the kingdom, and lately a great fire razed Dorchester to the ground."

"There is no need to sound so contented, Mr. Lacy," Elizabeth said.

"It is a matter neither of contentment nor sorrow," Lacy protested.

"You give a strong impression to the contrary," she chided him.

"It is not chance that such mishaps have occurred in a land that has forsaken true religion and shaken off obedience to the pope," he said. "The people are being punished for their faithlessness."

Brigge threw the letter into the flames and looked at his neighbor. "It seems we live in severe times," he said, watching the paper shrivel in the fire. "Every man with whom I have conversation talks of the world as a place of havoc and discord where people must be coerced, caged and punished."

"I sometimes ask myself what manner of Catholic you are, Brigge."

"A poor one, as I am a poor man, in every respect."

"Then you will recant when they come for you?" Lacy said, an edge creeping into his voice.

"I have sworn the oath of supremacy," Brigge reminded him. "I attend their church as the law requires."

Lacy huffled in disapproval. "Such shows of conformity are no longer sufficient for the persecuting kind who now hold sway," he said. "They will be satisfied only with confession and recantation." He put down his pot and became solemn. "They will require that we betray each other. To refuse to go gadding to their drear services merits but a fine. But it is a felony to attend mass and to shelter a priest carries death. With no more than a few words a man might easily have another hanged."

Brigge listened to Lacy's smacking lips and finger-sucking and searched his neighbor's face for subtle meanings. But all he saw there was as innocent and foolish as the sounds of his contentment.

"All the more reason for prudence in conversation," Brigge said.

"Indeed," Lacy said nervously. "Quite so."

When their visitor was gone, Elizabeth said, "Will we be safe?"

"If we do not meddle with them," he said, "they shall have no reason to meddle with us."

The following morning a messenger brought a packet bearing the laurel seal of the town's government. It contained a peremptory summons to attend a meeting of the Master and governors, to which Challoner had subscribed in his own hand: *I trust you will allow one who loves you to say do not neglect to fulfil this letter's command, for your own sake and mine, if for no other reason.*

o   o   o

BRIGGE WENT TO find his shepherd. There had been some losses during the worst of the gales and the frosts, but fewer than Brigge had feared, and with the days continuing so mild the lambs and their mothers were thriving.

They sat together on a flat rock above the pasture. Brigge looked Starman over. He appeared monstrous and ridiculous, a pathetic, wizened creature. The hair of his mustaches, the only hair he had that still grew, did something to hide the creeping putrefaction of his nose, but there was no mistaking the other ravages of the disease, the scabs that crusted his hands and neck, the lesions on his face.

"You told me, did you not, that you were once a soldier?" Brigge said.

"Not by choice, your honor. I was pressed and taken to Boston and then to London in the army of Count Mansfeld."

"You were part of the expedition to the Palatinate?"

"I went to Frankenthal in the count's army to rescue the poor Protestants of Bohemia from the papish armies of the Spaniards and the House of Austria."

"You fought in a very exalted cause."

Starman heard the sarcasm with which Brigge had recklessly clothed his comment. "The cause, I have heard, was noble, as you say, your worship," he replied carefully. "As for my fighting, I did all I could to the best of my capacity, and all my comrades and tent-fellows did the same. But calamity overtook us. The half part were killed, among them many captains and gentlemen, and of the half that were left living the greater number were cruelly afflicted with hurts and hunger and other sufferings. I was one of the many tormented with diseases, and had part of my leg shot off besides, as you see, which has left me lame and impotent so that I am hardly able to maintain myself."

"Why did you not go home to the fens on your return?"

"I made my way there as best I could, your worship, begging carters and carriers to take me, and some bore me small portions of the way, but arriving at last at the house of my half-brother Exley, I found him, like all the poor commoners of the fens and marshes, much oppressed by the great landlords and undertakers who were draining the land. They indicted Exley in Star Chamber for tearing down enclosures and fined him five hundred marks, the which sum he never saw in his life, and never will see. With his wife and family he was put out of his cottage with no choice but to seek settlement elsewhere in the company of other dispossessed men of the fens."

"Many would have been glad of the opportunity to escape the fens."

"Indeed, sir. Many have it that the air of the fens is notorious and unclean, and the life there so uncivil that people say, to describe a fall in the world, that a man goes from the farm to the fen and from the fen to Ireland."

"What happened to the boy you said you would bring to look after my sheep?"

"Are you not content with my work, sir?" Starman asked, suddenly made uneasy.

"You have worked well," Brigge said. "I am curious about the boy, that is all."

"The boy is dead, sir. He died in his sleep."

Brigge would have doubted the truth of this but for Starman's strange air of probity. He said, "I should have been notified."

"To what end, sir?"

"To the end of holding an inquest on view of the body," Brigge said sharply. "To the end of summoning a jury to determine the cause of death. This is the law, and in failing to notify a coroner you have broken the law."

"May I ask, sir, what your honor and his jury think they would have discovered?" Starman asked.

Brigge considered the inconvenience of the journey to the squatters' encampment, the summoning of a jury, the disinterment of the body. To what purpose? To find that a vagrant boy died hunger-starved? The law had nothing to say about the death of a boy by hunger and neglect. That was the business of men's conscience and charity.

As Brigge was about to return to the house, Starman, with much hesitation and great courtesy, asked if his honor would be kind enough to let him have a book to pass the time with.

"Do you know how to read?" Brigge asked, surprised.

"My father, who was a glover, sir, and is now dead, was most careful about the education of his children. Even my sister had some instruction, while I and my brothers were sent to the free school and there learned to read and write and had some education in Latin, Greek and mathematics besides."

Later, Brigge had James Jagger bring Starman Mr. Dalton's *The Countrey Justice* and a treatise on mortal wounds and injuries and how they might be recognized.

Seventeen

BRIGGE WROTE BUT DID NOT SEND HIS LETTER TO THE HIGH sheriff. His reluctance to do so was because of Katherine Shay; he could not rid himself of his doubts. Quirke had lied to him about Susana Horton, and Doliffe's conduct suggested the constable had something to hide. Brigge was torn between his resolution to withdraw from the snares and tricks of the world and his desire to uncover a truth that might discomfit his enemies, a truth he might yet have need of if he was to keep himself and his family safe.

In the week before Easter he held three inquisitions, one falling on the other in quick succession. The first two were uncomplicated: a man from Bradford who died with great suffering eleven days after a kick from a horse, and a nine-year-old boy who fell from a dovecote in Northowram while climbing with his friends. Lives extinguished in a moment that was not in any way extraordinary. Brigge felt intensely the fragility of being.

The third inquisition was a matter of greater intricacy. One Thornton, the constable of Padside, a place of no great moment beyond Wharfdale, came to Northowram, interrupting the inquisition there, in search of a coroner. He informed Brigge of the death two weeks before of a woman who had already been buried, it being held that she died naturally. But, certain informations coming to light, the story had gotten vent that she had been killed by a beating from her husband, and now the people were very desirous of a coroner coming. Brigge, who had hoped to return to the Winters after concluding the inquisition on the fallen boy, reluctantly followed the constable on the long road to Padside.

As they traveled on their way, Adam attempted to engage Brigge in talk of Dorcas and asked directly whether his master had fulfilled the promise he had made that he would press Adam's suit.

"I will speak to her when the time is right," Brigge answered brusquely.

Adam was silent for some moments. "When will that be?" he asked at last, his voice eager and intolerant. "She threatens to go, to leave the Winters and seek work elsewhere."

"She has nowhere to go, Adam," Brigge said. "Be patient and you will have what you want."

"Perhaps you do not want her to marry me," Adam said.

Brigge's heart skipped a beat. "I cannot think why you should say so," he said. He gave Adam a look to challenge him if he dared, to utter any suspicion he had of his master. The boy said nothing.

"I have given you my word," Brigge said to reassure him. "I will speak to her when the time is right."

⊙   ⊙   ⊙

IT TOOK NEAR the whole day to arrive at the place, which was very remote and obscure. There was a small, melancholy chapel, half of wood and half of stone, a half-ruin in whole, and some poor tumbled cottages standing at the crossways of foul and unregarded streets where rubbish, ashes, filth and excrements lay.

Brigge went first to the cottage of the husband whose wife was dead but, it being but a shanty of earth and timber like all the other habitations and too small and noisome to accommodate the jury and witnesses, he moved them to the tippling-house at the far end of the town, a low, mean laborer's dwelling with the sign of the Lion but at least with room enough for their purpose. He ordered the parlor cleared, and the drinkers that were there went out to the garden where they were content enough to sit on the benches, discoursing loudly and smoking their clay pipes.

When all was ready, Brigge ordered the husband brought forward along with those who accused him. He was a handsome, well-shaped young man with dark hair and dark brown eyes, very clear and tender, with a humble and sober demeanor.

On his oath he said his name was Robert Hewison of Padside, husbandman; his age was twenty-nine. He was born in Kendal and had come to Padside three years before to marry Mary, his wife, who was now dead. They had lived very happily and peaceably together, as his neighbors would swear, and his wife had never complained against him but said what a fine husband she had and no woman was better cared for. As to her health, she was sickly and always delicate and suffered swellings to the legs and feet, and lately these pains had tormented her so grievously she was hindered from walking and sometimes fell down for the pain and more than once hurt herself in her falling.

As Hewison spoke, Brigge began to perceive that his pleasantness and humility were a fourbe, that he was in truth boastful and spoiled.

"How did you come to find your wife dead?" the coroner asked.

"Returning from my labors on Saturday," Hewison answered, "where I was scouring the water courses, I found my wife in bed sore afflicted with grievous pains to the head. The following morning, being Sunday, she was not able to go to divine service but stayed in her bed and suffered much from vomiting of ugly stuff."

"Did you call any of the neighbors to the house when your wife lay in this condition?"

"She wanted only to rest undisturbed and not have the meddling of others, saying she would recover her health if left alone."

"No one saw her in that time?"

"When she did not improve, I went to fetch her sister Hannah, your honor, who came on Wednesday a short time before my beloved wife died."

The coroner noticed a woman in a white coif and blue petticoat standing next to the constable. She burned with the desire to speak out and be heard. Brigge assumed her to be the said Hannah.

Brigge gave Hewison a straight, hard look. "Did you beat Mary with your fists or feet, causing her to die?"

"I swear I did not. I loved my wife and cherished her and did never strike her," Hewison replied, his brown eyes full of gentle reproof for the injustice of the question.

"It is not difficult to see he is a liar," Adam whispered when the coroner left off his questioning of Hewison.

"No," Brigge said. "The difficulty will be in hanging him."

◦ ◦ ◦

BRIGGE CALLED FORTH Hannah Smith of Padside, twenty-eight years of age, spinster, to give her evidence. She was small and plump, quite unlike the description the coroner had had of her dead sister.

"When did Robert Hewison come to fetch you to see his wife?"

"There never was a day when Robin Hewison ever fetched me," she replied, casting a hard glance at her brother-in-law. "I went without invitation to speak with my sister, having not seen her at prayers. Robert Hewison would not have me enter the house and threatened me that if I did not go away he would see that I should suffer for it, but I, persisting, got inside."

Brigge looked to Hewison. "What do you say to this?" he asked.

"It is not true, your honor," Hewison protested.

"Mary told me that Robin Hewison, her husband, had killed her," Hannah shouted out. The people in the room murmured and hawked. "She told me he had returned from his work much distempered in drink," she continued, "and had beaten her to pieces as he had never beaten her before in her life and that she feared he would be the cause of her death."

"This is a lie!" Hewison shouted out.

"Did you see any bruises on your sister's person?" Brigge asked Hannah.

"She showed me marks on her stomach and legs where he struck her," Hannah replied, "and put her hand to the back of her head saying the blow she had had from him there would kill her."

Hewison again called out that she was lying, that she had always harbored him ill will because he had married Mary and not her.

"Robin Hewison knows the truth of what I say," Hannah shouted back. "He offered me five shillings that I would have at Michaelmas if I should hold my peace and say nothing."

"Did you accept his promise of money?"

"I accepted nothing from him."

"Why then did you not go to the constable?"

When Hannah hesitated in her answer, Brigge asked again, his voice severe and impatient.

"I did so at the request of my sister."

"How so?"

Again Hannah hesitated and again Brigge reprimanded her for her evasion.

"When Mary was on her deathbed," she began falteringly, "she said that she forgave her husband for she loved him and that when she died I was not to meddle or have any coroner, for God was able to reward them according to their dealings."

"By concealing this you have committed a crime," Brigge said. "Are you aware of that?"

"I pleaded with her and told her she must have justice, but she made me swear, saying if I forgive not him, how shall I be forgiven of God?" Hannah turned to her brother-in-law, and when she pointed at him, her finger shook and her voice trembled. "Robin Hewison has always been heady, rash and fierce. He is a despiser of others, conceited and arrogant. He is a common alehouse-haunter and a bastard-getting rascal."

She broke off to sob. When she found her voice again, both it and her anger were colder. "Since his wife's death," she said, the words bitter in her mouth, "he has neither mourned nor even given show of grief but has been with his friends drinking and playing at cards and boasting that now the shrew is in her proper place let her scold the devil for she cannot nag at him."

Darkness had fallen. The constable, jurors and witnesses were anxious to get to their homes. But the coroner would not adjourn the inquisition, allowing them time only to have their supper.

⊙　⊙　⊙

THE ALEHOUSE-KEEPER brought small beer to drink and halfpenny loaves of buckwheat and barley. The man would have loitered so that his fat lips might carry gossip to nourish the prating mouths outside, where it seemed the whole township had gathered, but Brigge bade him be gone with angry hard words and so he went, very quick his step and dismayed his look. The bread was stale and coarse and the butter near rancid. Brigge ordered the door of the parlor left open for air, but all that entered was the fuddled gaze of the drinkers, their pots in their fists, their clay pipes in their stained lips.

"Hannah has no evidence against the husband," Brigge said to Adam as they finished their supper. "At least none sufficient to return an indictment of murder."

"Perhaps the neighbors will have more hard proofs."

"Unless they saw the actual strokes he laid on her that killed her, he will go free."

"And you are content for that to happen?" Adam said, indignant.

"It is the law," Brigge replied evenly.

"Then I say the law makes mockery of justice. The man is plainly guilty."

Brigge looked over at Hewison, who sat by the constable and would not eat, posing as too distraught to heed the pangs of his belly. The coroner finished his meal and called for more candles. He directed the constable to bring the next witness forward.

This one and the following were friends of Hewison's and swore that they never saw him mistreat his wife, and that Hannah Smith her sister was a disputatious and scolding woman, a troublesome and turbulent neighbor who quarreled much and who did all she could to defame her brother-in-law of his good name.

After these Brigge heard some neighbors who took Hannah's part and were very strong against Hewison. In their account he was by common fame a notorious drunkard who spent his time and money in alehouses in the company of his friends and lewd women, to the great neglect of his wife and scandal of the neighbors. Several deposed that they had seen him at divers times and places—even once during divine service, in full view of the congregation then present—set upon his wife and beat her cruelly. None, however, claimed to witness the fatal assault, if indeed there had been such a thing.

Finally, the coroner called the curate of the chapel, a mere youth, earnest and trying hard to conceal the uncertainties he had of himself and his place. He eyed Brigge balefully. He was, the coroner perceived, one of the hotter sort.

The coroner asked if he had seen the body before it was buried and whether it bore any bruises or marks. The curate answered that he had no reason to look at any part of her except her face and hands and these, as far as he was able to perceive, had nothing suspicious about them.

The jurors complaining at the lateness of the hour, the coroner adjourned the matter until morning. Adam got up to leave with the rest, but Brigge asked the boy to sit and drink with him a while before they retired to their beds.

"In Moses' time," Adam said, "the Jews would have taken Hewison and stoned him to death."

"Is that what you think we should do to Hewison?"

"I do not think any man would object that it was unjust."

"You were not always so severe and passionate in your opinions, Adam," Brigge said.

"I did not then see that Satan was abroad in the land," Adam said.

"You believe so?"

"It is evident," Adam insisted. "And yet those ordained of God to keep the peace sleep. Kindliness and charity will not do. The sword, which God gave to magistrates, must be used with energy. If not, the Devil will be Lord."

"I think perhaps you exaggerate," Brigge said.

"This is the argument of the faint heart," Adam retorted.

"Is that what you think of me, Adam? Am I one of these faint hearts?"

Adam hesitated to answer. Brigge searched the boy's face for his true feelings. They were not well concealed.

"If you feel this way about me," Brigge continued, "why do you continue in my service, in my house?"

"You have always been kind and loving to me," Adam said slowly.

"So you overlook my faults, as you see them, out of gratitude?"

"Yes."

Brigge nodded slowly. "But these faults, they are serious, are they not?"

"I believe those who have power and sit by and do not act will be the ruination of the commonwealth unless they change their ways."

Adam was quiet for some moments; then he asked, "If the Jews were right to stone to death a man like Hewison, why are we not justified in the same?" When Brigge did not answer, Adam said, "You recoil from the terror of such a punishment?"

"The terror comes not from the severity, Adam," Brigge said at last, "but from the justification."

"What do you mean?"

Brigge drained his pot and wiped his mouth. "What does it say about men that our only just recourse is to spill more blood?"

"It says we are not afraid to do the Lord's work," Adam replied.

Brigge's head felt thick from the drink. "How long will gratitude allow you to overlook these derelictions?"

He did not expect an answer and got none.

The candle flared and flickered its last. He gazed at the flame until it extinguished itself.

Eighteen

WAKING IN THE NIGHT, THE CORONER WENT OUTSIDE TO THE
garden and, taking his easement, heard shouts and uproar nearby. Finishing his business, he took his sword and went out to the way in front, where
he found Adam and the tippler roused from their beds by the agitation. It
was the dark time of the moon, and shapes and shadows slipped by like
phantoms while men with torches ran here and there, shouting oaths and
threats. A shadow loomed over him, and Brigge leveled his sword against
the belly of a man who brought himself up to a sharp halt.

"I will let your guts about your heels if you come any nearer," Brigge
said.

"Stay your sword, sir. It is I, Thornton, the constable."

"What are you doing, Thornton? What is this havoc?"

"Neighbors have come running into town," the constable said in great
agitation, "having heard sounds of a great fight on the road to Knaresborough."

The young curate came running up, his shirttails flying, a pistol in his
hand. "The papists have risen!" he exclaimed. "Now must we stand
together or we will be put to our deaths!"

The Padside men took up the chorus that the papists were up and they
would fight rather than have their throats cut by Jesuits and Irish savages.

Brigge laughed loudly and, turning back to the alehouse, said, "I leave you to stand together then. Goodnight."

"Where do you go, sir?" the curate called after him.

Brigge stopped and, turning, saw the curate had leveled his pistol against him.

"I go to my bed," Brigge said evenly, "as you would do well to go to yours."

"So you might murder us the more easily?"

"What do you say?" Brigge said, taking an angry step forward.

"This man is one of them!" the curate cried. "He is the notorious papist John Brigge!"

Brigge swore at him and called him a fool and a coward. The argument went quickly from less to more and the Padside men gathered, carrying torches and armed with sticks, staves and pikes. Among them were jurymen who, only hours ago, had sat before Brigge in full acceptance of his authority. Now they were impassioned and goaded and very ready to set upon him.

Brigge felt Adam's shoulder against his and, glancing down, saw a dagger in his clerk's hand.

Turning to the constable, the curate said, "This man cannot be left at liberty. He should be put under restraint and taken before a justice."

The constable licked his lips but did not speak. Someone lunged forward to stab at them. Adam swung his knife, and the man withdrew himself into the crowd again, though not before Brigge had sight of Hewison's face.

The curate took aim with his pistol.

"Put up your gun, sir!" the constable said. "I will take them under restraint." Thornton turned to Brigge. "Give me your sword, Mr. Coroner," he pleaded.

"I will not be taken under restraint by you or anyone else," Brigge said. "Let any man who wants come close and he will see what he will have for his pains."

The curate urged the Padside men on. Brigge stood fast with Adam at his side. One or two of the neighbors made feinting strikes with their staves and pikes, and they circled the coroner and his clerk, ready to rush them. Thornton pleaded for quiet and reasonableness.

At that moment they heard a sudden cry and turned as one to see a man stagger forward, moaning pitifully that he was murdered. The neighbors hurried to the stricken man, save for the curate, who kept his pistol leveled at Brigge's heart.

"Come, sir," Thornton said to the curate. "Let us go, for God's sake!"

Brigge did not wait for the curate to put up his gun but pushed contemptuously past to follow the throng. He found a man collapsed on the ground, his face and hands all bloodied and his clothes torn, his chest heaving with the effort of his recent running.

"Who is this man?" Brigge demanded.

"He is Morrison, sir, the corn badger," the constable said.

The man fought to find his breath. Raising his hand, he pointed down the road. "They came out of the dark," he panted, "their faces covered, some wearing white sheets. They had swords and cudgels and threatened to murder me without mercy."

The cry went up that now it was proved: the Jesuits were coming to wreak slaughter.

◉   ◉   ◉

IT WAS LIGHT by the time they came upon Morrison's cart in a close near a watermill, men and women clambering over it like ants, and children by the back end and by its wheels picking grain from the grass where it had spilled. Others were making off as best they could with plundered sacks of barley and corn across their shoulders and backs. The curate raised his pistol and discharged a blast, knocking one man over, tumbling him from the cart, though he got up quickly again and broke into an awkward skipping run. The rest scattered, taking with them what they could. Most were so loath to abandon their booty they were apprehended with little effort. Some pleaded with their captors to release them for mercy's sake; others fought with their hands and feet and so struggling some got away, for there were too many to subdue them all. They were all men and women of the poorer, ignorant sort.

"Here are your Jesuits, sir," Brigge said to the curate.

He ordered the prisoners lined up by the cart. "Why did you set upon this cart?" he demanded of them.

No one answered, but one woman sniggered loudly in derision of him. She appeared not in the least broken or overcome, but, like the rest, wrought-up and defiant, though she like the rest surely knew that some of their number would hang for an example to the rest.

"Why did we take Morrison's grain?" she laughed bitterly. "Last summer oats were four shillings a bushel. Then they were six shillings and now they are twelve. I do not have twelve shillings, but I do have five children and so took for nothing what I could not pay for."

Her haranguing of him set up such a commotion in her fellow prisoners that the Padside men had a time to subdue them and make them quiet again. Brigge instructed the constable to have the prisoners conveyed to the town where, he had no doubt, the Master and Doliffe would see justice done.

"Come," Brigge said to the constable.

"Where do we go?"

"To the churchyard."

◎   ◎   ◎

THE EARTH AT THE top was mild and loamy, but the deeper the bury men dug, the darker the smell. Brigge knew this smell and would never be accustomed to it, to the dreams of worms and bones and decay it inspired. The grave-makers' work done, the coffin was brought up. Brigge led the way back to the tippler's parlor.

The jurors had taken their places on benches arranged to the left of the rough trestle table, prattling and hawking and much heated in their talk of the assault on Morrison the corn merchant. But they fell silent the moment Brigge and the bury men entered with the coffin. Brigge looked them over, lingering over the faces of the men who only hours before had seemed ready to kill him. One by one he stared into their eyes until they turned their gazes from him in acknowledgment of his power over them. Had he mind to, he could prosecute them for affray and riot, and they knew this all too well.

— 135 —

The smell was already noxious. Some lit their pipes to have the clouds of tobacco keep off the odor, others put handkerchiefs hard to their mouths and one or two had nosegays of rosemary and sage. The coroner ordered the coffin opened, and Thornton and one of the neighbors, holding their breath in their lungs, lifted the cadaver to the table. Hewison, Brigge noted, was very uneasy, not certain what lay in store for him, and sent Brigge pitiful pleading looks with his tender brown eyes as if the coroner were some wench into whose affections he could by his dolefulness insinuate himself.

Adam sent a questioning look as Brigge parted the sheet to uncover Mary Hewison's face. He gazed down on the body.

I was full fair and now am I foul
My fair flesh begins to stink
And worms find in me great prow
I am here meat, I am here drink.

It was not possible to tell from the skin of the face and hands, being now so discolored in decay, whether it was bruised by blows. Brigge put his fingers to the eyes, then peered into the nose. He opened the mouth. Flies crawled over the dead woman's lips and gums.

In my wanton breath an adder keen
My dazed eyes smart dim
My guts are rotten, my hair is green
My grinning teeth smart grim.

Waving the swarm away, Brigge peered inside, angling the candle for better light. Wax dripped onto Mary's face along with his sweat. Resolving himself, he called out to Adam that the front tooth on the left side was broken in half but that otherwise her mouth appeared undamaged. The inside of the lips, as far as he could tell, showed no sign of having suffered cuts.

Opening the sheet further to uncover her body, he examined with particular care her chest, stomach and sides. When he could discover nothing, he called Hannah forward to show him where she had seen the marks she spoke of. Hannah came up, averting her eyes from her sister's face. Taking courage, she leaned over to look at the body. She peered for some time.

"There," she said, pointing to the right side. "I think there is something."

Brigge could see nothing but the blotches and stains of the dead. He called the jury up to look for themselves. When they had satisfied themselves, he went on to inspect the legs. These appeared in some degree swollen, as did the feet, but whether from disease, decay or cruelty he could not say. The flies had settled again on Mary's face; they crawled over the cheeks and over the black lips and gums toward the promise of their fetid feast.

With the constable's assistance the coroner turned the body to survey the back, but to little purpose, it being as decayed as the front. Turning the corpse once more, Brigge, with his hands symmetrically placed, put his fingers to the head, feeling first at the forehead, then at the crown, then at the backside of the skull. Though at the left side above the ear he came upon a hard lump about the bigness of a hen's egg, which could as easily be the manifestation of disease as the result of assault, the skull wall did not appear smashed, but he knew that his fingers alone would never detect a fracture. The only sure method to discover such an injury would be to have the head without the flesh, for thus he had heard a dead man's broken skull ring unperfect, like an earthen pitcher with a crack, or a thread held between the teeth and struck like a fiddle string. But the law did not allow the opening of a corpse.

Finishing his work, Brigge pulled the sheet up over the dead woman, leaving only her face exposed. He turned to the jury. "From my examination, I have discovered no evidence of wounds or marks or bruises that came about by violence."

Hannah shouted in rebuke of him, calling the coroner blind, foolish and corrupt. But there was no mistaking the relief on Hewison's face. His friends winked and smiled at him, and there was a smirking lightness in his brown eyes which he could not hide.

Brigge then called Hewison forward. At first Hewison did not move, not crediting the summons. His friends became quiet.

"Come here," Brigge said coldly. Hewison approached the table slowly. "I ask you on your oath," Brigge said, "did you kill your wife?"

"I swear I loved my wife with my whole heart," he said, appalled that the accusation should be made just when he had thought himself free of danger.

Brigge stepped back to let Hewison see his wife's body. Hewison swallowed and turned his head away.

"Touch her," Brigge said.

Hewison looked up suddenly at Brigge, alarm coming to him with understanding of what the coroner was about. Adam left off his writing. The constable and jurymen were silent.

The curate came forward. "What papistical superstition is this?" he demanded.

There were shouts and dissensions from among the jurors so that Brigge had to bellow to be heard. "It is nothing of superstition," he roared, "Romish or otherwise." Still the commotion would not settle. "The authorities approving this as one of the proofs of murder are many and weighty," Brigge shouted out. "Mr. Dalton, a gentleman of very excellent learning and reputation, has written in his book for the instruction of justices of peace that when a murderer puts his hand on the corpse the victim's blood will flow anew. For those who will not accept the authority of Mr. Dalton, there is Sir Francis Bacon, the noble lord chancellor that was, a very learned author in both divinity, law and science, who held the same sign of murder to be evident. Who here will say he knows more than these eminent and learned gentlemen?"

The tumult began to subside. Brigge continued, quieter now, "In Erringden, five years ago, one Raistrick murdered his friend by drowning him in the river. I called on him to lay his hand on his dead friend and, as soon as he had, blood poppled in the corpse's mouth and came out of his nose. I was present at this, I saw it with my own eyes. So did the jury, and Raistrick, confronted with the proof, confessed the murder. I saw him tried at the castle. He was found guilty and hanged. God will not suffer murder, which is the most horrible crime, to rest unpunished."

"I have done no wrong, your worship," Hewison pleaded.

"Then touch the body if you dare," Brigge said. "The devices of men cannot be concealed from Almighty God."

Brigge gestured for the jurymen to come up. They and the witnesses gathered in a great crowd around the body.

"This is trickery and fraud," Hewison protested. He cried out and proclaimed his innocency and cringed wretchedly.

Brigge took hold of Hewison's right hand, which Hewison snatched back. But then, summoning his courage, he thrust his hand forward toward the corpse. It hovered above the right shoulder, trembling visibly.

"Touch your wife," Brigge said. Still Hewison could not move his hand to her. "Do as I say," Brigge ordered him.

Slowly, Hewison lowered his shaking hand.

"Keep your hand there," Brigge said when Hewison was about to withdraw his fingers after the merest brush with the stained sheet covering his wife.

Hewison looked at the coroner beseechingly. Eventually, Brigge signaled him he could take away his hand, which he did slowly and deliberately, in spite of his dread and revulsion, to show he had nothing to fear. A fly moved across Mary's lower lip.

The excited crowd surged around the body calling for more light, pressing right up to the table in such anticipation and excitement that the body was in danger of being toppled over to the floor. The coroner pushed through the crowd to lean by the door so that he might have clean air. He and Adam exchanged a glance, Adam's uncertainty about the proceedings evident from his expression.

"Blood!" Hannah suddenly exclaimed. "I see blood!"

The jurymen, one after the other, hesitantly at first but then with greater stoutness, affirmed they too saw blood flowing anew from the cadaver.

"Where? There is no blood!" Hewison screamed. "This is nothing but a trick! A papish conjurer's trick!"

The crowd contradicted him loudly and even his friends grew reluctant to support him. The jury found that Hewison had murdered his wife. Brigge ordered him sent prisoner to the town, where he would wait until produced for trial.

As Brigge put his signature to the inquisition, a bird flew into the house, causing great anxiety among those who saw it, for birds only enter human habitations to foretell a death.

○   ○   ○

AS THEY JOURNEYED home, Adam asked if the coroner had seen blood come forth from the corpse.

"The jury saw blood," Brigge replied. "That is the only thing of consequence."

"But did they see it?"

"They swear they did—did you not hear them?"

"I think they wanted justice done so saw what they wanted to see." Brigge shrugged.

"You would make justice the servant of such poor vision?" Adam said.

"You are conjectural, Adam, where I am merely peremptory." Brigge paused, as though unwilling to engage himself in such abstractions; then, not wishing his argument to appear insufficient and wanting to vindicate himself before his clerk, continued, "You and I agree on one thing at least: justice is poorly served by law."

"I would rather put it that justice is poorly served by weak law timidly applied," Adam retorted. "It is well served by sharp law rigorously enforced."

"You believe the deficiency can be made good with more and sharper law?"

"If law cannot make justice, who can?"

"Men," Brigge said.

"Men are capricious and passionate."

"And apprehend the world better because of it," Brigge said. "We see, as it were, around corners and in shadows. How do we do this? Because we do not depend only on our eyes. Consider Hewison. Apart from his alehouse friends, Hewison is a man not well thought of. The neighbors knew him to beat his wife. If they who knew him so well believed him guilty, should the law be a more exact judge?"

"Your argument surprises me."

"How so?"

"When what men feel becomes what is true are you not afraid that justice becomes very hard? Men are revengeful."

"What you say is true, but men also feel pity and so mitigate harshness where the law allows only severity. I once held an inquisition near Kippax—it was before you came to be my clerk. It was on the body of a child about the age of five years. The child's mother was utterly distraught in heart. She confessed in very plain terms, saying that her youngest son came to her and asked some victuals to eat and she, having nothing to give him at that time, casting her eye about, saw a knife on the table, which she took up and cut the boy's throat. She said she had no other quarrel with her son than that she had no food to give him. She said she was sorry and wished with all her heart her deed were undone."

"What became of her?"

"She went free from the inquisition."

"How so? She confessed to murder."

"She was a widow with four children. She had had no relief from the overseers of the poor for many weeks, she had no food. The people of Kippax knew all this. The jurymen from the town knew it. They found the child had died by visitation of God."

"Men are not always so merciful."

"We are imperfect and often susceptible to those who would stamp hate into our hearts," Brigge conceded. "But I would rather face men's heat than the law's bitter chill."

They were on the mountain in sight of the Winters when Brigge told Adam of his intention to renounce his coronership and write to the high sheriff to commend his clerk to the office. Adam professed himself amazed.

"I no longer have any taste for the work," Brigge said, "whereas you, I perceive, are hungry for it."

"I am eager to see justice done," Adam corrected him.

Nineteen

ELIZABETH CAME RUNNING OUT OF THE HOUSE AND TOOK
her husband by the hand and led him urgently to where Samuel lay in his
cradle. The wet nurse sat by, despondent and quiet.

"He has stopped feeding again and now will hardly suck at all," Elizabeth cried.

Samuel's eyes were large and distressed. Brigge cooed and made faces.
He thought he glimpsed a smile, and the kitchen maids said they saw it
too and Samuel would prosper now his father was home again. But the
child began to cry, a weak, hoarse, pitiful sound. Brigge gave him to the
wet nurse and watched as she attempted to put him to the breast. Samuel
struggled against her, squealing and making his body rigid and unyielding
before consenting to suck. He did not feed long, however, but seemed to
have his fill very quickly.

"So little," Elizabeth said gloomily.

"Better little than none at all," Brigge said.

But then the child vomited up what he had taken down. The little head
sank back, the eyes closed, one hand up near the face, the fingers closing as
delicately and gracefully as the petals of a flower when the sun goes down.

"He has turned against my milk, sir," the wet nurse said; she was close
to tears.

"No," Brigge said. "He will feed from you again, I am sure of it."

He led Elizabeth, who was plainly worn out, to their bedroom and made her lie down. He had much trouble to persuade her, and she would only consent to it if Samuel were brought in. At last she and the child fell asleep.

Brigge remained still in the darkness, listening to the breathing of his son and his wife. He felt a great tender rise in his heart. He had fallen, he had sinned, but in this moment he did not feel overwhelmed by shame.

Love God,
Fear God.
Falling down, despair not.

He looked at Elizabeth's hands resting palm down and motionless on the coverlet. He knew her by those hands. He put a fingertip to her wrist and traced a vein down to where it disappeared at the knuckle, then along the length of the long finger to the broken nail. He thought of the bird that had flown into the tippler's house.

Near midnight the kitchen maids crept in with the wet nurse behind them and asked if they might take the baby to see if he would feed, but Brigge said he still slept and bade them go to bed. The sleeping child's breath was shallow and fast, his color high.

During the night Elizabeth stirred and cried out, confused and afraid.

"Dear heart, dear heart," he whispered. "I love you."

"Such good words," she answered, reassured she was safe. "Do not stop your mouth up in the saying of them."

"I will not," Brigge said.

"I have sent for Father Edward," she told him. "Samuel must be baptized in case he is taken from us."

Brigge nodded; he was suddenly afraid for his wife, as one is for those who are so open to good and defenseless against evil. He wanted only to make her safe. He prayed that God would not take Samuel from them, that He would not submit them to that test. He doubted Elizabeth would survive his loss.

Antrobus had asked: *Where is John Brigge?* Brigge's reply was that he was here, in this room, in this house. Where he was loved. Where he loved. He would not move from here.

◦   ◦   ◦

WHEN SAMUEL BEGAN to stir, Brigge crept out of their chamber to bring him to the wet nurse. Again the child protested when put to the breast. Again he sucked for some small space of time only, and then became angry and pushed the breast away and could not be comforted. Brigge, unable to bear more of the sight, went to the parlor.

There he found a letter with the laurel seal. The terse lines were to inform him that he, by order of the Master and governors meeting together under the powers conferred on them by royal patent letters, was hereby deprived in perpetuity of all manner of authority, powers and privileges pertaining to the office of governor.

So they had not allowed him to renounce his office but put him out of it. Brigge let out a bitter laugh and read on. The letter concluded with an ominous summons: Brigge was to present himself without fail before the Master and governors to answer questions relating to his person and conduct.

When the Master had first urged Brigge to join with him in the remaking of the town and the reforming of the manners and lives of its inhabitants, Elizabeth had pleaded with her husband to consent to it though he had neither inclination for such a project nor ambition for the prizes or honors of office. But Elizabeth, ever a good guardian of his interests, prevailed against his doubts, saying he would have greater safety in among the governors than outside them. Now he was at odds with his friend and patron.

Brigge wrote some lines in reply, courteous enough, saying that press of business prevented him from coming to the town, though he would answer the summons as soon as he was able. He also wrote to the high sheriff to surrender his coronership and to commend his clerk Adam, a young man of excellent parts and learning, diligent, upright and of good religion, as one in every way suited to replace him.

Going to the kitchen to take his breakfast, Brigge gave the letters to James Jagger and told him to take the gray nag and go to the town for Dr. Antrobus. Then he asked for Dorcas to be brought to the parlor that he might speak to her privately.

Dorcas came in looking downcast and troubled. "How does Samuel this morning?" she asked.

"Neither better nor worse," Brigge said. "I have sent for Antrobus. God willing he will cure Samuel as he delivered him." Brigge placed his elbows on the table and clasped his hands before his mouth. "I promised Adam I would speak to you again."

"There is no need to speak to me," Dorcas said restlessly.

"Dorcas, please listen to me. Adam is ambitious and able. He will soon take my place as coroner. He is, I now perceive, a young man well suited to these times and he will prosper for that reason. He has a great affection for you."

"I have said there is no need for this," she repeated.

Brigge sighed deeply and rubbed his hands over his face, thinking how he might yet persuade her.

Then she said, "I have already decided I will marry Adam."

Brigge looked up sharply.

"Tell him he may come to talk to me," she said.

"What brought you to change your mind?" Brigge asked.

"I cannot stay here and have nowhere else to go."

"Do you feel no tenderness toward him?"

"I feel a great tenderness for Adam. We have been here in this house as though brother and sister. But that is what I feel, as a sister feels for her brother."

"You may yet grow to love him."

"I may," she said. "But I will never love him as I have loved you."

She waited to see how Brigge would respond. When he said nothing, she got up from the table and left the room.

Brigge summoned Adam and gave him his permission to speak to Dorcas. Adam thanked him with great profusion and declarations of love and gratitude.

That afternoon Adam announced to the household that he and Dorcas were to be married. Samuel's condition notwithstanding, Elizabeth and the kitchen maids baked cakes and puddings, and that night they drank beer and sack and toasted the pair.

Before they went to bed, Adam took Brigge aside to ask his permission so that he and Dorcas might go to Dr. Favour in the morning and arrange to have the banns read and a day for the wedding set.

"Of course you may go," Brigge said.

Adam looked around the room. "I shall miss this house," he said, "and all in it." He smiled at Brigge, then added, "I will never reveal anything of what I have seen here."

Perhaps Adam merely wanted to put Brigge's mind at ease, but Brigge thought the promise unnecessary and suspicious.

Adam was already on the stairs when Brigge called to him.

"While you are in town, would you perform a service for me?" he asked.

"I should be honored."

"Seek out Quirke—"

"The alehouse-keeper?"

"The same," Brigge said. "Discover the whereabouts of Susana Horton. Do so either by direct questioning of Quirke himself, or by the information of his friends and neighbors. Will you do this for me?"

"I will not fail you."

Brigge thanked his clerk and wished him goodnight. He found Dorcas in the kitchen.

"You are going to town tomorrow, I understand," Brigge said. Dorcas nodded. Brigge drew a deep breath before he spoke. "Dorcas, if this is not what you want—"

"It is not what I want."

"Then do not do it."

"May I ask you a question?" she said.

"Any question you want."

"Do you promise to answer truthfully?"

Brigge hesitated. "Yes."

"Do you want me in this house?"

"I want what is best for you."

Dorcas looked him directly in the eye. "Thank you," she said, and turned her back on him, pretending to be about some kitchen stuff.

"What, Dorcas?" Brigge said, exasperated.

"Nothing," she replied. "I asked you to answer me truthfully and you did. You do not want me in this house."

"I did not say any such thing."

"You did, John," she said quietly. "But I knew it already. When I enter the room, you shift like a thief. When I sit to eat at the table, you bolt your food like a dog."

"It is not true."

"It is time for me to go," she said. "We both know it."

Her gaze lingered on him a moment. Her eye was pleading and piercing. She pressed her lips together and stepped past him.

He saw them off in the morning. They would return together in three days, Adam said, as soon as they had spoken to Favour. Elizabeth and Dorcas embraced, Elizabeth smiling for the younger woman's happiness. Dorcas came to kiss Brigge. She squeezed his hand but said nothing.

Later that day Brigge found Elizabeth at her spinning.

"I pray Adam will be kind to Dorcas," she said, "and give her the love she had here."

She did not look at him but pretended to be intent on her work.

"The love she had here would not have sustained her long," Brigge said. "As Adam's wife she will have the comforts an ambitious husband can bring."

"You will miss her," she said. "There was always such great tenderness between you."

She gathered up a bundle of yarn.

"It was never so great as you think," he said at last.

He stayed while she worked. She said nothing more. When he came to bed that night, he could tell from her breathing she was awake. His heart was low and heavy. They heard Samuel cough and cry.

◦ ◦ ◦

IT WAS LATE in the afternoon of the following day when Antrobus arrived. Brigge led him straight to Samuel. Elizabeth described for the doctor how the child had been and what symptoms there were. She told him how that although the child had been slow to take the teat he had learned to suck well but now refused as he had before and also was hot and coughed and complained day and night.

"He is almost suffocated with phlegm," the doctor said on examining Samuel. "I will give him a lincture to relieve it."

Antrobus set out an array of bottles. He poured some drops of yellow-green-tinted liquor into a bowl and added a pinch of powder. Brigge recognized among the medicines nutmeg, fennel, scurvy grass, sugar, brooklime, and what he thought to be sage water; there were other things, both linctures, confections and syrups.

"Have you heard that Lister is now arrested?" Antrobus said.

Brigge answered that he had not.

"You seem unperturbed by the news," the doctor said, with a sidelong glance.

"My thoughts are presently elsewhere," Brigge said, glancing at Elizabeth. "Forgive me."

"As with Fourness, they have said nothing of Lister's supposed crime."

"That does not necessarily mean he has committed no crime," Brigge said.

Antrobus looked up accusingly. "What has Challoner promised you?" he said tersely.

"The only promise I have had from him is to expel me from the government of the town." Brigge saw that his answer had plainly taken Antrobus aback. "I thought you would have known," he said.

"No," Antrobus said. "Every decision has been taken into the hands of the Master's inner circle, from which I have been excluded. What will you do?"

"I had renounced my office in any case," Brigge said. "I want nothing more than to remain here at the Winters and, with God's grace, live quietly with my wife and family."

"I doubt that will be possible," Antrobus said.

Seeing how this was upsetting to Elizabeth, Brigge asked the doctor to leave off his conversation and concentrate himself on the cure of his son.

"Forgive me, Brigge, if I appear heated," Antrobus said. "But they have marked me down for destruction, which is a thing I find myself unable to contemplate quietly."

Antrobus said nothing more and set about his medicines, adding some sugar to his concoction, and began to stir the elements with a little silver spoon. "I will need help," he said.

Elizabeth took hold of her son. Antrobus instructed her in how to hold the baby so he might get down his lincture. He did so very ably, without fluster or mishap. He waited a moment to see the medicine was not brought up again, and then, satisfied Samuel would keep it down, began to explain to Elizabeth how to care for her son.

"Will he live?" Elizabeth asked.

"If he can be cured of his phlegm and made to feed, he should live," Antrobus replied, and seeing Elizabeth was not much comforted by what he said, he put his hand on her arm and smiled soothingly. "He has already shown himself in surviving so testing a birth to be strong and well made. He will live so long as you follow the course I lay out for his cure."

"I will follow it strictly," Elizabeth said.

Brigge squeezed her shoulder as he left with Antrobus and went outside to sit at the backside of the house. The kitchen maids brought them their refreshment.

"Next month Challoner and Doliffe will hold the special assize," Antrobus said, "at which will be hanged not only the usual rogues and delinquents of all kinds but men of good name and good principles like Fourness and Lister."

"You are convinced Fourness has committed no crime?"

"I am sure of it," Antrobus said, "and likewise I am certain of Lister's innocence."

"You may yet be surprised," Brigge said.

"And when I am arrested, Brigge, will I also learn to my surprise that I am guilty of some thing of which, though I search my conscience from top to bottom, I know nothing? Why do you refuse to see what is afoot? It is plain to a blind man that Challoner and his friends mean to tear down our liberties and construct a tyranny over us."

"I may be blind, as you say, but you, I fear, are dazzled by too bright a light," Brigge said.

Antrobus let out an exasperated sigh.

Brigge asked if he knew anything of Susana Horton. Antrobus frowned, trying to recall the name. "She was the serving girl at the Painted Hand who discovered the Irish vagrant's murdered child," Brigge explained.

"What of her?" Antrobus asked.

"She had, so her master alleged, gone to Burnsall to be with her sister and so was not present to give evidence. Without her I was unable to complete the inquisition."

"I know that Doliffe is most anxious to hang the Irishwoman."

"He cannot do that until the inquisition is done."

"Then he will find your witness so you may finish your good work, you may be assured of it."

"I requested of the constable that he have the girl brought back. However, when he showed no liking for the task, I went myself to Burnsall to fetch her."

Antrobus, now made curious, looked to Brigge to continue his story.

"She was not there," Brigge said, "nor, according to the neighbors, had she ever been in Burnsall."

"So the alehouse-keeper lied. Have him questioned again."

"I think it goes beyond the alehouse-keeper. I suspect Doliffe to be involved in the lie."

"In what way?" Antrobus asked, his eyes narrowing, his conspirator's mind searching for the possible advantages lurking in Brigge's story.

"I do not yet know," Brigge said.

Antrobus had plainly been hoping for more. His face, frozen in expectation of hearing something to Doliffe's detriment, relaxed again. Disappointment came into his eyes.

"It is my strong suspicion," Brigge said, "that there is something Doliffe wishes to conceal in this affair and that if I were able to uncover it the constable would be disadvantaged."

"To such great extent that he might fall from his power?"

"I think it possible."

"Do you know where this Horton is?"

"No. But I have sent Adam to discover her whereabouts."

"You trust your clerk to carry out your wishes?"

"Yes," Brigge answered.

Antrobus considered what he had been told. "I hope you will keep me informed of whatever he finds."

They dined alone together in the parlor. When they finished their meal, Antrobus administered more of his lincture to Samuel. Brigge saw no improvement in his son's condition. Elizabeth looked gaunt; there were dark crescents below her eyes.

Brigge led his guest to Adam's room, where a bed had been made up for the doctor.

"Where is Adam?" Antrobus asked.

"Gone to town to see Favour."

Antrobus became suspicious. "Be careful with Adam," he said. "He has lately become much enthralled by Favour."

"He has gone to discuss the matter of his marriage to Dorcas," Brigge said, "that is all."

"You may be sure Favour will have more interesting things to talk of," Antrobus said.

◦   ◦   ◦

IN THE MORNING Antrobus announced Samuel's breathing to be some-what eased and that the wet nurse should persist no matter how the child might struggle in getting him to feed. Elizabeth appeared in no measure reassured or certain of any improvement and was haggard through want of sleep.

Antrobus was anxious to return to the town, but Brigge detained him with a request. "Would you do me the kindness of examining my shep-herd," he said, leading him to the looker's cabin. "If you were able to relieve his suffering in any way, I would be most grateful."

Starman submitted to the doctor's scrutiny with a childish, uncomprehending, stricken look. Antrobus was fascinated by his afflictions and asked about both the great disease of his skin and the wound in his leg, how each had come about, what sensation he had there, what pain there was, what remedies had been prescribed, what cures he had tried.

Brigge left the doctor with his patient and went back to the house to see how Samuel fared. Elizabeth sat with him by the hearth, the firedogs and tongs at her feet. Still the child hardly sucked, but struggled and cried as had been his habit before.

Antrobus came to the house again, and Brigge took him to the parlor where they drank boiled milk and raisins.

"Your shepherd's flesh is badly corrupted," Antrobus said. "The scab you see on him, the beginnings of decay in his nose and palate, also the ringworms, the filthy odors, the corrosive ulcers—these are all manifestations of the same loathsome malady. In time the disease will invade his body further, corrupting his flesh yet more, eating his brain."

"Can nothing be done then to relieve him at least of his pains?" Brigge asked.

"There are treatments, but they are difficult and severe."

"Are you competent in them?"

"I have treated many suffering from this disorder. They are also costly."

"I cannot pay you now," Brigge said, "but if you would agree to take Starman as your patient, I will find the means to do so as soon as I am able."

"Why should you go to the expense of helping this man?" Antrobus asked. "He is a stranger, he is nothing to you."

"Be not forgetful to entertain strangers, for thereby some have entertained angels unawares."

"You think Starman an angel?"

"I think it unlikely," Brigge said with a smile. "Nevertheless, were you to take him under your care, I would account it a very great favor to me."

"Out of regard for you I would be content to perform whatever service I could," Antrobus said with finality. "But it is not possible. As soon as Doliffe has what he needs, he will have me arrested. I must look first to my own cure."

Brigge saw him off at the stables. When he was gone, he went to where Starman was watching his flock. They said nothing to each other of the doctor but sat in silence watching the lambs and the ewes.

At length Starman spoke. "It sometimes falls out a child that does not like the milk of one nurse will accept that of another," he said. "Perhaps if the women brought him another to suckle from, he would take the teat."

Brigge nodded but said nothing. He and his shepherd sat together on the flat rock until the sun went down.

Twenty

THREE DAYS LATER A STRANGE RAGGED WOMAN CAME TO THE
house and asked to speak to Brigge. The kitchen maids were for turning
her away, but she denied them vehemently and would not move from the
door, alleging she had come for a purpose but what purpose she would
reveal not to them but to the master alone.

She told Brigge she came from the encampment at the new bridge and
had undertaken the journey to the Winters at the urging of Thomas Starman. Brigge became suspicious. What business had Starman led her to
believe she would have here? The woman, who gave her name as Deborah,
answered that she had abundance of good milk. Brigge, not knowing anything of her character, told her to be gone, but Elizabeth, who overheard
their conversation from the house, hurried up and begged her husband to
have the woman enter. Seeing his wife so distraught, Brigge relented and
consented to have her come into the house.

The wet nurse sat at her usual place by the fire, a nipple between the fingers of one hand and Samuel's head in the other. The child, so weak and
wasted, still found strength to resist and the poor woman was plainly dispirited. Yet when she saw her rival—for she understood with a glance what this
new woman was—she became jealous and spiteful, and Elizabeth had to
coax her to release Samuel from her grasp. She fled the room in tears.

"There, mother," Elizabeth said to Deborah as she put the child in her arms. "Let him feed from you, if God wills it."

Deborah took out her right breast and offered the child to feed, but Samuel refused her and, in dissipation of the little strength he had left, made himself angry, stretching rigidly and twisting his head violently from side to side so it was all Deborah could do to keep him in her arms. The kitchen maids needed no further proof, but Elizabeth was prepared to be patient.

◎   ◎   ◎

THAT AFTERNOON Antrobus returned unexpectedly, bringing with him a chest containing rare medicines and secret remedies. The doctor spoke little. His humor was unusually somber and became more so when he saw Samuel, who still would not feed. He examined his stools, which were wet and foul, and Elizabeth plagued him with questions. Antrobus had no answers. He said only that he had done what he could and that they should wait to see if the child would take Deborah's milk.

Then, with no explanation of his change of heart, he told Brigge that he would treat Starman. Brigge thanked him most gratefully and had the shepherd brought to the house to take his cure.

For the foul scabs on Starman's head and in his nose and mouth, the doctor purged his body with pills and, after, used a decoction of guaiac, to which he added white copper and camphor. For the canker in his leg, he cleaned and cauterized it and made a lead plaster of the thickness of a thumb and ordered it worn for the space of twelve days, during which time Starman was to remain in a heated room and not be exposed to the noxious vapors of the air outside, already as heavy as it might be in August, corrupted with ill odors arising from the ditches and becks.

Antrobus refused dinner when he was done, saying he had business elsewhere, and asked if Brigge would accompany him some part of the way so they might speak together privately. He said nothing of any note until they were ascending the high pass.

"I have been dismissed as a governor," he said. "Scaife has been put in in my stead."

Brigge was astounded. "Scaife is an ignorant fool," he exclaimed.

"It is not his brains that commend him, but his fidelity to Doliffe and Favour. Likewise those who have taken the place of Fourness and Lister are men of no independence or judgment. They are told what to do and they do it—this is their real and only worth."

"We are better out of these entanglements," Brigge said. "We have no place among such dark politicians."

"I am a dark politician," Antrobus said, smiling for the first time since his arrival. It was a moment's levity only, a brief glimpse of the old Antrobus, cunning and calculating, the lover of intrigue. He quickly became again morose and inward.

"Did your clerk discover anything of Susana Horton?" he asked.

"He has not yet returned from town."

Antrobus shot Brigge a look. "He has been gone some time, has he not?"

"He will return soon enough."

The doctor's mind was always suspicious, but Brigge too had expected Adam before now and his own thoughts had already been turning distrustful and apprehensive. "If you should come upon Adam in the town," he said, "I would be obliged if you would send him home to me with all speed."

"I do not go to my house," Antrobus said. "I dare not. I am to be arrested today."

"On what complaint?"

"Why do you even ask, Brigge?" Antrobus said sharply. "No complaint was necessary against Fourness or Lister. Why should one be necessary for me?"

"You are wrong," Brigge said. "Fourness is accused."

"Of what?"

"Of sodomy and corruption."

"Never!"

"Challoner himself told me so."

"And you believed him?"

"I saw the informations with my own eyes."

"Perjured evidence!"

"They were credible witnesses," Brigge said. "Several accomplices have also already confessed." Antrobus was silent, not knowing what to believe. "Lister too, I believe, is implicated in the same horrible crime," Brigge said.

The horses snorted. The sky above was clear and blue, and though the sun shone, there was little warmth at this elevation in the mountain. Brigge pulled his coat around him and rubbed his thighs.

At last the doctor came out of his thoughts. "I do not know if any of what they say against Fourness and Lister is true," he said. "But if this is to be their pretext against me, I hope you know I am innocent of any such detestable thing."

Brigge said that he knew it well. "Where will you go?" he asked.

Antrobus seemed reluctant to answer; then he confessed, "To Lord Savile at Methley."

Had he said to the Devil himself Brigge would hardly have been less amazed.

"Savile has asked to see you too," Antrobus said; and seeing Brigge's astonishment, he continued, "He holds you in the highest esteem and is most desirous of making your acquaintance."

"You would combine with one who has committed so many outrages against justice and liberty as Savile?"

"To end the present greater outrages against the same principles?" Antrobus asked. "Why, yes." Brigge gave a dismissive laugh. "Savile has promised that should he come again into power he will put an end to the despicable oppressions of this unholy trinity of Challoner, Doliffe and Favour," Antrobus said. "He swore an oath in front of me that he will deal fairly and justly with every man. It is the only opportunity we will have to save the town, and ourselves. What do you say, Brigge? Will you come with me? Savile knows how to reward his friends."

Brigge looked at the doctor as if he were a feeble, deluded madman, but then understood that he was seeing Antrobus in his true light. He was only ever a conspirator, an ambitious plotter. It was Brigge's error to have forgotten this.

Below in the distance, Brigge could see the smoke of squatters' fires. "I will stay at the Winters," he answered.

"They will come for you soon, Brigge," Antrobus said. "You are to be arrested and brought to the bar and put on trial for your life."

Brigge laughed.

"You do not believe me?" the doctor said, keeping his voice peaceful. "Challoner has already instructed Doliffe to make an indictment of you. The constable has been taking informations from those who have much to say about you."

"Do you know who these pretended informants are?" he asked.

"The informations are being taken in secret. Doliffe has a very lively interest in uncovering conspiracies. Did you know there are five thousand papists in the town? Every one of them armed with daggers and ready at the command of the pope to slit the throats of honest Protestants."

"There are not a dozen Catholics in these parts," Brigge said with a dismissive laugh, "and the only conspiracy they are in is how best to stay at liberty."

"There are five thousand. Dr. Favour himself announced it. You may imagine how the godly people of the town are unsettled by the prospect of their imminent murder. They demand of Doliffe that he take all necessary measures to save them, which perfectly suits Doliffe's purpose."

"Men have more sense than to see devils where there are only shadows," Brigge said; he tried to sound confident, but he could hear the anxious pitch of his own voice.

"Do not rely on what you hope to discover about Susana Horton to save yourself, particularly now you have entrusted the task to Adam. The boy has new friends and they are no friends of yours."

Brigge thanked the doctor for his concern for him and for all he had done for his wife and child. He was polite and cold. Antrobus embraced and kissed him, then spurred his horse on without another word.

⊙   ⊙   ⊙

THE KITCHEN MAIDS hurried out to meet him, their eyes filled with tears. Brigge, his mood already dark, feared the worst, that Samuel was dead, and he leaped from his horse. The women could not get words to say anything but took him by the hand. From their manner as they went, Brigge began to understand that it was not grief but joy that was stopping up their mouths. Did they not say that all would be well? Praise God, their prayers had been answered!

They brought him to Deborah. She was nursing Samuel. Elizabeth stood over her.

"See how he feeds," Elizabeth said, smiling from ear to ear. "Deborah put him to the teat more than an hour ago and he has not stopped to draw breath."

There was laughter, women's laughter, full of relief and love and gratitude. A world made of such women, Brigge thought, would be a happy place; they wanted nothing more than that contentment and kindness should reign. But then, after he got over this great moment of happiness, he began to feel light-headed with anxiety. For now the child sucked, but would his cheeks keep up their happy work? Every quarter of the hour Brigge came to the women and every quarter of the hour their answer was the same: the child either sucked or slept contentedly.

The following morning Elizabeth and Deborah unwrapped Samuel from his swaddling and displayed his swollen full belly for his father to see and marvel at. Brigge went to Starman to thank him for causing Deborah to come to them. Brigge's head was in a turn and Starman's pleasure in his master's happiness was clear.

In the morning he gave the first wet nurse six shillings and thanked her and said they would always be grateful to her. Then he took James Jagger and selected a sheep, one past its prime, that had not lambed and would not, and slaughtered it and had the meat carried to the squatters at the new bridge.

Twenty-one

A STRANGER IN THE WAY, HIS FACE CONCEALED BY HIS HOOD, asked James Jagger to deliver this message, that if his master wished for pure water to come he was that night to leave a candle in the window at the back of the house. The boy repeated the message as he was given it. He did not know what it meant, but Brigge did, and so did Elizabeth. The kitchen maids' manner became sober and industrious and they set about cleaning and arranging the house. The household knelt together and prayed a *Pater Noster* and ten *Hail Marys*.

Father Edward came soon after midnight, stealing into the back of the house, as the thief in the night, where the door had been left unfastened. He asked if Brigge was certain there was none in the house who would betray him and Brigge swore the priest would be safe. He roused James Jagger and sent him to see to Father Edward's horse while the kitchen maids served roasted mutton and Elizabeth put out the best beer in the house.

Father Edward, whom Brigge had not seen for the space of a year, took his supper with them at the table. He was a black and red man, his high, choleric complexion and large raw red hands flashing against the darkness of his cropped hair and the opacity of his dress. His lips were likewise bright against his unshaved chin. He wore a gentleman's fine soft gloves and boots, and the name he went by was Maxfield. The kitchen maids moved as though the Savior himself had come among them. He ate quickly, refusing offers of more meat, put on his vestments and went to the parlor and closed the door so he might be private with each of them in their turn.

When he had heard their confessions, they gathered in the parlor. From his bag he removed a chalice and a cross. Elizabeth brought Samuel to the parlor. The child's look was tangled at being disturbed from his deep sleep, and he turned his head in quick curiosity but without alarm as they knelt and together heard mass and took the host, each of them that was of the faith and was able—Brigge, Elizabeth, Sara, Isabel and the boy James Jagger—while Deborah stayed abed in her room.

When the priest blessed them at the conclusion of the mass, Sara took the child out of his swaddling while Isabel went to bring a bowl of water. Then the little congregation stood together, and the priest took the child into his powerful hands and asked what was his name.

"His name is Samuel," Brigge said. Such pride he felt in this, such joy, that when he looked to Elizabeth to smile a tear came down his cheek. She reached out and put a hand to his waist to say she loved him and they were together and would always be.

A candle flickered at the movement of the priest's arm as he dipped the infant into the water and named him and baptized him in the name of the Father, and of the Son, and of the Holy Ghost. Samuel did not cry when the water came over him. The priest whispered in the Latin that by this baptism Samuel was received into Christ's flock, and that he did sign him with the sign of the cross in token that hereafter he shall not be ashamed to confess the faith of Christ crucified.

The priest returned Samuel to his father. Gazing down at the boy, Brigge saw his eyes, blue and with an ingenious, watchful cast from being more slitted than round, move carefully over his face. The hair, quite reddish at the birth, was turning fair like that of his mother, and the lips were very full. There were dimples in both cheeks.

Not more than two hours after he stole in through the back of the house, Father Edward was gone again. He left them with the prophecy that the days of their persecution would end, that it could not be otherwise, for every believer that was brought to the hurdle and dragged through the streets to the ladder to be half-hanged and cut down and boweled and quartered raised a cry to heaven that would have an answer. When he spoke, his eyes shone with fervor for his religion and a terrible burning passion to suffer for it. He blessed water for them and gave Brigge a little leather pouch with a precious relic of St. Christopher, which, put into the highest room of a house, would ward off all harm to it by lightning and fire.

That night Brigge and all in the house slept contentedly, and in the morning all reported their dreams had been sweet as honey. As Brigge was pulling on his boots, he heard Samuel, having fed and lying in his cradle, laugh a little hoarse laugh. All those in the room went quiet, then hurried as though on an unspoken command to the cradle to look down on the boy who, smiling up at his doting admirers, gurgled and laughed again.

◊   ◊   ◊

IT WAS ELIZABETH'S greatest joy to go into the little garden at the side of the stable and take Samuel on her lap. Here she rested and sometimes doted and dozed. Samuel was transformed, and all in such small space of time. Would that we who are old with years had a child's powers of recovery, they all said, then merrily talked of their stiffnesses and aches and poor eyes and ears. There was such bubbling and happiness with laughter and smiles and so much praising of Elizabeth's beauty and delight in Samuel's prettiness of behavior and appearance. His scrawny limbs were growing thick; there were creases at his wrist where the fat of his forearm met the fat of his hand. His cheeks were full and his eyes were quick and bright. His cry was loud and he sometimes vomited up stuff for feeding so hungrily. On these occasions there was some alarm, Elizabeth always fearing the worst, but Deborah was never flustered. She knew children and how they were to be fed and when and what to do when they complained and had colic and would not sleep. She appeared gentle and loving, but though correct and never forward with her master and mistress, she was of a close nature, speaking little and venturing nothing. How many children she had of her own or what had become of them, Brigge had no knowledge of, or of how she came to have milk and no child of her own to suckle.

Elizabeth observed the lamentable condition into which her garden had fallen. She would remedy it, she said, as soon as there was occasion, and plant vetches and onions, parsley, colewort and beans. She grew excited at the thought of the work before her and Brigge smiled indulgently. After a winter so full of hardships, so teeming with despair, the warm spring days Brigge and Elizabeth spent together were like a term in paradise. The kind of loving that comes from the threatenings of death is quiet and profound.

Brigge heard the short hard call of a mistle thrush and, looking up into a tree, saw the bird go anxiously from branch to branch. It called again, a dry clacking chatter. Samuel stirred in his basket, and Elizabeth took the child in her arms though he was still asleep. He complained at the disturbance and began to cry, and Elizabeth hummed and cooed to soothe him. Brigge saw a second mistle thrush come down from the sky in answer to the other's call, grasses in its beak, and fly off again with its mate. Brigge tickled his son so the garden was filled with the sounds of the gummy laughter of this angel dropped out of the clouds.

⊙   ⊙   ⊙

A LETTER CAME from Adam to inform Brigge that he was detained in the town on press of business, he now being coroner, and that he had taken lodgings at the Swan. He and Dorcas would be married in three weeks. He made no invitation to Brigge or Elizabeth to attend the ceremony, and he said nothing of questioning Quirke, nothing touching Susana Horton or where she was to be found.

Brigge did not care. Katherine Shay was no longer in his thoughts. Neither was Doliffe, nor the Master. In spite of Antrobus's warning, he began to think the storm he had feared so much had already passed over his head, just as the winter, with all its hazards, had passed. Sometimes it is hard for men when they are frozen to believe that when the cold season comes spring is not far behind and they will be warm again.

Lacy, visiting the house with his wife, reported that the special assize was still not yet held, it was said by reason that the Master, though pressed by Doliffe and Favour, had begun to have doubts of hanging so many. Every second man, Lacy related, now wore Savile's blue ribbon, and many prophesied that it would not be long before the old lord came back to begin his rule again. Brigge listened to his neighbor's tales, but with half an ear only. Brigge's son now fed and was growing fat. His wife was well and whole again. His ewes had lambs and the weather continued mild for his crop. This was the new design and order of things. When Brigge dreamed that night it was not of whores and lepers. No one offered him a key or looked to him to deliver or say anything, or lead or liberate any man. He had a wife and a son. His dreams were gentle. When a man is content, he does not hear the approach of calamity.

Twenty-two

BRIGGE RODE TO THE MOUNTAIN SLOPES TO FIND STARMAN. He discovered him in seeming familiar conference with a stranger. Coming close, Brigge saw the man to be Exley, the shepherd's half-brother. Exley carried his fowling piece and had the same dirty black breeches and tattered gray coat he had worn when Brigge first encountered him at the new bridge, but though his face remained broad, his body was much shrunken and, being not tall, he appeared scarce larger than a child.

On Brigge's approach, Starman's manner became suddenly fraught and meek, fearing a reprimand from his master. He whispered something to his brother and shifted a little apart from him, as though in hopes that these few inches might spare him hard words. Exley's countenance did not alter in the least way; he was reduced in bulk but his spirit remained scornful and possessed.

On another occasion Brigge would have questioned Exley as to what he did on his land, armed with a fowling piece as if he were hunting game, but he was no longer governor, nor even coroner, and was in no mood to be a lord over other men. He did not hail him familiarly, but courteously enough, asking how he did. Nothing flattered by Brigge's gentleness toward him, Exley said he did well enough, his tone as reproachful as if he had been offered insults and blows.

Brigge asked, still civilly enough, "How are the people at your camp?"

"Hungry," Exley replied, and mockingly thanked him for his inquiry.

"I will send them what mutton, grain and whey I can spare," Brigge said.

Exley laughed. Starman, caught between his master and his brother, looked uncomfortable, not knowing where to put himself.

"You are insolent, Exley," Brigge said, his patience at an end.

"Should I be grateful?" the vagrant asked, his voice sharp and angry. "Is it not enough for you that we must live as dogs on these blasted moors that are not fit for starved sheep, but must also give you thanks?"

Starman said quietly, "Mr. Brigge is a fine Christian gentleman who has often relieved our wants by his charity."

"I say he is no Christian who lets another starve."

"He has offered you meat and corn, Robert."

"A pox on him and all his kind!" Hoisting the fowling piece to his shoulder, Exley declared, "They think they are lords who can smite the poor famished people of this nation. They should take note that we are not so humble. Let them know that blood shall be met with blood, and fire with fire, that flames can consume the great houses of the rich as they can the hovels of the poor."

Exley spat on the ground and strode away.

"Your brother has a rash and troublesome spirit," Brigge said as he watched him go.

The two men inspected the flock. They found nothing to trouble them; there was no sign of the turn or the rot, for which Brigge prayed his thanks to God. Before long they would be washing the fleeces in preparation for shearing, and those to be sold for meat they would drive to market.

Brigge looked over his shepherd. Since his release from his cure, Starman had begun to take on the shape of a man once more, crippled to be sure and diseased, but no less than a man, with all that went of a man. Brigge questioned him about his infirmities and how the pain was, and asked if there was an improvement since Antrobus had attended him. Starman assured him that by the doctor's great skill he was much relieved in his body. Brigge had the sense that he was being gracious, not willing to criticize the doctor or appear ungrateful for his master's efforts. Still, Starman's outward appearance was undeniably improved, the ugly blains that had covered his head and face being much reduced and the mustaches he had recently grown hiding his nose somewhat so it was not easy to see that the nostrils were beginning to be decayed and eaten back.

After they finished their work, they sat on the grass to eat the cold mutton and apples Brigge had brought with him. Starman stared at the meat without taking any.

"Are you not hungry?" Brigge asked.

"I have appetite to eat," Starman said.

"Then eat."

"I will eat," Starman said, reaching for the food, "though my brother goes hungry."

"You heard me tell Exley I would send food to the encampment," Brigge said.

"You are generous and kind, sir, but I doubt there will be anyone there to receive it."

"Why not?"

"The reason for my brother coming to seek me out was because yesterday in the afternoon some men came from the town, led by the one who was formerly your clerk—"

"Adam?"

"It seems it was he, sir. He announced he and the gentleman that accompanied him, who was called Mr. Scaife, were governors of the town"—here Brigge could not prevent himself from laughing out of astonishment: Adam now governor as well as coroner? He had not been wrong to commend him to Dorcas as one ambitious and able and set for advance in the world—"and by order of the said governors had come to tell them they must leave their dwellings. My brother Exley and the other men were not then in the camp, being abroad to gather what food they could find, and on their return they discovered their cabins pulled down and the women and children crying lamentably in their ruins, saying that the governors had promised them that if they were not gone by morning they should return and set fire to whatever they found there."

Brigge listened but made no comment on what Starman related to him. After some moments the shepherd asked what he thought.

"Exley should gather his family and friends and set off to seek shelter elsewhere," Brigge said, "for Adam is most industrious in the pursuit of justice, and will keep his promise."

Starman looked to the ground and shifted uneasily. "If my brother cannot settle where he is and must move on, my place is with him."

"Are you a fool, Starman?" Brigge said. "Here you will have food and wages." Starman looked at him as though distrusting what he heard. "Do you think you will find better employment elsewhere?"

"No, sir."

"Well then?"

Starman considered for a moment. "I would be most content to remain in your service," he said carefully. "But I should like to ask your honor if in my stead he would keep another."

"Who?"

"Deborah," Starman said. "She has greater need of your bounty and is more deserving of it, being so devoted to your son."

"I know nothing of her," Brigge said, "nothing of her life before she took to tramping the roads."

"She was born in Essex, as I understand it, your honor," Starman said.

"Was she married there?"

Starman's voice took on a guarded tone. "I have heard it said she had a husband there," he replied.

"What became of him?"

"He was a bargeman and sometimes went to London about his work," Starman said, his voice evasive. "One day he went to London and did not return."

"She had children by this husband?"

Starman said nothing, and Brigge put the question again, frankly, so Starman would understand he was to answer and be plain with him.

"Two, your honor, as I have since learned," Starman said; he looked away over the mountain, hoping to avoid further interrogation.

Brigge persisted. "What happened when her husband did not return?"

Starman chewed his lip and dug at the earth with the heel of his shoe. "Having not the means to maintain herself and her children," he began slowly, "she had no choice but to solicit relief, which, it being a poor parish already blighted with a great many begging poor, she could get but little of and so left her house and took her children to London to look for her husband."

"Did she find him there?"

"She did not find her husband," Starman answered, "but had news of him from his friends, other bargemen from Essex, and so set out on the road to Bristol, thinking him gone there by what she heard from them. She and the children wandered west and reached the city, preserving themselves with roots and acorns and berries, but nor was he her husband to be found in Bristol and, she thinking that his friends had mischievously deceived her and that her husband might yet be in London, she resolved to return but fell ill in the way near Oxford and there remained very dangerously ill and at her wits' end and at a loss how to feed herself and her children."

"Is that where you came upon her?"

"I was with my brother Exley and two others who were then our companions, returning from Hampshire where we had work for a season, when we came upon her. She was in a most pitiful condition, starved and in a raging distemper of mind, roaring and railing, her tongue hanging to the side out of her mouth, so that even Exley, who is stouthearted and fears no man, would not approach her, saying here is the Devil come among us, but threw her scraps of bread as though to a dog which, she being in a great distraction, did not even eat."

"Did her children accompany her?"

Starman gave him a pleading look, begging not to be coerced in this of all things, but Brigge was stern with him.

"No, your honor," Starman said at last.

"What had become of them?"

Starman drew breath before continuing. "I knew nothing of any children until after we had made her calm and prevailed on her to eat," he said. "Then she cried for her children, calling them by name, and sometimes thinking she heard them call to her, or heard their cry, she would start off, hurrying into fields and forests saying she had heard them. In this manner I first learned Deborah to have two children, a boy and a girl, aged six years and four, as she later related to me."

"What happened to them?" Brigge asked, though he knew the answer.

"They died, your honor."

"How?"

"I did not ask of her then, and have never since."

Starman stared at Brigge directly on saying this, maintaining his voice firm to announce, as it were, that he had come to the end of what he would say, though his master would whip him for his silence.

Brigge watched the sheep. The sky was streaked with red and darkening. His own silence now made him complicit, not in the concealment of murder or misprision of felony, but in the ways of those of Starman's society. By their rule, a poor mad starving woman had ended the misery of her children. No murder had been done, no crime committed.

"How did she come to have milk when she first came to the house?" Brigge asked.

"She fell pregnant by one who ravished her in a field. The child was born in the wastes at the new bridge and lived two days before it died."

"Did she kill this child also?"

"No, sir. I am sure of it."

Brigge considered what he had been told. "She may stay as long as she wishes," he said.

He got to his feet and went to where his mare was tied to a bramble bush.

"Your honor must be careful in the promises he makes," Starman called to him.

"You think I would not keep them?" Brigge asked sharply.

"To feed and clothe the poor is beyond the capacity of a single man," Starman said.

Twenty-three

THAT NIGHT AS BRIGGE AND HIS FAMILY SAT DOWN TO TAKE
their supper, they heard a horseman approach. The light was fading and
they did not see who the rider was until he dismounted.

"Nathaniel," Elizabeth, turning to her husband, whispered, asking
with a glance what this visit portended. Brigge had no answer.

There was a moment's awkwardness at the door, then Brigge bade the
Master enter.

The tenseness in Challoner's comportment betrayed his urgent need to
talk, but he was too mannerly and modest to forget all civility. He compli-
mented Elizabeth on the fare she set before them. The pottage was flavor-
some and hearty, he said, though he scarce took a spoonful, and her beer
was as good as anything he ever tasted in London. He remarked on the
pretty Apostle spoons which she had from her father and on the painted
cloth hanging on the wall behind the long oak bench. Looking over the
poor plates, trenchers and cups, he said that latten and pewter were as ser-
viceable as silver and in any case less likely to tempt dishonest servants.
Then, noticing there was silver in the house, he picked up the cup Elizabeth's mother had given her when she was betrothed.

"But this is very beautiful," he said. He set the cup at arm's length the
better to admire it; in truth it was ordinary, particular only to Elizabeth

and Brigge for the occasion it was given them. "Beautiful," he said again, smiling at Brigge, a rich man pretending to envy the simpler domesticity of his poorer neighbor.

There is no better way for a man to get an advantage over another than by seeing him in his house with his wife. Abroad, even the humblest laborer can counterfeit himself a lord. Indoors, men are observed for what they are: children, with their favorite cups, and their chairs which must be this way or that, and everything just so. But there was no advantage to be had when Samuel cried and Deborah brought him to his mother. Challoner was plainly discomfited, not knowing how to look or where, or what to say. He admired the baby when Elizabeth presented him, but it was with half a heart that not even his perfect ceremony could make whole. Challoner had no son, nor would have. Even Elizabeth, rapt in her child, noticed the uncomfortable shift in the Master's demeanor.

After some insincere discourse about ordinary things the Master could no longer conceal his agitation. Brigge asked Elizabeth if Samuel was not fatigued. She said how happy she was to see Nathaniel again after so long, sending anxious glances to her husband as she did so. Brigge affected not to see them, but tickled Samuel in his chest and shoulders and gazed lovingly at his son until Elizabeth, the proprieties observed, took him and went from the room.

"You are a very fortunate man," Challoner said aloud before Elizabeth was out of earshot. "You have been blessed with a virtuous, discreet and dutiful wife."

Brigge understood his intent was to flatter Elizabeth further, a little trick to be thought of well by her, for men put greater value on reports of them given to others than related to their own faces.

"Elizabeth is a good wife to me," he answered.

"And now she has given you a son. Such faithful diligent women must be cherished."

Brigge said nothing; he was impatient for the Master to arrive at his meaning and wanted no more of formality and platitude, or of subtle disparagement. Challoner gazed at the table and played his fingertips over the grain of the rough wood.

"You disobeyed me, John," he said without looking up; he maintained his voice low, but his tone was sharp. "I sent letters commanding you to present yourself before the governors."

"And I wrote to you, Nathaniel, saying I would attend as soon as I was able."

"You left me no choice but to dismiss you from your office of governor."

"It was an office I no longer desired to possess, as you know," Brigge said. "Certainly my removal appears to have been a boon to my former clerk. I trust Adam is well?"

"Adam has already proved a most diligent governor."

"The vagrants at the new bridge swear to it," Brigge said.

"I had been told you were taking an interest in their condition," Challoner said. "I must confess it seems to be a strange preoccupation."

Brigge thought for a moment, then said, "When I first came upon them—it was as I was coming to the town to hold the inquisition on the Irishwoman Shay—I told them they could not put up cabins, that the land was not theirs to settle. One of them, a froward fellow named Exley, a dangerous-seeming, bold spirit, stepped up and answered me that they were Englishmen and must live somewhere. I could think of nothing then to counter his argument, nor can I now."

"The settlement is unlawful—that is the only argument you needed. I am surprised you were unable to find it. Exley and his band of vagrants must be removed from that place."

"Adam will doubtless see to it."

"Adam will do his duty."

"It is strange. When did Adam fall under Favour's spell? Why? No one in this house ever encouraged such vehemence and fanatic thinking."

"I dare say he grew so dismayed at the looseness he found here that he could stand it no longer."

"Looseness?" Brigge said with a tense smile.

"You know what I mean, John. You were ever one for turning a blind eye to the faults and sins of men."

"Yes," Brigge conceded. "Yes, you are right, Nathaniel. I learned it from my mother, I think. Do you remember her? You were always very respectful when she spoke. And what she said was that men must have mercy, for without mercy we are savages."

"Without law we descend to the level of the beasts. The law shall decide when mercy is to be given and when it is to be withheld."

"No!" Brigge said quickly. "The heart decides. The heart informed not by law but by sympathy and love. I am now more than ever convinced that an eye that is sometimes blind sees more justly than one that is sharp."

The Master made an expression of his plain disagreement, and also his despair at his friend's recalcitrance, pursing his lips and shaking his head slowly. He said, "You need look no further than your own words to understand why Adam chose to go from this house and come to join us in the town."

"I wish Adam and his new wife well," Brigge said.

"He will act as clerk when the assize comes on."

"When will that be?"

"The work is most urgent, but I have postponed it," Challoner said; he paused before continuing, "I did so because of you."

"How so?" Brigge asked, attempting to keep the smile on his face, yet made anxious by the directness of the Master's tone and answer.

"I wanted to give you time to save yourself," Challoner said.

"From what must I save myself?"

"You have spurned me at every turn, John," Challoner said, making his voice passionate, "notwithstanding the great affection in which I hold you and which I have always shown you. Do not spurn me now. Your life depends on it."

The self-pity and torment in the Master's voice were more than Brigge could bear. "Enough!" he cried out. "If I am to be undone, it is by your hand, Nathaniel!"

Challoner looked at him as if he was the most resentful ingrate in the world. "You know nothing of how I have striven to protect you," he said harshly. "When Doliffe first came to tell me of reports against you, any one of which would have merited an ordinary man's apprehension and examination, I told him I would not sanction anything against you until the evidence was clear. Had it not been for my care for you, you would long ago have found yourself languishing in the jail."

"What reports were these?"

"Be very careful in what you ask, John, for you may receive answers you do not like to hear."

"Am I to be one of Fourness and Lister's acolytes? Is that what Doliffe charges against me?"

"You know that is absurd."

"Tell me then, what are these reports Doliffe informed you of?"

Challoner glanced at the door to the passage. "You spoke of the duty you owe Elizabeth," he said slowly.

Brigge narrowed his eyes. "What has this to do with Doliffe?"

"Does that duty extend to fidelity?"

Brigge drew in air through his nostrils. His chest swelled and he felt his heart quicken. Shame welled up in him, but anger too. "A good husband is faithful to his wife," he said.

"It has been alleged you are an adulterer."

"Who alleges this?"

"Is this true?"

"Who charges me with this?"

"Adam. He claims you seduced Dorcas."

Brigge stared at Challoner. "What does Dorcas say?" he asked.

"Is it true?"

Brigge said quietly, "I have failed in many things, Nathaniel, and will answer for my lack in due time."

"You confess then?"

"I confess nothing. I say only that my private acts belong to my own conscience. It is for me to make amends, not for you—or Doliffe or Favour or Adam—to judge me."

"No, John, you are wrong. That is the old way of thinking, your mother's way of thinking. Our society is not the sum of people but the sum of acts, and every act, however trivial, however private, has meaning and consequence for the rest. You will be judged for your acts, and you will answer sooner than you think. No man is above sanction when he has broken the laws of the land."

"Moses' law has not yet been brought in," Brigge answered him, "unless it was done so very quick. He who has broken his marriage has not yet severed himself from life only to be regarded, as Favour had it, as a dead human being." Brigge brought his fist down on the table, rattling the plates and cups. He stared at Challoner. "Is this how you deal with a friend, Nathaniel? Is it the practice now to condemn men by gossip and calumny? Will you not answer me, Nathaniel? Not even to tell your friend whom you hold in such great affection that his very life is endangered by the revengefulness of a wretched mechanic of tyranny like Doliffe."

"No man, whatever he think of Doliffe, can impugn his sincerity."

"There is today too much pleading of sincerity," Brigge said. "Let me have men who are doubtful, who struggle with their consciences, who sometimes are confused by right and wrong, whose perceptions fail, whose troubled minds lead them this way and that and even to dark places they should not go. I do not care for these certain men who insist that what they feel is the truth as though their sincerity alone were enough to excuse their fanatic hearts. Doliffe's virtues bring suffering and agony in their wake. His sincerity is neither here nor there."

"What Doliffe does, he does honestly in the execution of his office and for justice' sake," Challoner said with exaggerated patience; then he added, "John, I must tell you there is something more, something that if proved will make you a dead human being as sure as if Moses' law were now enacted."

The Master's voice had more of pity and torment in it, but this time Brigge discerned his distress was without artifice.

"I have come to tell you that your neighbor Mr. Lacy and his wife were arrested tonight. They are infamous for their recusancy, having appeared before the justices and been fined on many occasions. However, they now stand accused of harboring a priest and for that they will pay with their lives."

Brigge was taken aback. "Was the priest apprehended?"

"Do you know this priest?" Challoner asked. "Have you kept him here at the Winters?"

Brigge said nothing. He felt like the prisoners he had interrogated who were so benumbed by their guilt and circumstances they could not think what to answer.

Challoner repeated the question, quietly, sternly, just as Brigge would have had he been the interrogator. When he made no answer, Challoner sighed and said, "Your silence will not save you. Lacy will confess. He will tell us what we wish to know." He spread his hands on the table and dropped his gaze. "I think you are a dead man, John."

"Get out!"

The men turned to find Elizabeth in the doorway.

"Get out!" she cried again. She went up to the Master. She trembled with rage and dread. "Leave us! Depart!" she cried. "You are not welcome in this house!"

Challoner, who had never shown himself capable of understanding or meeting the anger of others, who had always used his diffusing charms and appeals to reasonableness to arrest the progress of passions he found bewildering and undignified, was caught like an attorney without his brief. Speechless and made suddenly helpless by Elizabeth's wrath, he grinned foolishly and uttered some sounds to try to convey his amazement at what he had provoked and would have collected his hat and cloak to be gone but Elizabeth, who had told him so vehemently to depart, stood between him and his escape.

"I see you very plainly, sir," she said. "I see you for the hypocrite you are. You make your voice solicitous and sympathetic, but your heart is hard and unforgiving. You have won men over by saying they can be better men and love one another, but better men for you are the better sort, the rich and mighty who have all in their hands and yet want more. These are the men who have your love. Those who are truly in need of love and grace and pity, they go disregarded and reviled. From your rich friends you demand only that they continue as before, keeping all and sharing none. From the rest you demand that which they cannot give. You demand of them sobriety, thrift, truth, prudence, order. You demand industriousness and fidelity. You demand chastity and virtue, piety and obedience. You demand respect, discipline, hard work and prayer."

The Master began to recover something of his wits. "For this you indict me?" he said, incredulous. "Is sobriety a vice in your estimation, mistress? Chastity? Discipline? Why should such things not be asked of men?"

"Because men cannot give them!" Elizabeth cried. "Not in the measure you require. They are frail. And when they cannot answer your demands, you judge them and condemn them. But whip and prison all you may, you will not change men. They—*we*—cannot live to the rule you lay down. We cannot. We are not made thus."

"Your wife would make excuse for sin, it seems," Challoner said to Brigge. "You must find this quality in her most convenient."

Brigge said nothing to this jibe, but Elizabeth would not be bettered by sarcasm. "I acknowledge weakness," she said.

"Then you will never be strong!" Challoner cried back at her. His shout, his own high angry voice, the unruliness of his own passions, seemed to shock him.

"I confess it most readily," Elizabeth said. "We are frail, we are frightened, we are weak."

"Do not paint me with this brush."

"I do not," Elizabeth said. "You are plainly a supreme governor of your passions, Nathaniel, though I do not know whether to envy or pity you for it."

"Do you think I have not heard these objections before? I have listened to them many times. On every occasion I have asked a simple question. There are abroad in the land legions of beggars, there are delinquents and criminals of every sort, there are traitors and spies, there is vice, corruption, heresy and sin. My question is: what would you do? I have asked it of your husband. I have asked it of men a thousand times. Still I have had no answer. So, mistress, tell me what you would do."

"Forgive," Elizabeth answered him.

"This is your answer?"

"Govern men with clemency and caution. Overmuch sharpness and blood will draw upon you their hatred."

The Master looked to Brigge and made a short laugh in dismissal of his wife's plain idiocy.

"You have whipped more delinquents than Savile ever did," Elizabeth went, infuriated by his dismissing of her, "and Savile dearly loved the whip. You stock and bridle, you imprison, brand and fine. I have seen women hanged for stealing a shilling worth of corn or cloth from tenters in the gardens. I have seen children branded for taking chickens. This is not the way to order. By raising discipline and punishment to such heights you have set the people by each other's ears. One man reports his neighbor to the watch for lying drunk in a field. The neighbor reports the other for dallying with a serving girl."

"You would have men lying drunk when they should be at their work, you would turn your eyes from a man committing carnal sins?"

"Has your whipping made people better?"

"Can people not be made better then?" he scoffed.

"I think if they are to be brought to a better state it will be by kindness and charity," she answered.

"This is ranting Anabaptism. This is the doctrine of Hugwald and Müntzer and the deluded peasants of Germany who rose in rebellion against their princes."

"No," Elizabeth said, lifting the Bible they kept in the kitchen. She held it out to the Master and said, "If you care to look, you will find here this doctrine put into better words than ever I could utter." She went to stand by Brigge. "This is my husband, whom I know to be a good man," she said. "He is a good man yet you threaten that he should be hanged."

"Perhaps he is not so good as you think, mistress," Challoner said coldly. "Perhaps you do not know your husband as well as you think."

There was a silence for some space of time, Brigge not knowing what Elizabeth had heard or what she knew or suspected.

At last Elizabeth said, "I know my husband very well. And he shall have kindness and charity from me, as he deserves."

Perceiving her resolution, Challoner attempted a greater threat. Turning to Brigge, he said, "We know the priest who was at Lacy's house to call himself Maxfield. He is not yet in our power, but he will be found and he will face justice, as those who have harbored him will. That is the law. I hope for your sake that you have had nothing to do with this evil man."

Neither Brigge nor Elizabeth responded to him. Challoner, seeing his way to the door now clear, took his cloak and hat and went forward. He stepped outside into the darkness. Elizabeth let out a little cry, turned and ran to their bedchamber.

Challoner said, "Elizabeth thinks me a monster."

When Brigge did not offer to contradict his judgment, Challoner sighed heavily, his round shoulders fell. Brigge was about to close the door when he thought to ask, "What has happened to the Irishwoman Shay?"

"You surely have more pertinent matters to concern you now," Challoner answered. "As with the vagrants, I have never understood your interest in this woman."

"Does she still live?"

Challoner exhaled wearily. "For now she remains prisoner in the House of Correction," he said. "But I have asked Adam to see the matter brought to a speedy resolution."

"I went to Burnsall myself to search for the serving girl Susana," Brigge said. Challoner looked at him quizzically. "No man I spoke to there had heard of her or the sister she was supposed to have gone to visit."

"You were deceived then as to her whereabouts."

Brigge nodded slowly. "It appears so," he said. "The question is why."

"It is unimportant," Challoner said with a shrug. "It is nothing more than a distraction." He took a last look at Brigge. He said, "Why have you denied to save yourself, John?"

"I have denied nothing of the kind," Brigge answered. "Tell me how I may save myself and I will do it. I have no taste for martyrdom or sacrifice."

The Master merely shook his head. "Your son is very beautiful," he said, then added quietly, "I will protect you for as long as I am able."

Then he turned and went to the stable where James Jagger had put his horse.

Brigge closed the door. He listened to the clump of the horse's hooves. So well did he know his house and land, he could estimate precisely from the receding sounds where Challoner was: now on the stony path before the fields, now on the earth of the track that went between them, now on the marshy ground near the beck.

o   o   o

HE SNUFFED OUT the candles and went down the passage toward their bedroom. He could hear Elizabeth's crying. He thought his heart would break from the sadness he had inflicted. He opened the door in some trepidation, not knowing whether, now Challoner was gone, Elizabeth would turn on him to rebuke him. But immediately he stepped into the room Elizabeth came to him. Her eyes were red and lost. He took her in his arms and cleaved her head to his chest. He saw a strand of gray hair at her temple. He cursed himself aloud for the wretch he was and wept with her until she found his mouth and kissed him.

Twenty-four

AT A POINT IN HER PLEASURE BRIGGE SLIPPED TWO FINGERS inside his wife, this being how Elizabeth liked to have her due from him. But then, becoming aware of herself, she tensed her limbs and asked if it was well with him, if she still pleased him. He swore she did and gently coaxed her back to her enjoyment with flattering words and kisses. Nothing had changed in the way of her gratification. She was ever slow to the spasms of excitement, but when they came, she was left quite giddy. Then Brigge had his full enjoyment of her. She was flushed and happy. My wife is beautiful, he thought. Challoner was right in this at least: Brigge would cherish her in whatever time he had left. From the servants' room he heard the sound of Samuel coughing. He was about to rise when he heard Deborah's soft voice lull the child to sleep again.

◎　　◎　　◎

IN THE NIGHT he felt her come awake. She sensed he too was not asleep and raised her head to look at him.

"Have I made things worse with Nathaniel?" she cried.

"He had chosen his course before you spoke to him," he said, trying to reassure her doubts. "I pray he will take heed of the good things you said."

"I dreamed they came to take you," she said, "and the proofs they offered in your trial were the very words I spoke to Nathaniel."

It was her nature to be anxious. Brigge kissed her brow and put his arms around her. Her crying convulsed her whole body. "I dreamed I had killed you by my words," she sobbed.

Brigge told her that he would remember those words as long as he lived, and cherish every one of them, that no man had a better or more lovely wife. She became soothed somewhat at his words, but whenever his voice died away, she asked like a child that he speak to her, saying she had need of his voice. He recalled for her things of joy so they might share pleasant memories of people and places they loved. He told her the happiest occasions in his life were the day Samuel came safely into the world and the day he found her recovered from her sickness. She asked him to describe for her what had occurred during her labor, for she could remember little, and so Brigge found himself relating to her the arrival of Scaife to summon him to the town to view the body of the dead infant suspected to have been murdered by the Irish tinker Katherine Shay, and how on his return to the Winters he found her with the midwife and gossips in hard labor. It had not been his custom to speak to her of anything touching his work as coroner or governor, but he found himself relating the proceedings against Katherine Shay and the disappearance of Susana Horton, and he told her of the conversation he had just had with Challoner about the inquisition.

For the most part Elizabeth listened in silence, asking brief questions here and there. When Brigge had told all he could, she considered for some space of time. At length she said, "How strange that one so assiduous as Doliffe has not sought out this Susana."

He told her his thoughts had been the same. They said nothing more.

She was not content that he should sleep but kissed his neck and with her hands urged him again. Brigge became very eager for her. Nothing pleased or aroused him more than her pleasure and that she took pleasure from him, and he, thinking her abandoned to pure lust, as though it were May Day night again and they were reveling youths in awe of their own carnality and appetites, answered her heat and took her, forgetting himself, forgetting Challoner and Doliffe, forgetting the world. He existed in this moment only for her, to please her, to smell her sweat and taste her skin. Her paps were large and heavy, her belly round, and when she turned on her stomach, he rejoiced in her and the thought that she was his, that his hands could be free with her, that his fingers were invited to do their work, his tongue called and lured to where Elizabeth wanted it to go.

And in his enjoyment of his wife, in their recklessness together, she whispered something to him. He did not hear it plain, and before he could ask what she had said, she got a foot behind his leg and began to move under him.

He stopped his work, heart pounding, breath fast, and wiped the sweat from his face and searched her eyes. What had she said? She clung to him, was joined to him in every way it was possible for man and woman to be joined, so he could not think it was possible even for a red-hot needle to come between them they were so close.

He felt himself fall under the fetters of her arms and legs, pulling him down again on top of her. He tried to resist, keeping a hand on the bed to support himself, but she folded her limbs all around him and moved so that he had in no wise opportunity to part from her, nor wanted to be parted from her, from her heat and pleasure.

An hour before dawn Elizabeth fell asleep again and Brigge heard in his heart the thing she had whispered.

"Save us."

⊙   ⊙   ⊙

BRIGGE SLIPPED OUT of the room and into his fields. He stooped to inspect the ground, rubbing the dry soil between his fingers. There had been no rain and the hills around were as red as foxes. He searched the sky. It was clear of clouds. He smelled something on his fingers and brought his hand to his nose. His wife's smell. What would become of Elizabeth? Lacy or his wife could be induced to confess, by terror or promise. They would certainly implicate Brigge. But Elizabeth? Even now he could not make himself believe the Master would have her hanged. But Doliffe would have no scruple in this. Should he throw himself on the Master's mercy, recant and betray? Would the turning of conscience be sufficient to win their reprieve? Should they abandon the Winters and try to flee over sea and go to live as beggars in France? Should they take to the road and seek sanctuary in the anonymous wandering life of Starman and Deborah and Katherine Shay? Were these better fates than death?

Brigge turned and saw Elizabeth at the front of the house. She held Samuel in her arms and waved to him, and he came forward to meet them.

She appeared weary and her skin was hot to the touch, but she smiled on his approach. After their night together his heart was heavy and light, oppressed and joyful. He knew hers to be the same.

"You suspect there is something more to this business of the Irishwoman?" Elizabeth said.

"I do not know what it is," Brigge said, "or what it could be."

"You must find out," Elizabeth said quietly. "You must find this Susana and discover what she knows."

Samuel made a little animal sound as he yawned. There was mucus in his nose, which Brigge wiped away as he took him into his arms. He felt the thrilling warmth of the little body. He knew life to be fragile and happiness fleeting, but still, at this moment, in spite of all the present dangers, he could believe he had been brought to the perfect state: this, he thought, is all there is, all that is worthy of account. Man. Woman. Child. The means to feed, the means to make shelter, the kindness of others, and God's eternal, generous fount of mercy. He would do anything to preserve what he now had. He would do anything to save them.

Samuel coughed and more mucus came forth from his nose.

"I will find her," Brigge said.

◦　◦　◦

BRIGGE SENT JAMES Jagger to fetch Starman to him and, when the shepherd came, asked how his flock did. Starman said he had seen nothing to give him concern and had every hope the sheep would soon be good for wool and meat. Brigge considered his answer, then told him to wash and dress himself in a suit of good clothes he would give him, that he was to accompany him to the town.

While Starman prepared himself for the journey, Brigge went to take his leave of Elizabeth. He found her with Deborah and the kitchen maids, all the women having the same anxious appearance.

"Samuel has caught cold," Sara said.

Only an hour before he had seemed well enough, but now he coughed and spluttered; sadness swam in his eyes and he cleaved to the women. He cried and would not be comforted. When Starman came and announced himself ready, Brigge told him to wait and spent the morning by his son's side. Deborah alone appeared composed, affirming that children were thus, recovering and sickening and recovering again, and that Samuel was strong in heart and limb and they had no need for concernment. The evenness of her temper began to inflame Brigge and, recalling what Starman had told him of her, he had a sudden thought that she may have poisoned Samuel or in some other way caused him harm; but then, studying her closely, he saw her to be as troubled in heart as any of the rest. His suspicions lapsed though his fears did not.

In the afternoon, while Starman still waited, Brigge lit candles and prayed to St. Francis and to St. Anthony, the compassionate saints, the lovers of mercy. He and Elizabeth gazed at their son. The child's breathing came hard and his color was high.

"You must go now, John," Elizabeth said.

Brigge was loath to leave with Samuel so ill and would not do it and was angry when Elizabeth later again urged him to go before it became too late to undertake the journey that day.

"Time is short," she pleaded, "if our family is to be saved."

Brigge looked at his wife. Elizabeth's face was wan, her eyes tired and sad, her spirit downcast. He regretted his earlier show of annoyance and asked gently if she would not rest, fearing that she would make herself ill if she continued as she did. She refused him, as he knew she would.

He kissed her hand. "I am sorry," he said, "for the wrong I have done."

A tear came into Elizabeth's eye. "I know," was all she said.

Brigge went with Starman to the fold where his mare and the little gray nag were and had them saddled.

Twenty-five

ADAM WAS A MAN OF HIS WORD, AN EXCEEDING DILIGENT governor. At the new bridge they found the vagrants' camp pulled down, burned and effaced. There was no sign of Exley, nor of any man. Starman looked over the destruction as though he were a mourner by the graveside. What thoughts he had of what had passed there, or what questions he was asking of the fate of his companions who had lived there, he kept to himself. Brigge allowed him some minutes for his contemplation, or grief, if that was what it was, then called him on.

They set across the moor, the dry moss, thistle and grass crackling under the horses' hooves. Brigge explained what he was about, that he wished to find Quirke the alehouse-keeper and question him on the whereabouts of his servant Susana Horton. He told Starman they would have to enter the town without it being known, for it would be dangerous for Brigge to be found there. He asked if he had doubts of their going, but Starman professed his loyalty to Brigge and swore he would do what he could to assist him in his purpose.

"What do you think lies behind the girl's disappearance?" Starman asked.

"In truth, I do not know," Brigge answered.

"But you have some suspicions, your honor, do you not?"

Ronan Bennett

"I suspect she may know something of what happened on the night the child died, or was murdered," Brigge said, "and that what she knows is to the disadvantage of the men who would destroy me."

"What could this serving girl know of these powerful men?"

This was the question Brigge had never been able to answer. Yet by instinct and experience he knew something was being concealed from him.

"Do you suspect these men, or any of them, to have murdered the child?" Starman asked.

"I can think of no reason why they should," Brigge conceded.

"Perhaps you suspect one of them of having fathered the child and, being fearful of exposure as a hypocrite and bastard-getter, did away with his own son?"

Brigge did not answer. Starman had gifts of perception; he had always known it. Yet he did not welcome hearing his own suspicions spoken aloud, for now they were made audible, so was their foolishness.

"Had the Irishwoman been long in the town?" Starman asked.

"No," Brigge said. He fought down his growing irritation with the shepherd's acuity. "Scarcely a day or two."

Starman said nothing. He had no need. The conclusion was obvious: with Shay so recently arrived in the town, Doliffe could hardly be the father of her child. The idiocy of his undertaking was undeniable. Starman, sensing the looming shortness of Brigge's temper, left off further questioning.

⊙　⊙　⊙

AS DARKNESS FELL, they came within sight of Skelder Gate, but, perceiving the watch to be about and very vigorous, Brigge led Starman away, skirting the town, until they came to a place where the river could be crossed without their being seen, and from there to an unregarded passage through which they gained access to the town without they were challenged.

They made their way to Bull Green, a part notorious for its vices and sinks and stews, and there came to the sign of the Painted Hand.

The walls of the alehouse were high, it being among the largest of the

tenements. Brigge and Starman left their horses and went inside. The tipplers in the low, smoky room, men and women of disreputable appearance,
regarded them cursorily, those who noticed their entry at all, and went
back to their business. Some sat in groups of four or five around large
stone pots, others in couples, some of the men being very free with their
women companions. Some glanced at Starman and, perceiving his condition from the ravages of his face, smirked or whispered to their fellows.
Starman cast his eyes down and turned his head away.

"Pay them no mind," Brigge said. Starman mumbled that he would
not and pulled down his hat. Brigge glimpsed in his lashless, stricken eyes
the utter depths of his shame.

Brigge led him out of the way to a table by the back wall of the room.
He looked over the men, searching for Quirke. Many—the women as
well as the men—wore the blue ribbons of Savile's partisans. Some cursed
Challoner and the men who governed the town for their oppressions and
taxes. Others discoursed on the swarm of outsiders who came to settle in
the town and had but to ask for doles but were given them, while those
born here, and whose fathers were born here, were neglected and disparaged. One man spoke of the diseases lately found in the neighbors' sheep
and another of how if it did not rain soon their crops would wither, for the
weather was remarkable for its unseasonableness of heat after so bitter a
winter, at which there was much nodding and spitting and reminiscence of
previous hard years of hunger and want.

Brigge turned to see a man come through the curtain that separated
this room from the next. It was Quirke. He went to a bench where men sat
by a fire roasting a side of pork. Quirke brought them wooden cans and
blackjacks and sat to join their company as one cut meat from the roasting
and passed portions of it around his friends.

"There is the man we have come to see," Brigge said to Starman.

Brigge did not get up but was content to watch his quarry. He saw a
pair far gone in drink approach the alehouse-keeper to ask for use of a
room and saw Quirke nod as they stumbled to the stairs, the alehouse-
keeper's companions noisily offering the woman to perform whatever
duties were required of them should her lover be not a good doer for the

drink he had taken. On their going there was raucous laughter, mockery and coarse mime.

It was then Quirke became aware that someone was taking interest in him. He looked Brigge in the face. He was puzzled but gave no sign that he recognized him. Brigge did not move. Quirke whispered to his friends who, one by one, looked over. Still Brigge did not move but gazed at him steadily. Quirke attempted to compose himself, pretending to ignore Brigge. But after some minutes, with Brigge's stare yet upon him, he set his jaw and got to his feet and approached with one of his companions.

"I know you," Quirke said on coming up. He became agitated.

"Sit down," Brigge commanded him.

Quirke did not move but looked uncertainly at his friend.

"Do as I say," Brigge said.

"Stay where you are," Quirke's friend advised him. "This papist has no power to order you. He has been dismissed from among the governors."

"Sit down. You can choose to talk to me here or be brought directly to the Master where you shall answer for your deception of me," Brigge said. "It is your decision."

Quirke turned to his companion and dismissed him with a nod. The man hesitated, then went to rejoin his friends at the fire. Quirke sat across the table from Brigge and Starman.

"Where is Susana Horton?" Brigge said. "Do not lie to me as you did during the inquisition."

Starman tugged at Brigge's sleeve and, nodding, indicated that the one who had come over with Quirke was making his way to the door, doubtless to summon the watch or the constable.

"Let him be," Brigge said; then, turning to Quirke, said, "She was never in Burnsall as you alleged. I went there in search of her. Now tell me where she is."

Quirke had begun to sweat. His hands moved restlessly over his face; he rubbed his temples and put his fingers together again.

"Be quick in your answer," Brigge said, "or I swear you shall regret it."

"She is not here."

"Where is she?"

"She is in Langfield at the house of her aunt." Under Brigge's disbelieving stare Quirke swore he was telling the truth.

"Why did you say she was in Burnsall? Why did you lie?"

Quirke glanced nervously at the door. "She pleaded with me not to reveal where she was."

"Why?"

"I do not know."

"Why?"

"I swear I do not know."

"You are a rogue and a liar. Tell me why you said on your oath she had gone to Burnsall. Answer me!"

"She was afraid."

"Of what?"

Quirke shook his head, unwilling to say more. Silence had fallen over the room, the tipplers entranced and amazed by what they saw.

"Do not play with me, Quirke. Answer me," Brigge shouted.

"No!" Quirke said, rising to his feet and backing across the room. "You have no authority over me," he muttered.

Quirke turned and hurried through the curtain. Starman rose to follow him, but Brigge put out his hand to delay him.

"We will learn nothing more from him," Brigge said. "We must go to Langfield at once."

Some of the tipplers were already on their feet, ready to do violence. Brigge showed them the hilt of his sword to leave them in no doubts he would defend himself. And so he and Starman exited out of the alehouse without they were molested.

On mounting their horses they heard a great commotion of shouts and excitement which they assumed to be the watch coming to apprehend them. They set off as quickly as they could through the darkness, retracing their steps through the passage and across the river.

They followed a bridleway by the side of the river, picking their way carefully, for the moon was in its first quarter and there were clouds in the night sky. Arriving at Langfield before it was light, they tended the horses, then rested and slept. At first light Brigge woke Starman from his heavy sleep.

"Now we will see if Quirke was telling the truth," Brigge said as he mounted his horse.

Brigge sensed that the journey he had set out on when Scaife came to the Winters that freezing day to summon him to the town was at last nearing its end.

◌   ◌   ◌

THEY CAME TO a wooden bridge where, below, some maids were digging pignuts by the river's side. Brigge watched them awhile, then, leaving Starman on the bridge, descended to be among them. Coming into their midst, he hailed them and asked if they knew of one Susana Horton. The girls turned to one working among them. Brigge supposed her age to be sixteen or seventeen. Her open fair face was streaked with sweat and her brown hair was loosened under her coif.

Brigge came down from his mare. "Susana?" he asked gently.

"Have you come from the town, sir?" the girl said, her voice small and uncertain.

"Yes," Brigge said.

To Brigge's surprise she broke into a smile. Her teeth were white and her eyes were very blue.

"He promised he would send for me but did not say how long I should have to wait," she said, her voice growing joyous, "and with so many weeks passing, I did not dare believe he would keep his word."

"He is not a man to forget his word," Brigge said carefully, summoning a thin smile to his lips.

"I never doubted him, sir," she said earnestly, as though made anxious by her earlier words. "Do we go directly?"

"As soon as you are ready," Brigge said.

Again she smiled a great smile of contentment, as though her prayers had been answered, but then a look of concern came into her features.

"I must first go to Anna my aunt to tell her. She lives in that house," she said, pointing across the river to a dwelling on the far side.

Brigge nodded; he began to feel pity for the girl. She wiped her forehead, then wiped her palms on her petticoat. She ran to say farewell to her friends, which she did with kisses and embraces like one who, having come into sudden great fortune, was leaving a poorer place for a better one.

Brigge went up to where Starman waited, trying to think how he might continue to dissemble himself to Susana that she would reveal what he wanted to know.

"She thinks we have been sent by one she knows and has affection for to fetch her back to him," he explained quickly to Starman.

"Who?" Starman asked.

"That is what we must discover."

Her leave-taking done, Susana came up to the bridge. She flinched at seeing Starman.

"He will be overjoyed to see you again," Brigge said to distract her suspicions.

"Did he say so?"

"Often."

She let out a little laugh of happiness and skipped along.

"He regrets he could not come himself to fetch you," Brigge continued.

The look she gave him told Brigge she was beginning to have doubts and that he should tread carefully.

"What is your name, sir?" she asked.

"Brigge," he said.

"I have not seen you before in the town."

"I live at some distance from the town and am not frequently there."

"Where do you take me now?" she asked.

"Why, to him," Brigge replied with a warm smile.

Susana bit her lip and looked down at the broad river and the twisted waters boiling over the rocks. She said nothing more until they reached the other side of the bridge.

"Anna will be at her neighbor's, Mrs. Scargill," she said, indicating a house in the street ahead of them. "I will fetch her and return presently."

"We will wait for you here," Brigge said.

Susana left them and walked on.

"She suspects you, sir," Starman whispered.

Susana turned her head to look at them. She was young, little more than a child, but her instincts were sharp and she was not deceived by Brigge. She saw from his face that he had given up all pretense of being her friend. She broke into a run. Brigge hurried after her and easily overtook her. She began to cry.

"Who is he?" Brigge said, holding her by the upper arm. "What is his name?"

She would only cry and wail. People came out from their houses to see what was the commotion and what man this was that assaulted a child.

"I am John Brigge," Brigge said. "I have come to take Susana Horton to give evidence at an inquisition into the death of a newborn infant."

Susana let out a great scream and would have fallen faint to the ground had Brigge not caught her. He carried her to her aunt's house and, setting Susana in a chair in the parlor, found the said aunt, Anna, inside at her knitting. He told her who he was and what he had come for. "What is the name of the one Susana has been waiting for?" he demanded.

"I do not know, sir," Anna said. "I swear I do not. She never said his name and would never say it. I know nothing of him except that my poor niece claims him to be a gentleman that is very kind and loving to her."

"Has she received letters from him, tokens of any sort?"

"No, sir. And since she had no proofs of him, I would tease her and say there was no such man. But she was adamant there was and would rebuke my scoffs."

Brigge looked to Starman, triumph in his eyes. Who else could the gentleman be but Doliffe. Brigge felt light and free. His suspicion had been justified. He and his family would be saved.

⊙   ⊙   ⊙

SUSANA CALLED ON heaven to forgive her. Her aunt tried to be a comfort to her, embracing her and encouraging her as best she could, but Susana cried bitterly and begged that Brigge not have her hanged, for she was used and deceived by others and did what they told her because they knew better than she, but who these persons were she would not say and crumpled into tears and frenzy whenever Brigge pressed her.

Brigge waited until her sobs had subsided and she was whimpering in her aunt's arms. "How long were you serving in Quirke's house at the sign of the Painted Hand?" he asked.

The girl sniveled and chanced a look at him. He made his eyes gentle for her. "I went there at harvest last past," she said in a voice so quiet Brigge was scarce able to hear.

"Were you there when the Irishwoman, Katherine Shay, came to the house?" She gave a small, reluctant nod. "Do you remember the said Katherine," Brigge said in the same patient manner, "how she was?" Again Susana nodded. "Did you see that she was great with child?"

Susana neither spoke nor moved. "You must answer me," Brigge said. "Katherine was pregnant, was she not?"

Susana remained silent for so long that Brigge had given up hopes of her answer and was about to be strict with her and threaten her for her lies. Seeing the change in his demeanor, she said suddenly, "No, sir."

"She was not pregnant? You are certain?"

"She was not with child," she said, and began to screech again, pleading to know from her aunt if ever she would have forgiveness of God, her sin being so wicked.

"You must be truthful with me," Brigge said. "If you are false, it will go badly with you. Do you understand?" Susana sobbed loudly. "You had opportunity to see her clearly?"

Brigge had to repeat the question twice more before she could be brought to answer. "She was never with child when she was there at the Painted Hand," Susana sniveled.

"Do you know that Katherine Shay stands accused of murdering her child?" Susana whimpered that she did. "The child that you yourself found in a cupboard in the room where Katherine lodged?"

At this the girl went into convulsions and hysterical passions, and it was all her aunt could do to calm her.

"Who sent you away from the town?" Brigge said. "What is his name?" Susana begged him with violent and incoherent pleas not to press her but to leave her be. "Why did he send you away?" Brigge said. "Tell me, child. I promise you will come to no harm by him." She buried her face in her aunt's breast. "If you will not tell me now what I wish to know, I must have you carried back to the town where you will be compelled to answer me."

Susana flew into a passionate rage. She careered about the room, her eyes rolling. When Brigge attempted to touch her, she sprang at him to scratch at him and tear his hair and cursed him for a dog and a knave that was trying to murder her by his questions, and even her aunt, when she went to Susana to soothe her, received a stroke that made her nose bloody. Brigge took hold of the girl from behind and pinned her arms to her sides. She was neither thin nor plump; he felt her round high haunches in his groins. She fell forward, screaming at him to leave her, and so he gave her wish and left her to lie on the floor like a child in a fury.

"The child was yours, Susana," Brigge said, "was it not?" Anna looked up at him as though he were a devil. "It is true," Brigge said. "The child was hers."

Anna put her hands to her niece's face to hold her fast so she might look in her eyes. "Is this true, Susana?" she said.

Susana, her nose and mouth shiny with mucus and spit, her eyes red and wretched, cried that it was.

"Who was the father?" Brigge asked.

Susana shook her head, still in the grip of her aunt's hands.

"Tell me his name." Susana wailed that she would not tell him, and when he pressed her further, she seemed then to go into a fit, her whole body convulsed by tremors and gagging and choking at the mouth.

"His name is Doliffe," Brigge said loudly so she would hear his voice above her own screams. "The father of your child was Richard Doliffe, is that not true?"

Susana became suddenly quiet. She rubbed her red nose with her hand and sniffed. She wiped her eyes and became strangely calm.

"I know the truth of it, child," Brigge said. "Richard Doliffe, the constable of the town, got you with child, did he not?" Susana continued in her silence. "Did he come to you when the child was born?" Brigge waited for Susana to respond, but she said nothing.

Brigge sent Anna and Starman out of the room so he might be alone with her, the better to coax her to the truth. "Did he come to you at the Painted Hand?" he asked her gently when the others were gone. "Tell me and I will do all in my power to keep you from harm. Did Richard Doliffe come to you at the Painted Hand?"

She nodded her head a fraction.

"It was Doliffe who came?" Brigge said, his heart pounding in his breast.

"Yes," Susana said; her voice carried it in tones of childish but vehement bitterness.

"The child was his?"

"He was the one who misused me and got me with child."

"What happened when he came to you that night?" Susana seemed uncertain what to say. Brigge prompted her, "Were you abed?"

"Yes."

"With the child?"

She nodded her head.

"The child was alive?" She drew her upper lip into her mouth and sucked on it. Brigge said, "Susana, was the child living?"

She nodded her head again.

"What did Doliffe do?" She glanced uncertainly at him. "Tell me what he did."

Her eyes darted around the room.

"Susana," Brigge said in his kindest voice, "you know you must tell me what he did."

"He lifted my child from my arms," she began.

"Yes."

"And, laying it on a chair, covered its face with a pillow."

"He killed the child?"

She nodded. "I begged him not to do so wicked a thing and cried for help but no one came, and when I saw what he had done, I fell into a faint and never saw the child again."

"Is this the truth?" Brigge asked.

"It is God's truth," she said.

Ο   Ο   Ο

BRIGGE CALLED ANNA in again and told her to make her niece ready to journey to the town, then summoned the constable from his fields and directed him to keep guard over Susana.

Brigge had great need to take the air and move about and settle his agitated spirits. All would be well, all would be well. He trembled as he crossed the bridge with Starman.

"What will you do now?" Starman asked.

"We will take Susana directly to the Master and have her sworn and repeat before him what she has confessed," Brigge said. He could not conceal the delight he felt in the imminent downfall of his enemy. "Doliffe is destroyed," he said. "No one will believe him once he is revealed as a murderer. No accusation he makes against me or my family shall stand."

They walked some little distance from the town, Brigge almost dancing as he went, and were on the high moor above the river when Brigge heard his name called. When he turned round to see who it was that called him in this wilderness he discerned at once from the manner of his companion that it had not been Starman who had spoken. Yet he had heard his name called—*John!*—very clearly, though whether it was by man or woman he could not say, nor from what corner it came.

The air was still. Nothing moved, no bird or cloud or blade of grass.

Looking out over the moor, he thought he saw someone in the distance. "Do you see a woman coming this way?" he said to Starman, but for all Starman peered to see, he could devise nothing. "Do you not see her?"

"No, your honor," Starman said. "Who is it that comes?"

Brigge waited where he was, and as the figure came near, he saw it was Elizabeth. She came out of the air, from somewhere and nowhere, without covering on her head, dressed all in white, her hair about her shoulders, her face and eyes serene. She carried in her arms Brigge's son. The child was pale and did not move.

Brigge gave a cry and fell to his knees, unable to bring himself to look

— 198 —

up again. Starman bent over him and Brigge saw his face full of fear and anxiety.

"What is it?" Starman pleaded. "What do you see?"

Brigge jumped up and ran toward Elizabeth. He had not gone ten yards when he perceived she had vanished. He came up quick and looked forlornly about and called for his wife. His heart was wretched and tears flooded into his eyes. A spirit has no muscle, bone or sinew, a spirit is emancipated from all corporeality and so can know no dread. This was confirmed by the Ancients and is universally accepted to be true. Elizabeth could be quiet, but Brigge, who was solid and of flesh and blood, shivered violently with fright.

Starman came limping up and saw Brigge was deathly pale.

"As true as the Lord's Prayer, I saw nothing," Starman said to reassure and calm him. "Perhaps a shadow and trick of light on the moor deceived you."

"I must go home," Brigge said.

"What about the girl?"

Brigge put his head in his hands. Had he uncovered Doliffe's secret only to lose his son?

"Have the constable convey her to the Master," Brigge said, collecting his wits. "Tell him not to fail in his duty or he shall answer to me," Brigge said.

"Should you not accompany her?" Starman said. "Should you not be present to see that there is no meddling with the girl or concealment of the truth?"

"The Master is honest," Brigge said. "He will listen to the truth."

Twenty-six

SIX MILES FROM THE WINTERS, BRIGGE'S MARE THREW HIM and bolted. He fell to the ground, bruised in his back and right shoulder but otherwise unharmed. Starman gave chase and caught the horse. Removing the saddle, they found a sore about the bigness of a man's fist, red and livid, and no matter how they tried to calm her, the mare would not consent to Brigge's mounting of her again. They left the way to go on foot, leading the horses across mountain and moor and so shorten their journey. It was all Starman could do to keep pace with his master, for Brigge went angry and desperate, cursing aloud as he slipped on the sharp stones and pebbles that he should be kept longer from his wife and child.

As they were at last approaching the slopes where Brigge's flock was pastured, the sheep scuttled off, but one ewe stumbled and fell. Brigge halted to watch the animal pick itself up, swaying as though unsure of the ground. Starting forward again, it went first one way, then twitched to the left and turned right about. For a moment it did not move, but bleated twice; then, its legs giving way, it tipped and fell again. Starman hobbled to the giddy ewe, attempting to pull it upright, which, between its incapacity and the shepherd's own feebleness, was no easy thing to achieve; and once up, there was nothing for it to do but fall down. Starman left the ewe and went to another in a like condition, forelegs folded under it, hind legs helplessly splayed.

Brigge mounted Starman's little gray nag and rode down to the house, leaving the shepherd with the stricken sheep. There was nothing in his mind, no thoughts of what this portended for him or his family. He did not think of his debts or his ruin. He was benumbed, grief and despair beyond him.

○   ○   ○

THERE WAS NO one outside the house, no manner of activity. He did not hurry himself but very deliberately set about the horse's needs, providing water and oats and taking care as he removed the nag's saddle and blanket.

When he had delayed as long as he could, he started for the house. As he approached, the door opened and Deborah appeared in the threshold. He did not quicken his pace but went steadily on, his heart hanging in a trance.

This is the day I lost my son, he said to himself.

"I am sorry, sir," Deborah said when he came up.

Brigge halted at the door. Deborah's face was red and swollen from her copious crying. He looked into the kitchen, which he saw was empty, as lifeless as his child. Brigge took her hand to comfort her.

"I thank you, Deborah, with all my heart, for the care you gave Samuel. Without you, his life would have been still shorter and the joy we had in him still less."

He kissed her on her brow.

At once Deborah withdrew her hand and put it to her mouth. She was about to speak when Brigge heard from the house the sound of a child's crying. He looked at the woman, his mournful gaze giving way to puzzlement and panic.

Deborah said, "Samuel is recovered, sir."

Brigge's heart leaped with hope.

Then came understanding.

○   ○   ○

THE NEIGHBORS AND gossips washed the body and crushed rosemary and put sprigs in Elizabeth's hands, for the smell was rising as is common with women who die of the purples, and tied her ankles with footbands and bound her in the winding sheet she had prepared for herself before Samuel was born. The kitchen maids set out crosses and candles and tapers, and the faithful knelt before the corpse to pray a Pater Noster and De Profundis for the soul. Brigge kissed his wife's brow and put a penny in her mouth for St. Peter. Those uncomfortable at the performance of the rites quietly absented themselves to the kitchen, where they ate a dinner of cold meat and bread and sweet butter.

"The child recovered himself the day you departed," Isabel told him. "But as soon as he was well, his mother fell ill, a fever having come upon her very quickly. She was scarce able to walk for the pain she had in her belly. I saw she would not recover for she had death in her face. She was not in any way distressed in her mind but rather was calm, as if having seen her son recover she could leave this life content."

Brigge turned away and cried. Raising his head at last, he saw Starman come in and take off his hat and stand with his head bowed.

"She came awake only once after she fell into her delirium," Sara said, taking up Isabel's account. "Her eyes suddenly opened and she spoke, her voice very clear, saying that she felt well again and asked if her husband had come home. I answered you had not, and of a sudden she smiled and said it did not matter for she had seen you and you were safe. Those were her last words."

"When did she say this, what time of the day?"

"Early this morning," Isabel said, "not long after it was light."

"I saw her at that time," Brigge said. "She was bringing little Samuel to me. I thought it was to tell me the child was dead."

The maids crossed themselves.

"It was not for that she came to you, sir," Isabel said.

"She was coming to leave Samuel in your care," Sara said.

o   o   o

FATHER EDWARD ARRIVED with James Jagger. He wore a big gray hat so his face was not clearly seen. The kitchen maids came to usher him quickly into the chamber where Elizabeth lay. When those not of the faith had retired from the room, the priest consoled Brigge and prayed with him, then donned his vestments and sprinkled and censed the body.

"Almighty and everlasting God," the priest intoned, "we humbly entreat thy mercy, that thou wouldst commend the soul of thy servant Elizabeth, for whose body we perform the due office of burial, to be laid in the bosom of thy patriarch Abraham; that, when the day of recognition shall arrive, she may be raised up, at thy bidding, among the saints of thy elect."

Toward evening they set off, taking turn to carry Elizabeth's bier, to make their way to the chapel. The priest did not accompany them for the danger his presence would bring.

"Fly the country while you can," Brigge said to the priest at their farewell. "They have arrested Lacy and his wife and hunt everywhere for you."

The priest clasped Brigge to him with his large red hands. He said, "I live to do God's work. For as long as my life is useful to that work, I shall be protected. And when my death becomes more useful than my life, I will gladly give it."

Brigge wanted no more talk of death or sacrifice. "How have we come to this?" he asked. "How is it that good men divide and are at each other's throats and like to tear each other apart?"

"Those who walk in truth cannot go accompanied by those who peddle error and falsehood."

"I have heard Doliffe and Favour say exactly the same thing."

"A perverter of the truth will not scruple to claim it is he that possesses the truth," the priest said with vehemence. "He may deceive men, but his lies cannot be concealed from God Almighty."

Brigge felt a great tiredness come over him. "Save yourself, Father," he said. "Do not go to your death for the sake of such trifles."

Anger flashed in the priest's eyes, then passed as though he were making allowance for Brigge, for the suffering he was enduring. He spoke quietly but fervently. "These are no trifles. Good and evil contest for supremacy. The battle has only just begun. Men will die. I will die. It cannot be avoided. War is coming. It is on the horizon."

Brigge took a last look at the martyr before him, then turned to rejoin the little procession. The priest mounted his horse and was gone.

At crossways and forks they stopped and knelt to pray, as they had done when Brigge's mother was laid to her rest, leaving little crosses by the wayside before picking up the bier again and continuing their journey.

When they arrived at the chapel, the curate came to meet them at the stile, his look unwelcoming and cold. He stood reluctantly aside to allow the mourners entry into the church, where they set down the corpse and prayed in whispers, crossing themselves and knocking themselves while the curate performed the service they ignored. The bell tolled once and stopped, and Brigge went to the bell-ringer and demanded of him that he toll throughout as was fitting to mark the decease of a Christian. The bell-ringer hesitated but, seeing Brigge would not be satisfied otherwise, the curate nodded his approval and so the bells rang as in the old rite. Elizabeth was taken outside to the graveyard.

Brigge kissed Elizabeth on the mouth for the last time and the burymen lowered the body into the grave. Starman and Deborah threw flowers and herbs. The curate, offended at these superstitious enormities and able to withstand no more, withdrew himself from their presence.

Brigge whispered:

> *Man behold so as I am now, so shall you be*
> *Gold and silver shall make no plea*
> *This dance to defend, but follow me*
> *But follow me.*

And the others took up the chorus, murmuring:

> *Follow me*
> *Follow*
> *Follow.*

The earth fell on Elizabeth. The white of her winding sheet was first sprinkled, then covered as the clods came down.

Brigge made his way homeward. He prayed that in her final moment of clarity, when she came across the moor with Samuel in her arms, Elizabeth had not found him lacking in heart or soul or sympathy. That she knew she died loved by him.

o   o   o

RETURNING TO THE house, they passed the fields where the sheep were and saw how the turn had taken hold, so many animals now plainly infected. Brigge's flock was lost.

In the house Brigge gathered the neighbors and Deborah and Starman and the kitchen maids and, taking from his chest what little coin he had, he divided up his money and gave it to each person there, begging them to receive these doles in memory of his dear wife who was dead.

Starman hesitated before accepting and whispered to his master that he should preserve his money if he was to avoid ruin. But Brigge would hear nothing of it.

That night he slept fitfully but long enough to dream the thing he had not dreamed in many weeks. He was once again before the walls of the great city, the key he had accepted in his hand and now the warlike citizenry coming upon him, the leader among them holding aloft a noosed rope. Katherine Shay appeared at his side. She said, "Fear nothing from them. You shall be protected." "How shall I be protected?" Brigge asked the Irishwoman, to which she gave no answer and was gone again as suddenly as she had come. The armed men stepped forward. The first blow they gave woke him with a fright so sharp he thought his heart would never stop pounding.

It was almost dawn. Resolving in his mind what he should do, he rose from the feather bed he had shared for so many years with Elizabeth. He dressed himself in simple homespun clothes.

In the kitchen Samuel was asleep. Not wanting to disturb the child, he knelt by the cradle and whispered, "Your mother has passed from this life and you will never see her again on earth. Do not cry over this, Samuel. She has flown like an arrow to heaven and there we will one day be reunited with her."

He directed James Jagger to get ready the gray nag, telling his household he had business in the town. The kitchen maids put up great lamentations and begged him to stay, but Brigge would not be dissuaded. Starman said he did not trust the Master to deal justly with Brigge though Susana had told him all, and pleaded that he might go with him. Brigge refused all offers of accompaniment, saying he would go alone. He went to the stable and saddled the nag, the mare yet being beyond use.

Leading the horse out, he found assembled all of his household—Samuel, Deborah, Starman, James Jagger and Sara and Isabel—with their bundles about their backs. Since he would not remain at the Winters, they would go with him.

Twenty-seven

The women took turn to ride with Samuel, the rest going on foot, even Starman, who limped, though he made no complaint about his leg or the difficulty of the journey.

At Skelder Gate they were challenged by the watch who, seeing Brigge lead the nag with Deborah upon it and the child at her breast, became outraged that he went blasphemously in imitation of Joseph leading Mary and the Christ child from Bethlehem when they departed into Egypt. Brigge retorted they were no such thing and showed by his anger he would suffer no insult. The watchmen stepped aside to let him pass, one whispering with spiteful laughter that Brigge was well come and in good time, for tomorrow he would see hanged the very Jesuit he had harbored.

Brigge stopped. "The priest has been taken?" he said.

"He was taken this morning and will be hanged tonight. Lacy and his wife will swing also."

Another of the watch gloated, "And Fourness and Lister for the depraved sodomites they are."

All wore in their hats the blue ribbon of Savile but now also boasted sprigs of laurel with it. Brigge asked what it meant that these two opposite emblems should be mixed together thus, but the watchmen gave him only more scoffing and enigmatical laughs and proclaimed that all now would be well in the town by reason of the great reformation newly begun among the governors. Unwilling to collude in their making further sport of him, Brigge left off his questions, guiding those who followed him to the Lion, where he used to lodge when he was in the town about his affairs. There were blue ribbons and laurels in every window they passed and the streets were strangely quiet.

When the innkeeper saw who it was, he became alarmed and would have turned them away. But by his entreaties Brigge prevailed upon him to let Starman and the women have beds for the night, for they and Samuel were worn out from their journey.

Before he left them, Brigge commanded Starman to swear he would let no harm befall his son.

◎　◎　◎

AS HE PASSED under the arch at the entrance to the House of Correction, Brigge halted. Above, over the escutcheon where was inscribed the governors' apodictical motto—*And when was sin more plentiful?*—blue ribbons were draped, which caused Brigge much perplexity: what could it mean that Savile's emblem flew at the very seat of Challoner's government?

Banging on the door, he roused the keeper, who was amazed to see Brigge present himself here of all places. He stuttered his surprise and when commanded to bring forth the prisoner Shay, hesitated to obey, doubting Brigge's authority, but Brigge continued with him as though he were still a governor and coroner.

The keeper licked his lips and gathered his courage. "I am under strict orders, your honor, that the Irishwoman is to have no conference with any man," he said.

"Bring her to me at once," Brigge ordered him, his voice low and firm.

When the keeper saw Brigge would not be denied, he took the key from his belt and started up the stone stairs.

Brigge turned and entered the room where the Master and governors met. Everything remained as he had known it: the gleaming hard floorboards, the table in the center, the simple chairs around it, the unadorned walls. It possessed in perfection the very spareness and order Challoner had aspired to bring to the town. A brainsick fancy! Brigge should never have had any hand in the governors' work. He should never have allowed himself to be persuaded into their number. He knew—and had known from the first—what Challoner did not, that chaos beats in man's heart and is vital to it. It pulses his loins, it swims in his dreams. Easier to tame the wind than man, who is as turbulent, capricious, obdurate and selfish as dread and doct professors of religion maintain him to be, but also, which they do less, loving, merciful and selfless. Who knows better what man is than He that created man? It was Shay who had asked him if our Savior ordered for man's correction the whip and the prison. The Irishwoman had the right of it: nowhere in the gospels is this written. In place of the things of terror Jesus put into man's mind a glorious shining conception that would save him and raise him above the beasts and make him kind: *He that loveth his brother abideth in the light.* This is what the teacher taught, this is what is written for man. Had the governors been, as Jesus commanded his apostles to be, harmless as doves? Had they forgiven their brother until seventy times seven? Were they kindly affectioned one to another with brotherly love? Did they put brotherly kindness next to godliness and charity? *He that loveth not his brother abideth in death.* This too is written.

Brigge went to the stand to read the verse the Master himself had chosen at the first meeting of the governors to compensate with compassion, he said, the severity of the motto outside. *Charity suffereth long and is kind,* Brigge whispered from memory as he came up, *charity envieth not; charity vaunteth not itself, is not puffed up.* But what he saw was a new page and this injunction: *Thou shalt give life for life, Eye for eye, tooth for tooth, hand for hand, foot for foot, Burning for burning, wound for wound, stripe for stripe.* This too is written.

The keeper entered at the door. Brigge brought up the candle to have a view of the thing that was with him. He was accustomed to the sight of men kept prisoner for long spaces of time, but even he was aghast at the Irishwoman's condition. She was shrunken in girth and height, so wasted in her body that it was hard to credit she had ever had the carnality and voluptuousness Brigge remembered in her. Her hair was matted and coarse, her color ghostly.

Brigge directed the keeper to bring her a posset, then, supporting her by the arm, led Shay to a chair at the table where he saw by better light that some teeth at the front were broken and others gone. From these and other signs he could tell she was suffering from the scorbutic fever. Her breath stank.

He pondered long her dreadful state. "Forgive me," he said at last.

She peered about as though confused by things that were ordinary, the chair she sat on, the window, the candle.

"Do you know who I am?" he asked.

On hearing him she cocked her head like a bird. He was uncertain of her intellectuals. She smiled, exposing the horrid blackness in her mouth. "For what do you ask forgiveness, Germanus?" she said in a hoarse whisper.

Brigge had to work through her words as he had at the inquisition when he first heard her speak, and she repeated herself when she saw him unable to interpret the sounds of her tongue.

"It is I, Brigge," he answered her. "Do you know me?"

"I know you very well, I think."

When he had understood her, he continued, "I have spoken with Susana. Do you remember Susana?"

Her eyes moved like those of a child when questioned as to a thing of which it is uncertain. She said at last, "The poor child at the alehouse."

"Yes," Brigge said, encouraged that she had sufficient perception to remember; he went on, "She told me the dead child was hers."

Her gaze and attention wandered away again. Brigge called to her, speaking her name several times, but still she paid him no mind. He inhaled deeply, thinking of how he might persuade her concentration.

"Mistress, you will hang," he said quite brutally, "unless you tell me what you know." She continued to observe her surroundings as though they were strange and rare. He said with force, "If I am to save you from the rope, you must help me."

"Yes, yes," she said, turning to him at last. "We must all help one another. This is a good lesson you have learned, Mr. Brigge." Of a sudden she held out her arms. "Unfasten these chains," she said. "Let me go free from this place."

Brigge shook his head slowly. "That I cannot do," he said.

"But Germanus, do you not remember Germanus who could not bear the suffering of poor prisoners? He worked miracles so they might be free."

"I am not Germanus and have not the power to make locked doors fly open nor chains to fall off. If you are to have your freedom, it must be by the law of the land."

Katherine Shay shook her irons in demand that he free her. The keeper knocked and came in with Shay's drink of hot milk and ale. Brigge helped bring the can to her mouth. She sipped at the drink but would not take it down, being too rich for her constitution. Though he encouraged her, she begged to be spared from drinking more.

Brigge waited until the keeper was gone again before he continued his questions. "I know you gave birth to a child before you came to the town," he said.

"You think I was delivered of a child, Mr. Brigge?"

"From the evidence of your body you could have done nothing else. What became of that child?"

"Set me free, Germanus."

"I am laboring to set you free and shall do it if you tell me what I need to know."

She laughed, a raw, mocking, exulting sound. Her eyes were as big as saucers. "You wish to know what I know?"

"I must know it."

"This is what I know: *If thou seest the oppression of the poor, and violent perverting of judgment and justice in a province, marvel not at the matter: for he that is higher than the highest regardeth; and there be higher than they,*" she said. "This is what I know, Mr. Brigge, and is all you need to know."

"This is vanity, mistress, for which there is not time," Brigge said, despair coming into his voice.

"*This is also vanity,*" she said. "*He that loveth silver shall not be satisfied with silver; nor he that loveth abundance with increase.* How is there no time for this? This is the word of God."

"I know it, Katherine, and believe it with all my heart," Brigge said, taking her hands in his and leaning closer so she should know his sincerity. "But there are other things I must know, the things of this world. Will you not tell me what happened? Susana came into her labor. Was it suddenly? Did it take her by surprise?" She did not reply or give any sign that she understood him. He continued, "Did Susana smother the child? Did some other person do that deed?"

What little concentration she had now seemed to be slipping away. His voice growing desperate, Brigge said, "Did Doliffe come to the alehouse that night, the night Susana gave birth?"

Her eyes narrowed. She said, "Doliffe?"

"Mr. Doliffe, the constable. Do you remember him?"

"A bitter, harsh man," she said.

"Doliffe was the father of Susana's child," Brigge said slowly. She gave him a strange look, unbelieving of what he told her. "Susana confessed it to me," he continued. "She named the constable as the one who got her with child. The constable wants to see you hang, Katherine, but we shall turn things upside down and have him revealed for the hypocrite he is."

He waited for her to answer or merely acknowledge what he said, but she did not. He lifted the posset again and encouraged her to drink. She ventured to sip, then took the rest down very quick, the milk running down her chin and dripping onto her lap.

Brigge heard sounds from the hall and made out the keeper's voice. Going to the door, he pressed his ear to it.

"Good milk," Shay called from the table.

Brigge, straining to listen to what was being said outside, quieted her with an impatient wave of the hand. He heard a man's steps and a door open and close.

Brigge came back to the table. "Listen carefully," he said. "The keeper has sent for the constable. We do not have time to waste. Did Doliffe come to the alehouse? Did you see him?"

"The poor child came suddenly into her labor," she said. "She was in the room next to mine, and hearing her cry out several times, I rose from my bed and went to her."

Her gaze was away again. Brigge put his hands on her shoulders. "Go on, Katherine," he whispered. "What happened then?"

"I had seen her in the day several times since coming to lodge in the house, but did not know she was with child, her belly being not large, and well hidden by her shifts and petticoats. So seeing her much tormented with pains, I said I would go to summon others in the house, but she confessed what was the cause of her suffering and begged me to tell no one, and so I sat with her to comfort her."

"Did you deliver the child?"

She did not answer for some moments, then shook her head. "The poor child's labor was very hard and blood coming forth and she in great agony, I went at last against her will to fetch the tippler."

"Quirke?"

"If that is his name."

"What happened then?"

"He came to the room where Susana lay and, she seeing him, she began to cry for fear of what he would do to her. He would have had me leave, but I said I would stay and let him attempt to throw me out and he would see how I would repay him for his efforts."

"Did Quirke say anything?"

"The tippler was much agitated and very troubled," she answered, "saying that she would ruin him by having this bastard."

"Did he mention Doliffe by name?"

"He did not mention any man," she said; she continued, "The child came forth of a sudden, a boy child."

"The child was alive?"

"A fair child it was. I was the first to hold him, and giving him to his mother, Susana only screamed and would not at first even look on him but then by persuasion did accept to receive him in her arms."

"They must have smothered him. Who else did you see?" Brigge said, his impatience rising.

"My work being done and returning to my bed, I saw nothing more, but only heard the voices and footfalls of those who came during the night."

"Did you see Doliffe come to Susana?"

"I saw no man other than the tippler," Shay said with a shrug.

Brigge gazed at her. She appeared not to care, or perhaps not understand, what the deficiency of her evidence meant for her.

"Why did you not reveal any of this when you appeared before the
inquisition?"

She smiled, an odd cracked smile, and leaned toward Brigge and said
in a confiding whisper, "When you set me free, Germanus, I will lead a
crusade."

"Why did you not reveal that the infant was Susana's?"

"And have the poor child brought to the place where I was? To see her
suffer thus?"

"You were prepared to hang for her?" Brigge said, scoffing. "That is
very noble."

"No!" she said sharply as though Brigge were an idiot. "I would never
hang. I am to lead a great crusade," she continued, her voice rising. "We
will not go to fight. We will not raise our hands against any man. We will
go from village to village and town to town. They will be humble men and
women since great lords and prelates will not bestir themselves to our
cause. But all may go who desire it and who keep the rule."

Brigge got to his feet. "What rule is this?" he asked wearily.

"The rule is, first: the pilgrim will go barefoot. Second: he will not
sleep within stone walls. Third: he will preach mercy, brotherhood and
peace." Roused by her vision, she reached for Brigge's hands, rattling the
reckons that bound her. "The pilgrim will go as our Savior went, taking
thread and needle and a hat and a staff."

Brigge had a sudden recollection of the dream he dreamed when he
had fallen into his fever while returning from the town. He remembered
receiving two coins, one of silver and one of gold, but also a staff. "What
do these things signify?" he asked.

"When Christ was on earth, he kept a thread. This was charity, which
sews and binds. The needle was his penance, the hat his crown of thorns."

"And the staff?"

"The staff he took was the wood of the cross on which he rested on
Calvary," she said, recognizing from Brigge's look that what she said had

a meaning for him. She pulled at his hands. "You will come with me, John, and preach brotherhood and peace and mercy. You must sing this hymn. Listen and keep the words in your heart."

She sang:

> *Mercy, eternal God*
> *Peace, peace, O gentle Lord*
> *Look not upon our errors.*
> *Mercy we call upon*
> *Mercy be not denied*
> *For mercy we implore*
> *Unto the sinner, mercy.*

She sang the hymn three times more and made Brigge repeat the words. He did so only to pacify her, and she began to sing again. Brigge went to the door. The keeper was waiting outside as though maintaining guard.

"Return the prisoner to her room," Brigge said.

The keeper went and raised Shay from the chair.

"Should you falter, John," she said as she was led to the door, "only remember this: *The profit of the earth is for all.*"

"What is that the runagate says?" the keeper asked. "She claims to interpret the word of God?"

Shay rounded on him, shouting, "Hear what I say, you foolish fart-sucker. I have listened to great divines discourse and dispute the meaning of what is written in the Holy Book. But even a drunken wittol and speakarse such as you can know the meaning of so simple a promise: *The profit of the earth is for all!*"

The keeper smarted under her rebukes, and Brigge knew he would have struck her to keep her tongue still had he not been there.

"You are kind, Germanus," she said as she passed Brigge. "You are very kind."

The keeper pulled her away, she scolding him in her raw hoarse voice all the way to the top of the stairs. Brigge listened to the receding sound of her fulminations and footsteps and to the voices she provoked that called out from their imprisonment, souls in purgatory crying to heaven.

He left quickly, before those the keeper had sent for had time to come.

◊ ◊ ◊

THE AIR WAS WARM and gentle and carried the prisoners' cries outside. There they were mixed with other sounds Brigge could not at first apprehend. Then, listening with greater attention, he thought they were the noises of wild jubilee, as of drums and timbrels and trumpets. He started toward where he perceived the celebration to be when, out of the shadows, came a figure so swift and noiseless that Brigge had no time to draw his sword before he was overtaken.

"John," a voice said in urgent whisper. "It is Dorcas."

Brigge glanced about the dark street as though fearful of being set upon by those Dorcas had brought with her.

"There is no one here," she said when she saw what was in his mind. "Every man goes to Bull Green to see the celebration."

"What cause do they have for celebration?" Brigge asked.

"They have double cause," she said. "The town's government is newly remodeled and the priest that was captured is to be executed. You must go away from here, John. The governors have been told you have come to town. Do not let them find you here."

"I have business to attend to. Goodnight," he said. "My greetings to your husband."

At his mention of Adam, Dorcas dropped her head. She said, "I have heard report that Elizabeth is dead."

"I buried my wife yesterday." Dorcas's eyes filled with tears. "Why do you cry?" Brigge said in goading tones.

"By reason of the love I had for Elizabeth," Dorcas replied. "She went to her death without I could beg her forgiveness."

"She forgave me who committed the greater sin," he said, his voice becoming less strident, "so perforce she forgave you."

He stepped away from her. She called after him but he would not stop. Running, she came up to him and caught his sleeve.

"Do not be cold with me, John," she said. "Do you imagine I have betrayed you? Is that what you believe?"

"Challoner came recently to my house to tell me I was accused of adultery."

"Do you think it was I that accused you?" she said, her eyes wide with indignation.

When Brigge made no answer and she perceived she had been right in her suspicion, she stepped back from him to look at him more plainly and accusingly. They heard the approach of men in celebration, banging tabors and playing at trumpets, but neither Dorcas nor Brigge moved.

"I know you never loved me, John, as I loved you," Dorcas said. "Or that you ever would love me as I wanted to be loved. I know what every woman who yearns for a love she cannot have knows: that I should suffer for it, that the embraces you gave me would in the end bring me not closer to your heart but further from it. But I never thought my punishment would be to be mistrusted by you, to be held so fast in your discredit."

Her words tumbled out, ardent and honest. When they were finished, she cried and turned and ran from him. Brigge called after her. He started to give chase but, turning at the bottom of the street, ran into a crowd of men and women, all in high spirits and with blue ribbons and sprigs of laurel in their hats. They hailed Brigge without they knew who he was. "Do you not go to Bull Green?" they cried. "What keeps you here, brother, on this great day?"

Another company came from another street, swarms of people joining together, tributaries of a great river of reveling men. Brigge struggled desperately to weave and veer and slip out of unwanted embraces to follow Dorcas, but one with the shoulders of a smith and powerful strong hands took Brigge by the arm. His face was cheerful, vehement and fanatical. "Is it not a great day?" the man said. "Now shall there be order and good government, and honest poor men who labor hard and live by the commandments and yet were neglected will at last be given their due!"

Brigge was swept along.

Twenty-eight

AS THEY CAME INTO BULL GREEN, BRIGGE SAW THE SCAFFOLD
and ladder. A great roar went up. Men cheered mightily in demonstra-
tions of joy and threw their hats in the air, and others waved laurel
branches and scattered bay leaves by the handful. Brigge at last freed himself from his unwelcome companions and was about to go in search of
Dorcas when he heard the clatter of horsemen.

The crowd ceased their cheers and a reverent silence fell, so that
though five thousand or ten thousand or more souls were gathered in the
green, there was not the sound of a single voice. Then a great drumming
started, the reverberation and reecho entering into the chests of all those
who were there, filling them with passion and courage, and from the far
end of the green, from the direction of North Gate, came a second troop
of blue-liveried horsemen, their countenances solemn and proud. They
convoyed a great carriage of black and gilt and gold drawn by six magnificent black stallions. The curtains were back, but it was not until the occu-
pants drew level with where Brigge was that he perceived who they were.

He recognized first Lord Savile in a beautiful suit of black and azure
and a cloak of scarlet. The flesh of the ancient lord's face was wretchedly
phthisical and much spotted with age, and his eyes were dim like Isaac's.
In his time the great lord had appointed terror over men, but now, in his

ancient last days, it was as if terror was appointed over him, and consumption and burning ague that consumed the eyes, God's punishment for untold and terrible sins.

Opposite Savile in the coach Brigge saw Antrobus and one other. Amazed almost out of his senses, he stepped a little forward as the coach passed him, and the doctor, discerning some movement among those who were standing in the way, turned to see what it was. Their eyes met for a moment, then Antrobus looked away as if the man he had seen was nothing to him nor had ever been. The third man in the coach also turned his head to look back, and in his expression Brigge saw a momentary alarm. But then too Challoner turned away and the coach and its escort traveled on.

Brigge felt a tug on his sleeve and, coming out of his astonishment, saw Dorcas. "What is this?" he said.

"Did you not know?" she said. "The Master and Savile have allied together."

Brigge gazed after the coach in hideous fascination. The townspeople whooped and hallowed and whistled, and Savile's name was shouted with the same frenzy Challoner's had been in this very place not three years ago when the governors came into their power.

Dorcas called to his attention. "Go from here, John," she shouted above the roars, looking about in desperate agitation.

He hardly heard her, so fascinated was he in watching the coach. It made a circle of the green, then came through the crowd again to halt at the middle where a platform had been erected opposite the scaffold and where waited a deputation of the town with Favour and Doliffe at their head.

Favour came forward to receive the exalted passengers and bow his head to utter a prayer. All around, men began to go down on their knees in united show of piety and devotion. As they prayed, Dorcas gave him beseeching looks to pay her heed and be gone, but Brigge could not bring himself to leave so extraordinary a spectacle.

He heard the nasal quiver of Favour's voice. "The root of all evil, the greatest damnation, the most terrible wrath and vengeance of God that we are in, is willful blindness," the preacher intoned. "God open your eyes to make you see that lusts and appetites are damnable, to make you see that to tolerate the presence of sinners and evildoers among you is a foul disorder in a commonwealth. And yet you choose not to see. There are whores and you are blind to them. There are fornicators and you are blind to them, adulterers and you do not see them. There are vagabonds and masterless men who wander up and down the land inciting insurrection and teaching people by the example of their untrammeled loose lives to disobey their lawful heads and governors, and move them to rise against their princes and make all common and to make havoc of other men's goods—yet are you blind to them. Heretics and papists who conspire against established religion, the state and its loyal servants, who would overthrow all liberty and restore popish tyranny—yet you choose to turn your eyes from them."

Dorcas leaned to his ear and whispered to him. "I never denounced you, John, I swear it. Adam suspected what passed between us and confronted me on several occasions with bitter accusations. He suspected me because I could not dissemble passion for him, or love, and a man always knows when another holds the heart of his wife. Each time I denied what he put to me and swore I would not marry him if he continued with these questions. I lied to him. I lied to a man I esteemed and cared for. And I lied to Doliffe when he came to put me to the test. One day I shall pay for my lies."

She put her hand toward Brigge's.

"I know it was wrong but I do not regret it," she said. "I lied then and I would lie now because of what is in my heart. I would do all in my poor power to keep you from hurt."

Brigge took her hand and squeezed it.

The vicar's preaching had come to its climax. "The time for blindness is past," he was saying, and he pointed to the carriage before him in which Savile sat with Challoner and Antrobus. "It is time to see. The men who have come to do the Lord's work will root evildoers from your midst and pursue them wherever they lurk, for such evil men are an affront to God's sight and cannot be suffered to live."

The crowd amen'd Favour fervently.

Dorcas whispered, "You must go while you can, John, while there is yet time."

He saw that she was not false, that the care in her eyes was not play. "I have come to see justice done," he said, "and I will not leave until I have seen it done with my own eyes."

There was a rolling of drums and the crowd fell silent. Looking up, Brigge saw a cart being driven into the green, a hurdle trailing behind it, and brought to a halt. The prisoner was cut and taken from the hurdle and pushed forward to the scaffold. Though he was too far to see his face, Brigge recognized Father Edward from his size and shape. Brigge pushed forward through the throng. Dorcas came after, clutching at his coat. He could not make out what words Favour used to rebuke the priest, being too far distant, but got close enough to hear the priest return the reproach, saying he was going to be delivered from all his sufferings and enter into the joy of the Lord.

Brigge got to some thirty paces from the scaffold but could go no further for the press of people. He saw the priest mount the ladder and make the sign of the cross, at which there was much jeering and hawking. The priest began to speak but Doliffe interrupted him sharply, "You have not come here to preach, but to die! Better you use the moments you have left to prepare yourself."

"I have no need for further preparation," Father Edward replied. "My whole life has been for this moment."

The priest took the noose and kissed it. "Precious collar," he called out.

Brigge would not watch longer but dropped his gaze. He heard the familiar voice again. "Thy yoke is sweet, thy burden light." Then there was a great roar as every man and woman assembled there applauded the hangman for turning the priest off the ladder.

Brigge stumbled, feeling he was about to collapse to ground. He kept his feet and found himself looking into Dorcas's eyes. He put a hand to her face. "If I was ever unkind in my thoughts of you," he said, "I hope you know it was because of the lack in me. Forgive me, Dorcas," he said, kissing her face, "for all that I have done against you."

She smiled a small smile at him. Then her eyes, looking beyond him, froze in a sudden expression of alarm. Brigge turned to follow her gaze and found Adam and Scaife with armed men of the watch. His arms were pinned and his sword removed from his belt.

Adam gave his wife a violent, accusing look before pushing Brigge forward through the crowd. Brigge heard his name whispered and echoed by the blabber-lipped multitude, the rumor going up with the breeze that John Brigge the papist was apprehended. Then came the shrieks and cries as the priest was cut down and the boweling and quartering begun.

o   o   o

THEY TOOK HIM to the House of Correction, but it being overfull with prisoners, they put him in the storeroom, which had little enough of space, being new-stocked with coals and kindling.

"Tell the Master where I am kept," Brigge said, "and have him come to me."

"Who are you to summon a beggar to you, let alone the Master?" Scaife sneered.

Brigge ignored the fool and addressed Adam. "He will wish to speak with me. I arranged to have brought to him the serving girl Susana Horton. He will by now have spoken with her. I have further information touching Horton's evidence that he will wish to hear."

"What prattle do you have to relate, sir?" Scaife demanded.

"Adam," Brigge said, "for pity's sake, do this for me."

The boy stared at him with hard eyes. He said, "I doubt the Master will have inclination to come to you."

"Adam, do not let whatever suspicions you have of me stand in the way of what justice requires. Fetch the Master to me, for what I have to tell him is of the greatest consequence."

Adam said nothing but looked rather downcast and uncertain.

"You will have opportunity to tell him tomorrow," Scaife said, "when you will be arraigned before the commission on which the Master sits with Mr. Doliffe and Lord Savile." He smiled mirthlessly. "You and those skeptics, heretics and reprobates like you who disparage the truth and mock the great work we have undertaken here will learn what justice is.

Evildoers may hide from other men, but they cannot escape those guided by a higher authority, whose eyes see all and whose conscience will not be satisfied other than by a final cleansing of the earth."

Scaife stepped out of the room. Adam hesitated to follow. When he spoke, his lip trembled and he seemed on the verge of tears. "My wife was very familiar with you," he said. "She has always denied that anything untoward ever took place between you. Does she tell the truth?"

Brigge made no reply.

"Tell me!"

"Are you content with Dorcas?" Brigge said. "Does she please you?" He waited for Adam to answer; when he did not, he said simply, "If she does, turn your eye from whatever past fault you suspect."

"And if I cannot?"

"Then accept that your contentment is over."

Brigge was left without candle or any light save the little which came in at the small barred window high up on the wall. He moved a foot from side to side to clear an arc where he might rest. He sat down with his back to the wall and waited for the door to open again.

◎   ◎   ◎

HAD ONE HOUR gone, or two or three? He could do nothing to estimate the passage of time. Perhaps only minutes had passed when the door opened and Challoner appeared at the threshold. The Master turned to dismiss the keeper, took a lantern and stepped inside to be with Brigge.

"I am sorry to see you here, John," he said.

"I am the sorrier, Nathaniel, believe me," Brigge said; then added, "Did you enjoy your ride in Savile's carriage?"

Challoner drew in his breath, a weary man who has once more to vindicate himself before the stubborn though he has had enough of rebuke. He said, "You know the town was in great tumults with men at such variance and strife they were almost brought to a civil war. To bring an end to these dangerous and lamentable times, we have allied ourselves with Lord Savile. It is nothing perverse, nothing strange. Why should the two most powerful factions be at each other's throats? Small points of doctrine may separate us, but, ultimately, we share the same principles, do we not? We believe in order, prosperity and good government; so does Savile. We believe in discipline, property and good religion; so does Savile."

"I can still remember your speeches condemning Savile for a pernicious, corrupt man, a rack-renter and monopolist, one who put his own interests and those of his friends above the town's," Brigge said. "Those were very pretty speeches, Nathaniel. I remember how people cheered them."

"I could not say so at the time," Challoner said, "but I always maintained a great admiration for Savile. He was, whatever opinion you might have of his dealings, and I do not believe they were as bad as some would have it, a very great leader. Now we are joined, our government will be stronger and the town more united."

Brigge gazed at Challoner; he searched for winks and tokens of sarcasm in his friend's face. He found none.

"I sent Susana Horton to you," Brigge said. "You have examined her?"

"I have," Challoner replied so levelly that Brigge was momentarily taken back.

"Well?" he prompted.

The Master merely shrugged.

"Did she not tell you the dead child was hers? She was the mother, Nathaniel," Brigge said, peering at Challoner, the feeling of unease growing in him. "She was the mother and Doliffe the father."

Brigge waited for the Master to confirm what he said, but Challoner only shook his head as at the ravings of a maniac outcast.

"She confessed it to me, Nathaniel," Brigge said.

"I know exactly what she has confessed," the Master said.

"Then you know the child was Doliffe's."

"No, John," the Master said.

Brigge became animated. "Susana Horton confessed it," he said.

"She confessed what you wished to hear from her, John," the Master said. "You put into her mind a strange and tangled story, which she repeated back to you because she divined it pleased you. The truth of the matter is not so dark. It is plain and ingenuous. It was Quirke who made the girl with child and it was he, unable to perform the deed himself, who solicited another to do away with it."

"It is a lie!" Brigge exclaimed. "Doliffe is the father. He did away with the child!"

"Quirke has already confessed. He also conceived the idea of fixing blame upon the Irishwoman, she having confessed earlier to Susana that she had given birth on the road and the child dying only the day before. You would have discovered it for yourself, John, had you not been so resolved to find cause to condemn Doliffe."

"You are in concert with him," Brigge said. "You are trying to save his neck."

Challoner shook his head as though he were sorry to have disappointed his friend by his news.

"You esteem Doliffe a fanatic. I say you are mistaken in this belief, but I understand why you, who appear so loath to correct fault where you find it, should think it, for Richard has ever been zealous in God's causes. But what I do not understand, and will never concede, is that you should think him a hypocrite. He is a just dealer and lives by the Word. He holds it dear. It is his guiding light. He has never, to my knowledge, gone contrary to it nor has had any spot of infamy attached to his name. I would sooner accuse myself of murder than point the finger at him for even the smallest misdemeanor. If I am discontented with any man, it is with you for seeking your own safety in the ruination of one of the town's most honorable and loyal servants."

Brigge knew he was lost. "The jury must be appraised of Quirke's confession," he said. "Shay's innocency must be made known."

"The matter will be dealt with tomorrow by the commissioners of assize. All three—Susana, Quirke and the rogue who did the murder— have been apprehended. They are prisoners in this very building and will hang for their crime."

"And Shay will go free," Brigge said.

"She is a dangerous incendiary. For the people's safety she must remain where she is."

"She will not live long where you have put her, Nathaniel," Brigge said. "Let her go free. She has fantastical and misshapen opinions. She is strange and brainsick, but she will harm no one."

The Master shook his head in denial of him. He waited, as though preparing himself to deliver hard news. He said, "I am sorry, John, but you are beyond my help now. You will be arraigned tomorrow."

"On what charge?"

"The harboring of the Jesuit that was executed tonight."

"I deny it," Brigge said.

"Lacy has implicated you and will give evidence tomorrow," the Master said.

Brigge could not find words to say. Challoner moved to the door. Once outside he turned and said, "Will you embrace me, John?"

Brigge came up to the door. Challoner smiled sadly and benevolently as Brigge approached. "I have in my heart nothing but sorrow and grief," he said, holding out his free hand for Brigge to take.

"I cannot call you a betrayer, Nathaniel," Brigge said. "I cannot call you hypocrite or knave. You are neither arrogant nor boastful."

Challoner's look was serious and moved, as was fitting for the hearing of such a tribute.

"I cannot call you anything," Brigge continued, "because I do not know who you are, and that makes me an even greater fool than I already believed myself to be for ever having faith in you."

The prisoner pulled the door to, entombing himself in darkness. He found space on the floor and fell at once into a deep and dreamless sleep.

Twenty-nine

HE WAS WOKEN BY URGENT VOICES CALLING FROM THE STREET and saw by the window that it was still dark outside. He listened, trying to imagine what could be the cause of such alarm but did not move, as though he sensed something dreadful and did not dare rise to confront it. He became sensible of how uncomfortable hot it had become in the chamber, and he wiped the sweat from his brow. The air had grown heavy and thick.

At last, the hubbub and frenzy rising, he climbed the shifting coals and, pulling himself at the bars, got up to the window from where he saw an orange glow in the sky. His head was still unclear from the sleep he had been disturbed in and, still stupefied, he did not at once comprehend what his senses were telling him. Only when he heard the terrified screams from the prisoners above in the main part of the House of Correction and heard their pleas and entreaties that they be let out and not suffered to roast did he understand there was a fire.

Fear clutched at his heart. He again saw the vision of himself as a child standing at the hearth, held by the fascination of the flames, his mother chiding him that the fire would consume him, as though she had known even then that immolation would be his end.

He dropped down from the window and stumbled to where he thought the door to be, the coals rolling under his feet to make him unsteady. He pitched forward. Gaining his legs again, he went on only to feel his palms on the stone of the wall. He moved his hands about in desperation to discover the door. An ember came in at the window, sailing into his room with the grace of a delicate bird. He shouted for the keeper, for any man to come to his aid. He pounded the door with his fists, begging someone to come. He cried and called for Elizabeth to come to him. He called for his wife and called for his mother. He called for Samuel and he called for Dorcas. He sank to his knees.

When the horror in his guts took him from his tears, he got once more to his feet and turned back for the window, climbing and sliding over the coals as he went. The bars he took hold of were now hot to the touch. Smoke came into his nose and mouth so he choked as he called at the window to anyone outside who might be there.

Brigge's scorched hands lost their grip on the bars. Rising on his fours he spluttered and retched. The room was now full of smoke.

In this blindness and suffocation Brigge struggled to fight down his terror. The thought of death was not new to him. What did it matter that he was called a few hours sooner? He would be hanged in any case. All he could do now was pray for the strength to die well, as the priest had died. He resolved to use the last minutes he had in this life to prepare himself for the next. He said a Pater Noster and heard in the murmur of the prayer the consolations he sought, the promise of life to come.

Brigge's time of pain had come; he would find the courage to embrace it. He fixed his mind on Elizabeth and saw her as she was in their garden with Samuel in her arms during the short time they had in paradise together. How beautiful she was and how happy. How he loved her then. He begged forgiveness for being the occasion of pain to her, then, bringing his hand to his mouth, kissed it as though it were her brow.

Brigge's head was giddy; the strength in his arms gave out. He fell into the coals and lay still.

◎   ◎   ◎

HE FOUND HER not in the garden but on the mountain overlooking the bleak beauty of the Winters. She was smiling as she came to embrace him.

Her hair was dark, her eyes clear and bright, her skin fresh. Stretching out a hand, she showed him how his estate prospered. Looking down, he saw Starman with his flock, so many ewes and wethers he had never seen; and in the field that stretched from the house to the beck was a lush swaying crop of oats.

He became suddenly alarmed and, looking about, asked where Samuel was.

"He is not yet come to join us, John," Elizabeth said gently. "He has life left to live and will live it well."

She drew him to her, saying, "Do not be frightened, my love. Here you are safe at last."

◎   ◎   ◎

WHEN HIS EYES came open, they discerned a man's heavy dark jowls. Brigge sucked in some air and at once vomited. Wiping his hand across his mouth, his lips and tongue became grimed with coal dust, and he spat and hawked to rid his mouth of it.

The keeper stepped back and looked to a man Brigge could not quite devise.

"Can I go now?" the keeper pleaded.

He dropped the key into Adam's hand and ran off as swiftly as his great bulk allowed. Brigge stumbled to his feet and saw they were in the street before the House of Correction. He retched violently.

When he had breath again, he looked about in wonderment and horror at the advance of the flames. "Thank you, Adam," he said. He thought he heard the squealing of pigs; but, listening with more care, he realized it could be nothing other than the cries of the roasting inmates.

"The town has been attacked," Adam said in wonderment and horror. "Our enemies have struck."

A strong wind was up and it whipped the flames toward them. People ran for their lives. The whole town, it seemed, would be consumed. Behind them the roof of a house collapsed in on itself and flames jumped from the windows.

Adam gazed at Brigge. "Get away from this place," he said; his voice was low and bewildered. "Men will be dazed by what has happened here, but they will soon find their anger again and will seek revenge."

"Why would they revenge themselves on me?" Brigge said. "I have nothing to do with this."

"We live in bitter times and the world is divided in two: those who live inside the godly nation, and those outside. Inside is righteousness and strength. Outside is barbarism and terror. You chose to live outside."

"I chose rather not to live inside," Brigge said.

"It is the same," Adam said. "There is nothing in between."

The front of the house whose roof was gone now toppled to the ground in a motion like the felling of a great tree. It crashed to the street, causing hot dust to come up in clouds, sending sparks and embers everywhere. Brigge and Adam hunched their bodies and closed their eyes to protect themselves. Brigge felt his skin pricked with small burns.

When Brigge opened his eyes, he saw Adam was already walking away.

"Adam, wait!" Brigge shouted. "Where do you go?" Brigge hurried after him and took hold of his arm. "You must open the jail."

"I have freed you," Adam said harshly. "Make good your escape while you may."

Some men ran past, one of them his hair alight and screaming. Adam went after them.

"Adam!"

When Adam was gone a dozen paces, Brigge saw him drop something from his hand. Running up to where he had been, he looked down in the dirt and soot and saw the key the keeper had left with him.

○   ○   ○

HE DID NOT know that he would ever find the door, so thick and dangerous was the smoke. And when he came to it, he was almost overcome by the noxious air; he became faint and dropped the key and thought he had lost it until, scratching and raking the ground in a frenzy, he came upon it again. From inside there was silence and he feared the inmates might already be dead. He fought to make his trembling weak fingers do their work and unfasten the lock.

They poured out, retching as Brigge had retched, staggering and falling and some dragging others as they made their way to the stairs. He called for Katherine Shay, but there was no answering call. He questioned those who stumbled to their escape where was Shay, where was she held, but no man paused to tell him.

Fighting his way to the stone staircase, he went up through the choking smoke to the floor above where there were small rooms and private quarters. The heat here was still greater, for the roof was on fire and timbers and slate crashed around him. Taking the key, he attempted to open the first door, struggling with the lock. Then he heard pitiful cries from the far end of the passage. With his arm up to shield his eyes and face, he hurried to where he thought the cries were.

"Katherine?" he shouted, and called her name again and again. Every time he opened his mouth, he felt it catch as the noxious smoke came into his throat and choked him. Hearing a weak call from behind a door, he set to it with the key. The lock was scorching to the touch and Brigge burned his hand as he wrestled to open it.

Inside was Shay, loaded with chains, black with ash and smoke, so overcome she could not walk. Brigge pulled her up, a light burden in despite of her reckons, and carried her to the stairs.

Coming out of the jail after them, he found the prisoners in the street. He saw Lacy and his wife. He saw Fourness and Lister and others he had seen when Katherine Shay had her followers among the prisoners. He saw Robert Hewison and Quirke, the keeper of the Painted Hand, and Susana Horton. Some were hardly able to walk and were helped by their fellows, others with stouter hearts and stronger legs ran away at speed to save themselves. He heard the name of Germanus invoked, and some said that Katherine Shay had promised one day a saint would come to liberate them. They stood about, trepid and in awe of him who had freed them. "Which way do we go?" one asked.

"Why do you ask me?" Brigge answered sharply. "Go your own way."

Thirty

BRIGGE'S COAT FLAPPED ABOUT HIM IN THE WIND AS HE HURRIED down Cheapside to reach the Lion and Samuel ahead of the flames. He went into Petticoat Lane where, at the woolshops, those coming from the north end of the town joined with those coming from the west. A horse cart loaded with goods came at them and Brigge had to jump so as not to be run down. He ran through the market, where the conflagration had not yet taken hold.

Beyond the cornmarket the smoke began to thicken again. Brigge closed his burning eyes, and when he opened them, he saw he was not where he thought he should be and realized he must have turned off the way into an alley or courtyard. He knew the town well, but everything was so utterly changed that he was confused and, turning about, looked for a sign by which he could discover where he was. That he should be lost in a place he knew so well added greatly to his terror. It was like walking into his own house and not knowing it; if that could happen, then the whole world had to be falling in on itself.

A woman ran past him with chickens swinging in her hands as she went. Flames exploded from the small house at the foot of the alley, and Brigge felt a blast of heat sear the skin of cheek and neck on the left side. He wheeled about and hurried into what he thought must be Bull Green, but he was sure when he saw it that it was not.

What street was this? He did not know. Was it possible he was in some other town? Had he fallen insensible in the jail of one town only to wake up in another and witness it consumed like Sodom? Brigge had to put his arm across his face. His skin was blasted and he felt his eyeballs horribly shriveled, so that even to open them for a moment seemed to risk them being burned in their sockets. The houses on both sides of the street were alight, and the flames billowed along the thatched roofs, whipped by the wind; he was in a tunnel of fire. Horses and pigs screamed; the air was full of firedrops. He saw smoke rise from his coat and became afraid his clothes would catch light.

Out of nowhere someone passed him a bucket, and he threw the water at the wall of flame, hardly conscious of what he was doing. He might as well have thrown the water into the sea for the difference it made, and he could only stare at the flames and the flakes of fire swirling up into the air.

He felt the bucket snatched from his hand and this brought him out of his daze. Looking back along the street, he saw men with ropes pull down a house in the fire's path. Men and women hurried from doorways carrying infants and pots and chairs and chests. A brick chimney crashed to the ground only yards from where he stood. Smoke and dust came out in a great cloud and left him and those around him blinded and choking violently and covered in ashes. He could only put out a hand to find his way.

He did not now know in what direction he was headed. Toward the fire? Away from it? He was jostled and pulled and he pulled and jostled as desperation overtook him. He was aware of a horrible sensation, something underfoot, yielding yet hard in places, unmistakably flesh and bone, a body, a human body. Someone had fallen, and to make good his escape Brigge was prepared to crush the unfortunate wretch, to squeeze his guts, smash his skull.

Brigge stumbled blindly on, falling more than once. He tripped over an empty bucket and, when he realized what it was, went back to pick it up and take it with him, thinking he had a duty to preserve whatever might be of use in fighting the fire, and so made his way half a mile or more carrying an empty bucket until he reached the open spaces of Little Green and Bull Green, where men and women lay on the grass to recover their breath amid the screams of the burned and mutilated.

He gathered himself for the strength to go on to make his way to the Lion and Samuel when he heard his name called. They were ghosts who approached him—Starman and women and the little boy James Jagger covered with white-gray ash, and Deborah shielding Samuel as best she could. There were oaths and curses and rumors and cries. There were cries that the woolshops were in flame, that the fire had now spread west of the market, that the whole town would soon be engulfed and no man and no woman would escape. The detested name of Exley the vagrant was on every man's lips, and some said they had heard with their own ears Exley threaten to set the town on fire for revenge.

Brigge shepherded his family together and said they must go while they could, for in the morning there would be wild justice. As they went, they found fat Lacy and his wife who, terrified out of their wits and fearful of being pointed out and killed, begged to come with them. They came to the end of the green, meaning to strike out for the moors and mountains north of the town. Brigge took Samuel in his hands and kissed him. The child felt hotter than he had ever done in his fevers and Brigge became seized with the need for expedition.

He turned to Starman and the women. "Go up by Back Street and Snidal Lane and leave the town by that road. Do not let any man prevent your going. Wait for me beyond North Gate and I will come to you."

Lacy was very quick to be off with his wife, but the kitchen maids were loath to go from him.

"Why do you not come with us?" Isabel cried.

"I must stay to give what assistance I can," he said.

They would not go until Starman persuaded them for Samuel's sake and promised them they would all be reunited but that they must go quick before the flames arrived at this part of the town.

The first spots of rain came on when it was still dark.

○   ○   ○

BY FIRST LIGHT it was raining as heavily as during the worst of the winter. The fires began to die down from the great dampness and having run their courses; by midmorning they were entirely extinguished. Brigge walked among the people. All men were the same, specters of ash and amazement, powdered over with dust, walking spirits and visible ghosts, and he went unrecognized.

From the cornmarket to South Gate, from King Street in the west as far as the Causey in the east, the town had been destroyed, turned into a heap of blackened timber and ashes. The stench was there, the smell of roasted flesh and decaying, distended guts. Some were so badly disfigured their bloated limbs had the ruptured, crannied texture of charred wood, and the flesh of their heads was scorched back to the teeth and skull; others seemed hardly touched by fire at all. Brigge had seen men to their graves by apoplexies and blastings, by sudden blows, by water and fire, by every kind of instrument and agency, man's and God's. Nothing on earth is as feeble and frightened as man, and nothing more deserving of compassion, of charity.

The air smelt densely of woodsmoke and on the wind charred scraps still floated. He passed people with the broken, vacant looks of soldiers of a defeated army going in search of shelter and food. At the market men were already laboring to clear away the waste and wreckage, and the gravediggers skulked with their handcarts and spades. Men's talk was swiftly becoming terrible and wrathful. The town would be revenged, the City on the Hill rebuilt, its light restored. All swore they would not rest until those who had set the fires were called to account to receive such punishment as would terrify evildoers everywhere. There would be no mercy, only bitter revenge. When Brigge asked who it was they would revenge themselves on, the people rounded on him and threatened him with blows for the impertinence of his question and asked who he was. There was no need to ask who was guilty. The guilty were those who were their enemies: the papist gentlemen who armed their servants and went by night conspiring to murder them; the Irish who came in hordes from over sea, landing at ports and beaches, then setting out to claim the land for their own; the vagrants and rogues and counterfeit Gypsies who wandered the roads stealing and plundering men's goods, striking fear into the hearts of honest men; the armies of emperor and pope that ravaged the poor people of Germany; traitors who lived in their midst and succored those outside who would destroy them. These and others were the guilty ones and would pay for the wickedest deed that was ever done by man. Reason and skepticism were the mark of the faintheart and the traitor. Brigge heard extravagance and absurdity. He heard the panting of tyranny. He saw that in the town at last all were now united where for so long they were warring and at each other's throats: the great merchants and wealthy clothiers and drapers and yeomen with poor laborers and spinners and tallow-makers. Some lived well and some did not and some would eat tonight and some would not, but differences of rank, wealth and degree had melted in the fire. All were now united and would be revenged. *War is coming,* Father Edward had prophesied. *It is on the horizon.* Brigge stole away from men and made for the wilderness.

◦   ◦   ◦

BRIGGE FOUND HIS family among the hordes of those refugeed by the fire on the moor beyond North Gate. James Jagger had the nag with him, which he had led from the stable at the Lion at the first soundings of alarm. The kitchen maids Isabel and Sara were there too. And Lacy and his wife, and others of the jail. They were, all of them, waiting for Brigge, and when he came up to them, they asked him where he would lead them.

"I will not lead you to any place," he said.

He took Samuel in his arms and whispered loving words to him, then returned him to Deborah and put them upon the nag. He took the rein and led the horse, setting out for the mountains beyond.

Thirty-one

THE RAIN CAME ON AGAIN, A VERY HEAVY DOWNPOUR OF
water. Now will my sheep drink and my crop be watered, Brigge thought,
though he would never see his fields or sheep again. He spoke to Elizabeth
as he went, relating to her all that had passed and saying he was sorry he
had not stayed longer with her when they were reunited on the mountain.
And sorry too that he had looked for Samuel before his time. Brigge
grinned with happiness thinking of Elizabeth saying that Samuel had life
to live and would live it well. He would soon leave this life, and he would
be content enough to go knowing his son would live and prosper. He
glanced up at Deborah, who kept Samuel under her cloak, his narrow eyes
watchful and bright and showing no sign of fear or complaint at the
strange course his father was leading him. If Brigge was aware of those
who followed in his wake, he did not show it.

They came to East Wood in the evening. Mother Moore sat where
Brigge had last seen her beneath the gibbet, so still he imagined she had
not moved in the months that had passed since then. She rose on Brigge's
coming, clutching her son's bones in her hands.

"Where do you go, Mr. Brigge?" she called.

They found shelter in a barn and begged food and milk from the
farmer, which he, having tidings of the terrible fire, was content to give

them, though casting his eye over the company could not but think that the town had disgorged to him its most disreputable inhabitants. He offered to take the child inside and Brigge and Deborah too, but Brigge would not have it.

That night some crept up to where Brigge lay with Samuel. "Do you know me?" a woman asked him. He gazed at her thinking he had seen her but where he did not know, only that it was in some other life that now had neither meaning nor worth to him. "I am Joanna Henry and was among those apprehended for taking grain from the cart of Morrison the badger," she said.

Another said, "I am Charles Denton, whipped and sent to the jail on the order of the governors."

"I am Alice Cartner, whom you bridled and stocked."

"I am Quirke, who got Susana with child and caused the Irishwoman who called herself Shay to be apprehended."

One more made his confession; he was very grave. "I am Robert Hewison," he said. "I killed my wife by beating her, the which thing you demonstrated to all the world."

They whispered it was he who had condemned them but had also delivered them, and who could he be but St. Germanus that Katherine Shay had said would one day come to free them.

Starman chased the fools from his master and told them to let him be and rest, then covered Brigge with a blanket and added his own blanket to the covering, and the kitchen maids came to be of comfort to him.

When they left in the morning, they found others in the way. Their leader was a woman, small, toothless, old and frail, who still carried on her limbs the chains of her imprisonment. Katherine Shay smiled on seeing Brigge. "I thought the crusade was mine to lead," she said. "But I was wrong, Germanus. It is for you to show us the way."

Brigge paid her no heed but walked on with his son in his arms.

⊙   ⊙   ⊙

BY THE NEXT night they were past a hundred strong, all of them miserable, poor, disordered creatures raked up out of the refuse of mankind, many with infirmities, a multitude of blind, crippled, hunchbacked, limping men.

o   o   o

THEY CAME INTO a small place where Brigge had never been before and did not know the name of. On seeing a ragged man with a dirty face lead the little nag and the woman and child upon it, the people came out and prayed, and some sought to touch Samuel and some fell on their knees and clutched at Brigge's feet as he went past.

Those with him sang:

> *Mercy, eternal God*
> *Peace, peace, O gentle Lord*
> *Look not upon our errors.*
> *Mercy we call upon*
> *Mercy be not denied*
> *For mercy we implore*
> *Unto the sinner, mercy.*

Starman sang the words and the others sang them too, and the people of the little place thrust bread and cheese and scraps of meat into their hands and pockets. Katherine Shay rattled her chains as she went, denying to have the smith break them, saying they were the marks of their suffering and their salvation.

Some of those who had squatted at the new bridge and who were dispersed and hiding in the mountains heard their singing as they crossed the moors and came to join them, so Starman was reunited with his friends. He asked them of Exley and what news they had of his brother, but no one knew what had become of him, or whether he was dead or alive.

At the next parish they came in to, some of the women went ahead so that when Brigge and Deborah and the child entered into the town they hosanna'd him and threw branches and saplings in his path. Men came from the fields and women from their work to ask who it was that came among them, and when they saw this great army of poor penitents and sinners, their hearts were touched and they gave food and drink.

Mercy we call upon
Mercy be not denied
For mercy we implore
Unto the sinner, mercy.

On the seventh day, at the instigation of Katherine Shay, those who followed Brigge demanded of him that he reveal himself to them and speak to them and tell them what he would have them do. Brigge would have no conversation with them and struggled to escape their demands and imprecations. But they got him in a corner and confronted him. Brigge would only say what his name was, which was John Brigge and no other. His dwelling was at the Winters, he said, though he could not return there and never would live there again by reason that there were those who would destroy him if they found him, and since he could do no other thing, he would go from place to place as he had done this last week for as long as his life was spared, which he did not think would be long. He said they were fools to have any expectation of him or put any hope or faith in him, that he was neither teacher nor guide but was no more or less than they were themselves. He said they should go their own way, for he could not take them to any place that was better than where they then were, which was waste and high moor with nothing but rags for their apparel and stale bread for their bellies. Whereupon there was great crying out and lamentation, and men and women came forward, crying that he should not leave them or they should be lost, and nothing Brigge could do or say would persuade them otherwise.

Seeing they would not leave him in peace, he waited that night until they were asleep and crept to Deborah and Samuel and led them and the little gray nag and slipped away. But Katherine Shay led the pilgrims to overtake him not a mile from where he left them and with tears and mourning beseeched him not to desert them and so brought him back to their camp.

Brigge dreamed again of the key he was given. In the morning he spoke to Shay and asked what was the key for. She answered him that he should take the key and go forth into the world and have courage and speak and men would listen to his words.

Brigge roused those who were with him. Coming slowly into their blear-wits, they gathered around him. For the first time Brigge took proper note of who there was: Lister, Lacy and Fourness, Isabel and Hewison, James Jagger and Denton, Henry and Cartner, Sara and Deborah, and to all of these and the others who were among them he said no one of them was without guilt and some among them had committed foul deeds and terrible acts, and he confessed he was one of these. He said they were forsaken but they would find fellowship with those that lived in cabins and dens and caves and in the desolate corners of the earth, and in their brotherhood and fellowship they would find first forgiveness and then life.

Before they started on their way again, remembering the enjoinder of Katherine Shay, he made them throw away their shoes and vow they would never sleep again within stone walls. Lifted in spirit and with happy hearts, they tramped fields and highways and bridle paths and tracks. The sun was kind to them, neither searing their skins through its force nor chilling them by weakness. At night they made fires and slept on beds of moss and bracken.

They came to a large town in the north and, as was their custom, the women went ahead to strew branches on the ground before Brigge and Deborah and Samuel. The townsmen left off their work and, coming upon them, said, "What is this that you do?" When Katherine Shay answered that they should be happy and not make show of such displeasure, they fell into a distracted rage and threw stones and excrements at the pilgrims.

One came up to Brigge, who carried on though rained on with hard blows, and stopped him and said, "Who are you that goes in such mockery of our Lord?"

"I am John Brigge," Brigge said, "and no other. This is my son and this his nurse."

So saying, Brigge tugged at the rein, but the one who stopped him raised his club and brought it down on Brigge's crown. Brigge sank to his knees. The blood dripped on the road before his eyes. His head swam and bile came up into his throat. Then he got slowly to his feet, took up the rein again and went. All round, the townspeople beat the pilgrims and pursued them from the town, scattering them in every direction.

◎ ◎ ◎

WHEN THEY HAD gone far enough to be safe from the crowd, Brigge stopped and sat down on the road. Deborah helped him, binding his wounds and setting him on the horse, she taking Samuel in her arms as she led the nag.

Katherine Shay found them. She took Brigge's hand in hers and held it close. As pilgrims came by in ones and twos, making their way as best they were able, she bade them halt until Germanus recovered himself.

The hours went by and the pilgrims, fearful they would be attacked again, were restless to be gone. And so Katherine Shay took her leave of Brigge with a kiss and, her fetters clanking, led them away to continue their crusade.

At their going, Brigge fetched a sigh for the sadness he felt in his heart. The pilgrims went as doves, but war was coming, it was on the horizon. Cities would crumble, men would die. There was nothing to prevent it.

◎ ◎ ◎

AT NIGHTFALL TWO men came out from the hedge, one of them Robert Hewison, the other Quirke. Deborah called on them to help her, but they, seeing Brigge to be dangerously sick, threw him from the nag and made off with it.

In the morning Starman, one eye closed from a blow and his left hand broken, found them hiding in the hedge. He lifted Brigge, now unable in his whole body, and carried him some little way, but could go no further. A gentleman passed them and gave them some coin and felt such pity for them that he took off his coat and gave it to them. Afterward some carters came, and Starman paid them with the gentleman's money to load Brigge on their cart and carry him to a doctor. When they had gone as far as they would go with him, they lifted him from their cart and placed him on the road. Starman and Deborah wept as they watched over him.

By morning Brigge was recovered. His head was cleared and his wounds healed. He felt such extraordinary strength in his heart and limbs that he marveled at it as though he had fallen asleep an old man and woken a young one. He climbed the mountain with bounding steps and called for Elizabeth. Below, his sheep grazed contentedly and Starman waved to him that all was well, and in the fields the harvest was nearly done, the ripe corn, as high as a man's middle, being gathered into the barn. He was so joyful he lay down on the heather and gazed up at the gentle sky.

Someone leaned over him, and though Brigge saw the man's mouth move, he heard no words. A second face appeared full of concernment and promise, and she gave a sad smile and reaching to her side brought up a beautiful, incomparable child, its belly full, its mouth wet and white, a happy gurgle of contentment in its throat. The mouths moved again. Brigge heard some muffled sounds they were making but still could not make out any words.

He felt wetness on his cheek and saw the man and woman above him were crying, their tears dripping onto his face. Then he thought he heard someone call his name, gently and sweetly, and striving to turn his head, he felt his cheek stroked. He wondered who it was that called his name.

Then Elizabeth came to him. She took his hand and put it to her breast and whispered to him that here there was mercy and all men who sought it should have it.

Acknowledgments

The lengthiest acknowledgment of the sources and inspirations that have gone into this novel would still be incomplete, for, as anyone who studied Tudors and Stuarts at school will know, the literature on the political, religious, social and economic (not to mention local) history of seventeenth-century England is vast. Nevertheless, I must cite a few of the most important.

Apart from the obvious contemporary voices—Aubrey, Baxter, Clarendon, Cromwell, Evelyn, Fox, Lilburne, Pepys, Wallington, Winthrop and others—I owe debts to the modern work of, among others, James Cockburn, A. G. Dickens, Conrad Russell, Keith Thomas, Keith Wrightson, and, of course, Christopher Hill. I have also benefited from Peter Clark and Paul Slack (eds.), *Crisis and Order in English Towns, 1500–1700*; David Cressy, *Birth, Marriage and Death: Ritual, Religion and the Life-Cycle in Tudor and Stuart England*; Stevie Davies, *Unbridled Spirits: Women of the English Revolution, 1640–1660*; Eamon Duffy, *The Stripping of the Altars: Traditional Religion in England, 1400–1580* (the source for many of Brigge's "prayers"); R. F. Hunnisett, *The Medieval Coroner*; William Hunt, *The Puritan Moment: the Coming of the Revolution to an English County*; Ronald Hutton, *The Stations of the Sun*; Robert M. Kingdon, *Adultery and Divorce in Calvin's Geneva*; Iris Origo, *The Merchant of Prato*; Joan Thirsk (ed.), *The Agrarian History of England and Wales, Vol. IV, 1500–1640*; David Underdown, *Fire from Heaven: Life in an English Town in the Seventeenth Century* and *Revel, Riot and Rebellion: Popular Politics and Culture in England, 1603–1640;* and John Watson, *The History and Antiquities of the Parish of Halifax.*

John Brigge performed inquisitions in the West Riding of Yorkshire in the 1640s and '50s, the records of which are now lodged among the gaol calendars, indictments and depositions of the Northern Assize Circuit in the Public Record Office/National Archives, London.

Many years ago, I discussed this material with Alan Betteridge, Ian Roy and John Smail, albeit in a very different form. I hope they will not object to the use to which I have put their knowledge and expertise.

Which brings me, lastly, to the acknowledgment every novelist working with history must make that when conflicts arise between historical fact and the demands of the novel we tend to settle them in favor of the latter. This is a work of fiction.

About the Author

RONAN BENNETT was born in 1956 in England and brought up in Belfast, Ireland. After moving to England as an adult, he went on to receive a Ph.D. in history from King's College, London, where he now lives. He writes regularly for the British and Irish press, and is the author of *The Catastrophist*, two earlier novels, and several award-winning scripts for U.K. film, television and radio.